SEX IN THE SAGAS

Óttar Guðmundsson

SEX IN THE SAGAS

Love and Lust in the
Old Icelandic Literature

SKRUDDA

2016

Sex in the Sagas
© 2016 Óttar Guðmundsson

Translation: Wincie Jóhannsdóttir
Cover design: Hafsteinn Michael Guðmundsson
Cover painting and other illustrations:
Jóhanna V. Þórhallsdóttir
Photos:: Finnbogi Helgason, Jóhanna V. Þórhallsdóttir
and Steingrímur Steinþórsson
Illustrations from Melsteds-Edda: Jakob Sigurðsson

Originally published in Icelandic as
Frygð og fornar hetjur in april 2016

Printed in Sweden
Published by Skrudda ehf.
skrudda@skrudda.is
www.skrudda.is

ISBN 978–9935–458–49–0

This book is dedicated to the most important women in my life: my mother Fjóla, my wife Jóhanna, my daughters Edda, Kristín and Helga Þórunn, and my sister Steinunn.

Contents

Introduction

No period in Icelandic history so radiates glory as the time from the settlement to 1262, when the King of Norway came to power. *Landnáma* (the Book of the Settlement), *Íslendingasögur* (The Sagas of Icelanders) and *Sturlunga* (The Saga of the Sturlung family) all deal with this period and describe the complex lives and struggles of the first settlers and their descendants.

These books are the country's most important contribution to world literature. They provide insight into the difficult life that awaited the settlers who crossed the ocean from Norway, stopping in Ireland and elsewhere along the way. Here we will be enquiring into the private lives, close relationships, loves and sex lives of these people. The Sagas do not reveal much directly about these aspects of life, since their Christian writers were expected to say as little as possible about love games and bed antics. According to the church's teachings, lust was a dangerous phenomenon which led folk astray, off the narrow path of Christian virtue.

We can often hazard a guess and speculate as to what went on in people's private lives. What were the sexual mores of the time? What do legal records have to say about sexual relationships? What was allowed and what was not? How did the Nordic gods arrange their sex lives? How did the sexual habits of men compare to those of the gods? Did the gods obey the rules of men or were the rules different in their part of the world?

I have been a practicing psychiatrist for many years, and use that experience to examine the relationships between the sexes in the mythology, the *Íslendingasögur* and other books of the period. A few years ago, I published *Hetjur og hugarvíl,* which dealt with psychological and spiritual problems in the Sagas. In this book, I will be examining the sex lives of men and gods.

How did those cousins, sex and love, get on in the male-dominated society of the *Íslendingasögur?* Relations between the sexes are seldom mentioned. Sexual intercourse is never described and other loving caresses are rarely mentioned. The stories are first and foremost about the upper classes who controlled everything; less is said about the ordinary people of the country. Sex will have been important in that time as it always has been. The imminence of death and uncertainty about one's own existence function as an aphrodisiac or large doses of Viagra.

The authors of the Sagas are not forthcoming about sex and emotions and make little of love relationships or courtship among the young. There are many reasons for this, not least the inimical attitudes of the period to sex and women. People were still very alive to Eve's original sin, which they saw as the cause of man's exclusion from Paradise. This was ample reason to be wary of women and their deceit. These hostile attitudes to women are found throughout the Sagas. The writers were men who served the church, so they had a limited experience of women and feared them.

Women and History

The history of humanity is just over four million years old. Relics of tools that indicate some thought and organisation are two and a half million years old. Man developed and progressed over time. Many thousands of years lie between the making of simple tools and a deeper understanding of the origin of life. Of course, our ancestors were clear as to motherhood, but paternity escaped their notice for several thousand years. There was probably a long period during which people did not understand the connection between sex and conception, and indeed, there were no restrictions on fertility. Modern feelings such as guilt and shame did not bother those first humans. Nor did they deliberate about such concepts as ethics and morality. Marriage, sometimes called the "moralisation of sex", did not exist.

Greater knowledge about conception and the roles of the genders didn't come until pre-historic times, after 12000 BC. Man was a wandering race, travelling about the earth in smaller and larger groups, staying temporarily in some lush valley. People started dividing the labour. The man took on hunting and fetching food while the woman saw to cultivation. Not everyone was suited for heavy work, of course. Men were stronger and women weaker so the natural division of labour was based on physical qualities, though there were exceptions. The occasional woman could use a spear as well as a man and hunt better. Some men were better in the fields than out hunting. A certain division between the roles of men and women came about early in man's development and the sexes probably cooperated better at the dawn of civilisation than they did later on. In humankind's fight for its life in a harsh environment, both sexes were important and probably of equal standing. People shared everything; water, food, fire, shelter, and the genitals of the adults. Men and women took part in a flexible sexual order which modern man might call group marriage. This system was necessary for the species to survive all the adversity they faced. Women got pregnant and bore their children and pregnancy was the only form of contraception. The children were the offspring of the group or society.

Group marriage was acceptable while sexual behaviour was governed by spontaneity and the heat of the moment, without any moral element. Once the secret of conception had been revealed and the concept of

11

property emerged, however, the days of group marriage were pretty well over. It has actually never worked, despite a number of experiments. Last century's hippy movement preached peace and free love, but did not find general support and ended up on the refuse heap of history, like so many other failed social experiments.

Group marriage came to an end due to humanity's growing understanding of itself and its own existence. No one actually knows how it happened. We can imagine that better weather and changes in farming methods led to people staying longer in each place; abandoning little by little the wandering that had characterised humanity up to then. The ice age was over and the ice caps that covered the northern hemisphere slowly drew back, revealing arable land. Winters grew milder and summers hot, so people settled in one place and started farming instead of hunting. Life became more organised and predictable. They started watching their flocks instead of roaming the woods and mountains to hunt. And suddenly, the penny dropped.

Let us imagine a certain shepherd watching a ram service a ewe. When it has finished, it does not lie down to rest as a man does, but looks for the next ewe. This goes on and the ram often manages to service several ewes in one day. A few weeks later the shepherd notices that these particular ewes are beginning to swell and he realises that this is due to the behaviour of the ram. Up until now, he had thought that life quickened by itself in female bellies and had nothing to do with sexual activity.

Suddenly he grasped the connection between ejaculation and pregnancy. He was well aware of his own ability to have intercourse with females, but he had not understood that that activity was the start of all life. That women's bellies did not swell of their own accord, that a man's semen was needed for that to happen. Little by little he came to understand that a woman of child-bearing age could become pregnant at certain times, because of only one man at a time and could have one child a year. The man, however, could inseminate many women every day of the year. Until they made this discovery, men had probably undervalued themselves and overvalued women, who they believed could have children without extraneous help.

Men had now understood semen and their own importance in creating children. This was one of the most significant discoveries man made about his own existence. The creative power of semen brought men closer to God and their own immortality, which Adam had botched back then when he ate of the apple. Men could create life which made them like gods. Now they realised that they lived on in their descendants, thus ensuring the eternal duration of their own talents. After this, the importance of semen increased century by century and came by degrees to be of ultimate importance, as Aristotle maintained. The word "seed" occurs 222 times in the Old Testament where it is deemed so precious that it must not be deposited anywhere but in a woman's vagina, where life could quicken. Throughout ancient Greece there were statues of erect penises which reminded men of their superiority and women of their subservience. The phallus became a kind of religious symbol for fertility and longevity, being both the avenue and the vehicle for semen. Without the phallus, semen was useless and without semen the phallus was powerless.

Philosophers were fascinated by semen and its power. Men's ability to produce semen distinguished them from women and made them superior beings because it was they who created life. Women were characterised by their inability to produce semen; they received where men gave. Men bestowed, women received. This made all the difference. Men went bald because their brains and semen were more splendid than those of other living things. Women didn't go bald because they were in essence like children, who couldn't produce semen. Eunuchs didn't go bald because they had changed from men into women and were thus deformed. Some went so far as to maintain that women were deformed men. The clitoris was an underdeveloped penis. Semen became the source of much self-aggrandisement where men appropriated the leading role in increasing and maintaining the race. Many drew semen as lots of little human beings,

all dressed up, ready to enter the world. A woman had very little role in the conception and creation of a new human. Her role was to provide nine month's accommodation for this little human that sprang from the semen, but she mattered very little otherwise. In Old Norse mythology, the father of the goddesses is always named but the mother very seldom. This comes from the old belief that a child is in fact complete in the man's semen.

Men had long exceeded women in terms of strength and stamina. With the addition of the new knowledge of the importance of semen, men gained even more power. They became sensible of their own superiority to women. This theory eventually established itself and became a major precept of religion and society for a great many centuries. Men claimed the power they thought they needed, and thus began *"patria potestas"*, the patriarchy which characterised all the ancient civilisations and later the *Íslendingasögur*. Their power came directly from God. In the religions of the world the main god is usually male and behaves accordingly. He naturally favours his fellow males in their endless battle with the opposite sex, conferring on men the godlike right to control women. Polytheism is usually a miniature version of the lives and households of humans. The man is the head of the house, controls and commands, the woman is subservient though she may show signs of independence.

There was, however, one hitch. A man could never be completely certain as to the paternity of the children born to his wife. The child might just as well be the offspring of his brother, his cousin or his best friend. A woman could, without her husband's knowledge, open her vagina to anyone and this fact eventually became men's principal worry and obsession. The Bible's story of the treachery of Eve and all her daughters did not soothe men nor give them more confidence. Because they assumed that women were prepared to betray them, men drew up all kinds of laws to ensure their jurisdiction over their women's vaginas and wombs. Possibly all legislation and rules relating to marriage and sex could be said to have the sole purpose of ensuring children's paternity. Men could not bear the thought that a child might be wrongly attributed to them and did everything in their power to prevent it. Any woman who lied about her child's paternity was to be cruelly punished. A wrongly attributed child was an attack on the immortality of the supposed father, who brought it up as his own. In time, this became the worst nightmare of patriarchy.

Men were in a difficult situation. They had dominion over their women, they were stronger than them, had the godlike right to control and command them, but even so could never be certain that they had fathered the children their wives bore. The seeds of suspicion had been sown. Women were not to be trusted and were prepared to betray their husbands. This has affected the entire cultural history of mankind. The misogyny of the *Íslendingasögur* and oppression of women was built on an age-old foundation of cultural, religious and evolutionary history.

The Impact of Religion

Any attempt to understand our ancestors' attitudes toward sex must include an examination of their religions and ideologies. The heathen polytheism of Northern Europe had a good deal in common with the Greek and Roman religions. The gods were in many ways similar to men; they were both noble and vain, mischievous and tolerant, forgiving and vengeful. They were endowed with the same virtues and vices as humans so the world of the gods and their way of life mirrored human existence. The gods had the same marital strife, got sulky or jealous, argued and took revenge. What set them apart from men was their immortality and godlike attributes, not their behaviour otherwise. Lust governed the lives of gods as well as of men.

The Christian God of the Old Testament, on the other hand, was more distant and more perfect than the heathen gods. Jesus Christ was more human than God Almighty, but lust played little part in his life. The children of men found it difficult to identify themselves with God and his son because they were so holy and virtuous.

The book of Genesis tells how God created woman, describing a complex procedure in which the Lord Almighty put the man to sleep, took one of his ribs and replaced it with flesh. He then formed a woman from the bone and led her to the man. They were both naked and felt no shame. What followed was the tragedy of the fall from grace and humans were driven in disgrace from Paradise.

We all know what led up to that, since the story is so often told. Adam and Eve lived happily in Paradise until a sly snake tempted Eve to eat of the tree of the knowledge of good and evil. She handed the fruit to Adam, who took a bite and then they were shown out the door of Eden like badly behaved guests at an election rally. Eve's crime was disobedience. Adam's was to listen to his wife and obey her.

Men were advised to keep their wives silent, as we read in both the Old and the New Testaments. A man was meant to control his wife and this could best be done by not listening to her. The Old Testament provides the basis for the Western patriarchy where it is imperative that men have full control of their wives.

Greek Mythology

Greek mythology had a great many gods all belonging to a large family. The gods were immortal and lived on Mt. Olympus, but often visited the earth to spend time with mortal men, whose behaviour they emulated. The gods were imperfect, frail, vain and often laughably childish. They were crafty and used deception to confuse people and gain their ends. They were full of sexual energy, had sex with each other and with mortals and were in constant competition as to who was stronger and most beautiful.

Zeus, the foremost of the gods, was reminiscent of a self-satisfied, self-confident, sex-obsessed womaniser. He slept with goddesses, nymphs and young men and would do anything to get hold of tasty flesh. The goddesses shared these qualities, so life on Mt. Olympus was characterised by energetic sex and emotional chaos, where adultery and dishonesty went hand in hand. The whole world has ever since been fascinated by

Greek mythology. A myriad of authors and scientists have sought inspiration and paradigms there. Sigmund Freud was a specialist in Greek mythology, where he found names and credibility for various theories of his.

Old Norse Mythology and Sex

Man creates the gods in his own image and according to his view of life, his dreams and desires. They deal with the same doubts and limitations as man himself, and ponder the same urgent questions about the meaning of life.

Sex shapes the life and existence of the gods as it does man's.

The Nordic people had complex legislation dealing with sex and interaction between the sexes. It is noteworthy that the gods totally disregarded these laws and behaved like amoral sex addicts. In the world of men, they could have been sentenced to exile or huge fines for many of their crimes. This discrepancy between the laws and the behaviour of the gods is interesting and may reflect the reality of the age better than the Sagas themselves, which are permeated with Christian attitudes. Possibly the mythology gives a more realistic picture of people's sexual behaviour than the stories.

The main sources of Old Norse mythology are the *Eddukvædin* and *Snorra-Edda*.

Here we will look briefly at some of the major gods in *Valhöll*, their sexual behaviour and relations between the sexes.

A major farmstead in a nameless region

The world of the gods in *Valhöll* is reminiscent of a major farmstead in a beautiful valley in the countryside where all sorts of people, of higher and lower class, mixed together. The farmstead was allegedly run by the head of the family, the prominent farmer who maintained full authority over

Valhöll. *The goat Heidrún stands on the roof and gnaws the tree Léradur. All the pictures in this chapter are from the Melsted Edda, illustrated by Jacob Sigurdsson, 1765.*

the farming. His wife considered herself to more privileged and important than the other women. The children and their spouses had places of their own on the farmstead where they had built their own houses, did their farming and brought up their children. There were plenty of workers on the farmstead who did all kinds of jobs for family members. Life there included ordinary irritations that sometimes made people break into groups and gang up on each other. On this farmstead, love and sex flourished as they do wherever people come together. Adultery was frequent, and both men and women often woke up in beds other than their own. The problem here was how closely people were related, which meant they shouldn't actually have sex. The people of the farmstead chose to ignore this and gave their sex-drive free rein. For the transcriber of the mythology, *Valhöll* was a kind of Paradise where sexual dos and don'ts weren't in effect as they were in the world of men, where you weren't allowed to do anything for pleasure.

The enemies of our farmstead's household were rather vaguely portrayed farmers on other farmsteads who followed other ideologies and values. They were titans, giants and other riff-raff. There was tremendous enmity between the farmsteads and everyone knew that it would eventually lead to conflict. In that war everyone would lose, and that beautiful valley would be devoid of life. The situation was like a temporary ceasefire, or the calm before the storm. Life was a never-ending battle between the gods and their enemies. However, relations might be peaceful when it was a question of sex, because the gods often coveted beautiful damsels on the other farmsteads and always gave in to such appetites, causing all kinds of skirmishes to arise from such lechery. Let us look more closely at this world.

Prominent farmer and local potentate

The head of the household in *Valhöll* is the prominent farmer *Óðinn*, god of battle, knowledge and death. Like many local potentates in 18th century Iceland, Óðinn was tireless in his search for knowledge. He paid for a slug of the water in Mímisbrunnur with one of his eyes, so he remains forever one-eyed. Óðinn is greedy and cunning as wealthy farmers tend to be. He coveted the Skáldamjöður (Poetic Mead) which was guarded by giants. The story of this drink is complicated and bloody, characterized by deceit and death. Anyone who drank this mead became a prolific poet. Poetic skill was precious, so such a magical drink was especially desirable.

The prominent farmer Suttungur the giant, one of the enemies of the gods, was the custodian of this super drink. He had it bricked up inside a cliff and his daughter, Gunnlöd, was left to guard it. Óðinn did not let this stop him; he did a deal with Suttungur's brother, Baugi, and the two of them bored a narrow tunnel into the cliff. Óðinn then changed himself into a serpent and was thus able to crawl through the tunnel

Óðinn.

and into Gunnlöd's chamber. He charmed Gunnlöd, slept with her for three nights and then, in the shape of an eagle, just managed to get away with the mead. This story is sexual, since Óðinn seduced Gunnlöd, had intercourse with her repeatedly, and snuck away in the morning. The girl was left disappointed and weeping, ruing the day she trusted that treacherous, womanising farmer.

Óðinn's wife was *Frigg*. Instead of living with her husband, Frigg had a residence called *Fensalir*. They had one son. Frigg, as goddess of fertility and growth, was often appealed to in connection with childlessness and childbirth. This venerable old couple did not have a happy marriage. Óðinn was a lecherous womaniser who was on familiar terms with women both local and far-flung. He was also suspected of homosexuality in connection with his interest in magic. There are no stories of specific homosexual lovers but plenty of gossip about his interest in beautiful boys. Óðinn had an exceptionally good horse, an eight-legged hot rod of the fastest sort. There are many images of Óðinn with the horse Sleipnir, usually where both have raised members. Óðinn's weapon is the spear Gungnir, the phallic symbol of the god.

Óðinn cheated on Frigg and had numerous children with goddesses and giantesses. Óðinn fathered the god Heimdalurlur with nine mothers, who were all sisters. He had his son Váli with the giantess Rind after having raped or seduced her with magic or runes. The god Týr was

Reflections

Óðinn is the epitome of patriarchy, master of his house, a powerful god replete with manliness and lust who cheats on his wife and doesn't hesitate to use both violence and dishonesty to have his way with women. Óðinn is every man's dream, riding the classiest horse, a lady's man who has fathered the children of women and goddesses. He can seduce any woman using magic. He changes himself into a serpent or penis when he tempts and seduces Gunnlöd, so the moral of the story is that a stiff member will always get where it's going.

his son by the beautiful daughter of the giant Hymir. The list of Óðinn's children and mistresses is long and varied, and he was indeed prepared to take on any willing flesh, much as the local potentates may have done around the Icelandic countryside.

Frigg was the typical submissive wife who saw and accepted her husband's adultery and bastards by a variety of paramours. This made her symbolic of the Icelandic prosperous farmer's wife who sat quietly by while her husband performed in other beds. Might her counter move have been to cheat on her old man? Once, when Óðinn had been away for a long time and everyone thought he was dead, his brothers Vé and Vili split his inheritance between them and both married Frigg and went to bed with her. This was a love triangle involving two men having sex with one woman. When Óðinn returned, the brothers left Frigg in a hurry while Óðinn put on his pyjamas and crawled into his wife's bed as if nothing had happened.

The eldest son on the farmstead

The eldest son was *Thór*, god of the heavens and fertility, who encouraged the vegetation and greening of the earth. Thór was straightforward and simple, travelled a lot, got along with everyone and cared little about his appearance. He was in charge of security and was a danger to all enemies of the gods. Thór's home was Thrúdvangur where he lived with his wife, Sif, and their children, Módi and Thrúdur. Little is known, in fact, about their home life in Thrúdvangur, since Thór was constantly travelling and never at home.

Many a story tells of Thór's womanising as is traditional with lusty farmers' sons. "He's a chip off the old block", people would say. He lay once with the neighbouring giant Öskrud's 18 daughters, one after another, during a sex orgy. This caused a lot of talk and Öskrud was unhappy with his daughters after this revelry. Thór had his son, Magni, with the giant Járnsaxa after a one night stand.

Thór.

Eventually Thór's wife, *Sif*, decided to follow her husband's example and cheat on him. Loki Laufeyjarson, a sly and treacherous lad from a nearby farmstead, claimed to have had passionate intercourse with her and cut off her hair as evidence. This made Thór so furious he threatened to break every bone in Loki's body, but spared him when they finally managed to make a deal. Loki promised to get the dwarves to make replacement hair out of gold that would grow from Sif's head. Loki here appealed to greed in Thór, who decided to forgive the adultery when he saw the gleam of gold. This is reminiscent of the Saga period, when any man who had sex with a woman not his wife was forced to pay her husband or guardian a high fine. The atmosphere in Thór and Sif's farm was one of cool and stony silence when the subject of cheating came up.

Thór's hammer, Mjölnir, was his weapon, his attribute and, naturally, his phallic symbol. He used it to break the heads of the enemies of the gods. The giants of Jötunheim did once manage to steal Thór's hammer and it was an urgent matter to retrieve it. King Thrymir of Jötunheim said he would give back the hammer if he could have the goddess Freyja for his wife. He loved her from afar and would do anything to share her bed. She adamantly refused to marry Thrymir, so Thór decided to dress himself as a bride and pretend to be Freyja, though he feared he would be thought homosexual if he did so. The gods helped him dress as a woman and he set off for his own wedding with keys hanging from his belt, a necklace on his chest and a skirt fluttering around his knees. Loki accompanied him in the guise of Freyja's bond maid.

He managed to fool everyone in Jötunheim and trick the hammer out of them, though he almost gave himself away several times as his behaviour at the feast was anything but ladylike. He bolted his food, drank too much, belched and in no way resembled the genteel bride the groom had expected.

Óðinn preparing to enter Gunnlöd's cave.

Loki, as ladies maid, had to make excuses for this battle-axe of a bride, saying she had been so excited about the wedding that she had been unable to sleep for days.

It is astonishing that Thór should have been prepared to dress in women's clothing, considering that such behaviour was punishable according to Norse law, being considered a sign of cowardice and homo-sexuality. During the charade he was neither man nor woman or both man and woman. The mythology created an asexual being that was at the same time full of sexual energy. Thór signed on to the sex-change process of our time, where the boundary between the sexes is unclear and tradi-tional stereotypes are discarded. When he got his hands on the hammer, he returned to being your traditional man dressed in a woman's bridal trappings, swung Mjölnir with his usual enthusiasm and killed everyone at the feast, the groom, his friends and his family. Love was the death of the giant Thrymir, as it has been for so many others. Thus this marriage ended with a bang and a clatter before it started. Thór slipped into his natural sexual role once he reclaimed his phallic symbol.

Thór was like the good farmer's son who looked after his inheritance with exceptional loyalty. He was not as much of a womaniser as the head of the farmstead, since he was, after all, more interested in defence than sex. Thór was a self-centred, childish and violent character who had faith in his own strength. In the Edda, Ódinn and Thór appeared as allies who complemented each other. While Ódinn gained power over women with cunning and violence, Thór used his hammer. He was constantly travelling to protect the world from giants and other riff-raff that sought to create confusion and chaos. He was the epitome of masculinity, a universal cop waving his raised member at the world.

Njördur and Skadi

One of the smaller farmers on this big farmstead of ours was a distant relative, *Njördur*. He was a fertility god and god of fishermen and seafarers. The story of Njördur's bride is interesting and reflects the constant bickering between the gods and the giants. The giant Thjasi had kidnapped one of the goddesses, Idunn, who guarded the golden apples that were meant to keep the gods forever young. Loki Laufeyjarson had helped him commit the crime. Something had to be done because the gods were becoming old and senile and fast going grey when Idunn was not there with her apples. They soon realised that Loki was in some way responsible for this untimely aging and did not rest until they managed to reclaim Idunn with her apples. The giant Thjasi died a painful death in the struggle.

Family ties were strong on the farmsteads of both gods and giants. Thjasi's daughter, *Skadi*, rushed to the home of the gods, fully armed, to take revenge. The gods wanted to come to an agreement and as compensation for her father offered her the chance to choose a husband from among the gods. However, the condition was that when choosing, she would see only the legs of the gods. The gods here created an amusing party game where they strolled around bare-legged behind a curtain and the young giantess Skadi studied the legs. She chose the most beautiful, thinking that she had chosen Baldur, the most beautiful of the gods. This was not the case, however. They belonged to Njördur.

She and Njördur were married but were profoundly unhappy. Njördur wanted to live by the sea, Skadi up in the mountains. They tried a compromise of living nine days in each place, moving back and forth. But Njördur could not stand the howling of the wolves

The death of Thjasi.

in the mountains, nor Skadi the cries of the seagulls by the shore. Their marriage fell apart; this story describes a marital problem in the home of the gods which is in many ways similar to the problems of present-day people who live one in each country and try all kinds of compromises to save the relationship. This usually doesn't work any better than it did for the marriage of Njördur and Skadi. Eventually they solved it by living in an unhappy long-distance relationship, Njördur in Nóatún on the farmstead, Skadi in Thrymheimur in Jötunheim. The story of Skadi shows the situation of many women who end up with a man totally different than the one they thought they were marrying. In the *Íslendingasögur*, we find accounts of women who marry their father's slayer, as Skadi did. A woman is just any old plunder that the victor can do with as he likes.

Before Skadi and Njördur married, he had two children by his nameless sister. These were the twins and gods of fertility, Freyr and Freyja. Such children were of course morally out of bounds; it was strictly forbidden to have a child by your sister. This relationship may have been based on a real event, where a girl was given to her father's killer, an older man and father of two.

Freyja

Njördur's children and his sister had their farm on the farmstead of the gods. The best known was *Freyja*, the most exquisite and amorous of the goddesses. She was deemed the most beautiful girl in the district, greatly lusted after by the giants while she herself longed for both men and money. She lived at Fólkvangur (yet another smallholding) along with the cats that drew her chariot. Freyja's husband was Ódur, and their daughter was Hnoss. Ódur had gone away long before and Freyja still mourned for her husband and searched for him in vain. She hid her identity on these long journeys and used various names.

Freyja had a strikingly beautiful necklace called Brisingamen. She had once happened to see into a cave where four dwarves were making the necklace. She tried to buy it off them for gold and jewels but they said they would only sell it for sex with the goddess. She agreed to this and spent one night with each dwarf. When Loki told Ódinn about this, he forced Loki to get the necklace for him. Loki got into Freyja's chamber in the form of a fly. She was lying on her stomach, so Loki had to sting her to get her to move so he could reach the necklace. This is a sexual story, where Freyja slept with the four dwarves to acquire the necklace, and Loki stuck his stinger in her to get it back off her. Freyja went to Ódinn and demanded the necklace back. He refused, saying she had acquired it dishonestly. He had been Freyja's lover and treated her badly, as he did all his mistresses. No one seems to know why Ódinn wanted the necklace.

Freyja is a pitiful goddess of love. Her marriage is unhappy, her husband being lost. Her long wait for Ódur mirrors the reality of many women of the time. Men went on viking raids and were lost. Ships sank between Iceland and Norway so that many women will have had years of uncertainty as to the fate of their husbands and sons. Freyja never stopped hoping but searched constantly for her husband, even if she had minor love affairs along the way. The fact that she hid her identity during the search suggests that she suspected Ódur did not want to be found. Freyja would appear to have had a dwarf fetish, sleeping with four dwarves to get her hands on the necklace. Sex with a beautiful woman will buy anything. This goddess travelled around in a chariot drawn by cats, which underlined her lack of control over her own life, since cats can never be controlled. The life of this goddess of love is as complex and tangled as love itself. People would invoke Freyja in matters of love, as she was not only beautiful but had a varied sex-life.

Gefjun

Another goddess living on the farmstead of the gods was *Gefjun*. She was served by those women who died virgins. A woman's importance was greatly dependent on her fertility. A girl who died without having had sex got to serve Gefjun in the afterlife as compensation. What this service involved is never defined. Could it be that Gefjun was homosexual and was happiest in the company of chaste young women? There is no mention of young male virgins having such a sanctuary.

Freyr

Freyja's brother, the fertility god *Freyr, son of Njördur,* controlled the rain, sun and fruits of the earth. His wife was the giantess Gerdur, daughter of Gymir. Freyr saw her from his seat in Hlidskjálf and immediately fell in love. He sent his servant Skírnir to gain the girl's hand. Skírnir offered her all kinds of riches, such as eleven golden apples and a famous ring, if she would accept Freyr, but she steadfastly refused. He threatened her with all kinds of punishments if she would not marry Freyr, but she wouldn't give in. It was only when the threats became sexual that she gave in. Skírnir said he would deprive her of any pleasure with a man.

A dreadful troll, who would give her nothing but goat urine to drink, would get her to have and to use as he wished. He also threatened her with period pains, homosexuality and madness, until Gerdur saw the writing on the wall and agreed to marry Freyr nine nights later. Their son's name was Fjölnir.

Ancient sources often mention the rites of Freyr. The most famous of these rites were in Uppsala in Sweden, where they raised a giant phallus in honour of the god. The people prayed, sang and danced around the phallus. The historian Adam of Bremen said the songs were so immoral that he shrank from writing them down. Many other Christian writers maintain that women had shown provocative movements and sexual posturing. Sacred sexual relations or orgiastic sex were part of the ceremony, so these rites must have been quite exciting. A few small statuettes of Freyr have survived, most of which show the god with an erection, which is, of course, a fertility symbol.

Freyr becomes the embodiment of man's superiority to woman. The erect penis is endowed with power and magic that can conquer anything. It is noteworthy that despite all his sexual power, Freyr had only one son with his wife Gerdur, he was not as lustful as the other gods, so he seems to have preferred showing his penis to using it. Freyr got Gerdur through threats and mental cruelty, which did not bode well for the marriage. These perils reflect the reality for many women in the world of men. They experience mental and physical cruelty before and after marriage.

The worship of Freyr

In the Norsemen's worship of Freyr, the ancient worship of the penis is evident, as we see in the tale of King Ólafur helgi (holy) Haraldsson and his encounter with Völsi. Ólafur came once to a farm in Northern Norway where an old couple lived with their children, slave and other people. That autumn, the farmer's work horse had died. The slave cut off the horse's penis and the farmer's son took it into the common room and showed it to the people of the household. The mistress of the house took the penis, dried it and then brought it out every evening and chanted in its honour, naming it Völsi. Little by little, the penis became a god for the old woman and her family. In the evening they would pass it around and each of them would recite some amusing lewd verses. All of which strengthened Völsi so much that he could stand by the mistress whenever she wanted. When Ólafur came to the farm, in disguise, the lady of the house tried to get him to take part in the ceremony. She brought out the phallus and recited a verse. The King was angry, threw the phallus to the farm dog, and exhorted the household to Christianity. The old woman tried to rescue Völsi but failed. After much persuasion, the people of the farm were all christened, but Völsi ended up in a dog's stomach.

Loki and *Lokasenna* (Loki's Rant)

Of the residents in the home of the gods, *Loki Laufeyjarson* is the most difficult to define. In the younger myths he often reminds us of Satan himself, and indeed, one could say that Loki is the representative of evil in the home of the gods. He relates with the gods as equals. Loki has many faces and many different natures. He is definitely not a purely evil devil, rather a sly and mischievous trickster. Loki tricks the gods and breaks the rules they have made.

His sex life was complicated and his progeny dismal. He had three dreadful children with a troll-giantess named

Loki.

31

Reflections of a psychiatrist

It is difficult to infer much about the sexual behavior of Icelanders from the mythology. The gods were promiscuous and people in the Saga period saw reason to prohibit by law much that went on in Valhalla. Adultery by married women was, of course, forbidden by law and a husband was allowed to punish anyone who seduced his wife. Homosexuality was strictly forbidden and there were penalties for such behaviour. Incest was forbidden under pain of severe punishment. Despite being almighty and having power over land and sea, gods were like men, victims of their own libido which often worked against them and gave Loki a reason to abuse them and vilify in Lokasenna. Lust plays an important role among the gods as it does in the world of men.

The author of Lokasenna appears to have painted an exaggerated picture of his times, presented in a humorous context. It was easier to place this abuse in Loki's mouth as he berates the gods, than to speak out openly about his friends and neighbours. He knows that all kinds of adultery and immorality are practiced in the shelter of secrecy and cover ups. This he describes graphically but lets Loki do the talking. The author uses comic hyperbole, making the poem unbelievable while at the same time critical of the world of the old gods. The gods are made to look ridiculously vain and banal but also quite human.

But the gods honored certain core principles that also applied in the world of men. Patriarchy was absolute and men played the major role in the Valhalla dwellers' conflicts with their environment. The women were more often than not neutral observers of the conflicts and decisions of men, which they had to respect. The gods of the Greek and the Nordic people were different in many ways, but their family life was very similar, characterized by the man's total control in the home.

Angurboda (she who brings misery): the wolf Fenrir, Hel (lord/lady of the underworld) and Midgardsormur (earth-circling serpent), all of whom are involved in Ragnarök, the twilight of the gods.

Loki was actually also the mother of Ódinn's eight-legged horse, Sleipnir. Loki had changed himself into a mare in order to appeal to a stallion owned by the giants. When he saw the entrancing mare the stallion immediately got carried away with lust. He ran off as his erect penis directed, leaving the giants without a horse, so they lost this particular skirmish with the gods. Yet again the sex drive plays a major role. Loki's metamorphosis here is reminiscent of many stories in Greek mythology, where Zeus takes on the form of animals in order to carry out his plans. Loki leaves the traditional male role for a female role, switches from perpetrator to victim.

The death of Baldur.

In the wedding of Skadi and Njördur in Jötunheim, the gods were meant to make Skadi laugh, but it was not going well. She was unhappy with her bridegroom, feeling that her father-slayer had deceived her. The gods made various attempts to please the bride, but she was not amused. Then Loki tied a string around his genitals and got a goat to pull the other end of the string. They pulled back and forth screeching loudly and eventually this made Skadi laugh. In this case Loki was offering up his genitals to be laughed at, which makes one think of contemporary BDSM games, where people tie all kinds of things to their genitals for their own pleasure and the amusement of others.

Loki was the only one in Ásgard who had a lively sense of humour. In the poem *Lokasenna* (Loki's Rant), the Gods were at a party and got very drunk. Loki was kicked out for indecorous behaviour but he wanted to keep drinking and came back, like an obnoxious customer who has been expelled from a restaurant. They let Loki in and he began to castigate the gods. His critique was based mostly on rumours he said he had heard about them. The gossip about the gods had to do with homosexuality, lack of manliness and their wives' infidelity, all most ignominious. Loki's imagery was based on women and their lower body parts. He told each god/goddess in turn to be silent and then started his harangue. In this way he went on to deal with pretty much every single one.

Loki maintained the the daughters of Hymir had used him as a piss-pot and urinated in his mouth. This was of course extremely humiliating and the question is whether Loki is here referring to some surreptitious sexual practices. Loki appears to have known all about various piss fetishes which are familiar in modern day sex studies. He also reproached Njördur for having fathered Freyr with his sister, which was punishable incest. He accused Ódinn of sorcery and homosexuality, so the gloves were off. "Homosexual yourself", was Ódinn's answer, which tells us the gods' dialectic skills hardly reached the level of a high school debating society.

Freyja advised Loki to keep quiet lest evil ensue. But he paid no attention and carried on until Thór turned up like some bouncer, shaking his hammer in the face of the party-pooper. Loki gave up when confronted with the power and authority of the thunder god, backed away from the party and was permanently excluded from the society of the gods.

The influence of Christianity

At the meeting of the Althing in the year 1000, the Lawspeaker Thorgeir Thorkellsson godi (priest/chieftain) of Ljosavatn concluded, after careful thought, that Iceland should become Christian. He allowed, however, for people to dally with the old traditions, as long as they were discreet. They could still secretly eat horse meat and expose newborns to the elements and do various other things that were a matter of course in heathen times. Christianisation was peaceful and bloodless, and it probably took a century or two for this new religion to become firmly established. People were not eager to accept foreign control of the church and obey directives from abroad, not even in the name of religion. However, little by little, the church did come into its own, becoming the most powerful institution in the country for centuries. The two bishoprics were the country's capitals, and had the largest educational establishments and populations.

The Christian church had definite, negative opinions about sex and the sexual behaviour of its subjects. Straightaway in the first century AD, the Apostle Paul declared that celibacy was more pleasing to God than marriage. He did, in fact, admit that it was slightly better to marry than to burn with lust. The church's basic doctrine was that sex should be practiced for procreation only, not for pleasure. They said that all sex beyond the bare necessity was a sin and extremely unhealthy. The Íslendingasögur were written by Christians so Christian attitudes are widely evident in the books even though they describe a heathen period in our history. The authors of the Sagas could not comfortably speak openly or positively about sex, so they refrained from describing things of that sort.

The patriarchy of the Sagas comes from both heathen times and Christianity, which placed great emphasis on the subservience of women and the superiority of men and their right to make all decisions. According to the teachings of the church, lust was evil and it was vital for every Christian man to keep his desires under control. The fall from grace and expulsion from Paradise could be traced to temptation and lust. The Old Testament abounds in all kinds of instructions and prohibitions regarding sex. Warnings against women and women's nature are extensive and of course the fall from grace and its consequences was still fresh in the minds of those men. Heavy emphasis is placed on the superiority of the man and his role as controller of his household.

According to the church's teachings, sex could only take place when the purpose was procreation. People were not to have any other sex and men were forbidden to bestow their semen anywhere else than in the vagina of a woman where there might be some expectant little eggs waiting. Anal sex was strictly forbidden as were oral sex and masturbation. This brings us back to the belief in the godly power and sanctity of the semen that was entrusted to every man.

The church meddled in the timing of sex. Intercourse was allowed only on Mondays, Tuesdays and Thursdays. On Wednesdays and Fridays people were meant to fast; Sunday was of course totally sacred and Saturday was too near to Sunday. Intercourse was not allowed during menstruation, pregnancy, for 33-56 days after birth, 40 days before Christmas and Easter and four weeks before Whitsun. People were allowed to make love about three to four times a month on average, so there were restrictions on frequency. Anyone who broke these rules was in danger of bearing disfigured children and losing their own soul's salvation. The Devil was ever nearby. Not least in the marriage bed, where he tempted people to give in to their sex drive and turn a deaf ear to the message of the church. The church gained from the sinful living of its subjects because people confessed to all kinds of transgressions and their punishment would be fines as well as prayers.

Men of the church considered that love should first and foremost be spiritual, and the greatest virtue of all was the love of God. The cravings of the flesh came from the evil one and nothing was more important than triumphing in one's battle with him. Sex was for the purpose of increasing mankind and not at all for pleasure of any kind. All this will, of course, have influenced the authors of the *Íslendingasögur*. Occasionally they attempt to get around this negative attitude but they found it difficult.

The Spirit of the Age

The *Íslendingasögur* are largely about conflict and revenge. There was no actual executive in the country, and individuals had to protect their rights themselves with the help of relatives and chieftains. Whether it was possible to get men convicted of an offense and punished for it depended on your kindred. Public administration and power were entirely in the hands of men. This absence of a centralised executive was the weakness of this period and gradually brought the commonwealth to an end. The spirit of the age was characterised by a complete lack of respect for people's lives and emotions. Fathers got rid of their daughters' unwanted suitors by killing them. Cuckolded husbands did not hesitate to kill their rivals. Men would resolve conflicts and problems by getting rid of inconvenient players in the game. This was particularly useful for the rich and powerful who had no need to fear the revenge of the poor and vulnerable. The society of the Sagas was a society of the strong who could use violence without fearing consequences.

In the Sagas, honour was paramount. Men were constantly defending their honour with litigation or weapons. One can't help noticing how much of the violence in the Sagas was ignoble. Great heroes never hesitated to take advantage of greater strength, attack their enemies with a mob and kill them. Might was right, since there were no police or other recognised authorities. Victory belonged to him who had lots of cunning, lots of money, and no scruples about reaching his goals.

This was a society of insecurity and fear. Everyone had weapons and many did not hesitate to use them in even the paltriest of arguments. A man could condemn himself or others to death with a careless word or an unlucky joke. Conditions were perfect for humourless, touchy men who were easily insulted and always ready to defend their supposed honour with violence.

All that killing obviously upset the equilibrium of people's lives. After the burning of Njáll, Kári Sólmundarson killed almost twenty people in revenge. They were all farmers, providers, fathers, sons, members of society. This revenge left a great many fatherless children, widows and other survivors. Many productive men lost their lives, with associated changes in the fortunes of others. This is rarely discussed in the Sagas. Their main subjects are killing and revenge, not the reactions of mourners.

It was common for young Icelanders to go on raids with Nordic military kings and seafarers. They would sail their ships from Scandinavia, raiding in England, France and elsewhere. Swedish Vikings raided towards the east into Russia. Wherever they came, Vikings were particularly loathed as they were merciless butchers. They killed the inhabitants or enslaved them, stole any valuables, raped women and burned people's homes and churches. The evil deeds of the Vikings were well known throughout Northern Europe where people feared these visits like the plague.

The Vikings asserted that the more terrifying they were, the less was the resistance of the local people. Therefore they behaved with absolute ruthlessness and savagery as indeed invading armies have always done. They aimed to destroy 20 to 30 civilians for each fighting man who was slain, a standard maintained in wars ever since. The Vikings played all kinds of games to fill the locals with terror. They would throw babies in the air and catch them on their spear-heads, saying this was good for the children because that kind of death marked them as Óðinn's. There were all kinds of stories about the sex lives of these barbarians. They would rape any woman they could get hold of, so their violence was also sexual. Vikings would enslave women and sell them on to be sex slaves or otherwise serve their masters. The authors of the *Íslendingasögur* are very impressed by these raiding expeditions, calling them a maturing rite of passage for young men. Yet little is written about the violent, criminal activities of the Vikings on these raids. There is no reason to doubt that the Icelanders who participated in them enjoyed themselves, like other Vikings, murdering infants and raping women and girls. Some of the greatest heroes and noble gentlemen of the Sagas, such as Gunnar Hámundarson and Gunnlaugur *ormstunga* (worm-tongue), participated in such raids. Possibly their heroic lustre would be somewhat tarnished if their achievements on Viking raids were described in detail in the Sagas.

Sex on the farms

Human beings have never had much success in beating down the sex drive. The church had its rules and threatened excommunication and severe punishments while powerful men ignored these instructions and kept concubines and mistresses at will. But what was the everyday reality on the farms around the country. What about ordinary people?

All over the country were different sized turf farms, all cramped and crowded, where people were crammed together in a single skáli or *bad-stofa* (common room). These living quarters were very confined and people were always close to one another. Their beds, usually occupied by more than one sleeper, were lined head to foot along the walls, and many children slept together on a pallet. Although attempts were made to maintain decency, there was always the danger that people would stray into forbidden beds, guided by lust alone. There is no doubt that many illegitimate children were born in this society though they are seldom mentioned in the Sagas.

Strict rules as to the minimum property a couple must have in order to marry meant that many were unable to get married, but people did, of course, have sex lives then as always. Not all children will have been attributed to the right father then, any more than now, and it is likely that fertile farm owners made their farm hands admit to fathering children they had nothing to do with. Yet there are few accounts of such things in the Sagas. In fact, it would have carried heavy responsibility to maintain that someone was attributed to the wrong father, due to the many ramifications it might entail. In recent years, people have built replicas of the commonwealth period farms. It is interesting to see the accommodation that people put up with and imagine what it was like to live in these small, crowded farms. They were isolated, the darkness long and black, winters bitter cold and temptations of the flesh all around. People prepared for bed, undressed completely, placing their underclothes beneath the pillow, or slept in their linen. No doubt sexual tension was high in these common rooms where naked people lay within reach of each other under their blankets. Children witnessed the sex lives of their parents and others, sexual activity being difficult to hide in such a crowd. This brings to mind the claims of many psychologists that children never recover from seeing their parents having intercourse. Many people nowadays largely deny themselves a sex life for fear their children might accidentally see or hear their sexual activity.

People worked together in sel (mountain dairies) and the various out buildings, so there were plenty of opportunities to let their hair down and set emotions free. There are few accounts of such meetings in the Sagas, which seldom dealt with everyday life on small farms. History totters along like an unsteady toddler, treading the narrow path of temptation, punishment, emotions, love and hate, arriving little by little at the society we know best today. Many take some false steps but get away with it as usual.

In comparing the attitudes of heathen and Christian to promiscuity and having children, we see that they are quite similar. First and foremost, they were trying to keep down unlimited and untimely procreation. Everyone knew that paupers were a burden in the homes of common people. It was thus vital that such dependents were not having children that the society would then have to take responsibility for. The church clad its struggle against undesirable paupers in the dress clothes of doctrine, which heathens did not do. The church's way of preventing people from visiting each other's beds was to say that the sex drive came from the Devil. Thus it tried to scare people away from sex and direct them into the safe harbour of marriage. The problem was that the harbour entrance was blocked by various rules and regulations about minimum property and finances. Thus many had little chance of marrying but had to struggle with their sex drive in the high seas of impulse, emotion, and daily temptation. Some wandered from the path and the result was a child that grew up to be a farm hand on a prosperous farm only to get in trouble with his or her own sex drive when the time came. Adultery and bastards were a source of income for the church since people often had to pay fines for their sins if they were to have any hope of redemption and forgiveness. The church gained substantially from the sins it fought hardest against, which reveals a certain hypocrisy.

Marriage: ancient and modern

The Old Testament instructs a woman and a man to leave their parents to join together in life and have children and a family. This was the obligation the Lord of Hosts laid on Adam and Eve after the fall. The same is true in Norse mythology. The brothers Vili and Vé were walking along the beach and found two trees which they changed into a man and a woman. Óðinn gave them spirit and life, and they were called Askur and Embla. Vili gave them understanding and power and Vé language, vision and hearing. The gods dressed them in clothing and smiling they held hands as they faced life. All mankind comes from Askur and Embla.

In spite of significant changes in people's life circumstances, marriage has endured. It has withstood a variety of storms and other forms of cohabitation. Such forms as communes and polygamy have been tried, but the relationship between two people has turned out best. Marriage is a framework for the fertility of people who can work together for the good of the family. The rights of spouses and their heirs are defined in law. For centuries, men were expected to be totally in charge within the marriage, this being the basis of patriarchy. Much has changed over the centuries. In recent years, same-sex marriages have been consecrated, unthinkable only a few years ago. Divorce and remarriage are more common than ever. Nowadays, equal rights within marriage are considered a matter of course and patriarchy is in retreat. Today's western man, when he hears the words "marriage" and "wedding", envisages a bride in white and bridegroom in black promising each other eternal devotion in a beautiful church before a smiling pastor. In the ceremony, the pastor follows an ancient ritual, quoting the words of the Saviour on the subject of marriage. Nowadays, prospective married couples turn to many others than the church who have the right to marry them: magistrates, the heathen high priest or the representatives of various other religions. But the form of the ceremony makes no difference to the content and purpose. The bride and groom can be a man and a woman, two men or two women.

The bride and groom make their own decision to marry and their friends and family have little to do with it. Modern Western societies all agree that the choice of a spouse is the responsibility of the prospective partners, outside the sphere of influence of parents or other family. The parents of the couple usually do not know each other before their children decide to tie the knot, and are seldom consulted about it. People are expected to learn about love itself without the intervention of others. Modern parents are grateful if they are allowed to give a generous present and cover the cost of the reception, otherwise they have nothing to do with the preparation and execution of the wedding. Sometimes the father gets to lead his daughter down the aisle to the accompaniment of loud organ music, but such performances are in decline.

At the time of the *Íslendingasögur* and *Sturlunga,* it was most often

the fathers of the couple who made all decisions about the wedding and marriage of their children, and no one thought to base the marriage of two young people on such vague ideas as love and affection. Few even knew their meaning and considered love to be something of a curse.

Marriage should be based on reason, not some emotional foolishness, since the point of it was a contract between two families which would unite in the marriage of the young folk. They were not asked about the match and rarely even knew each other beforehand.

People's opinions about love were unlike those now in fashion.

Caritas (charity) was one of the three virtues of the Church (faith, hope and charity), characterized by love of God and one's neighbour, not the cravings of the flesh (*cupiditas*). Sometimes a marriage was said to be a lust-match where emotions (*lust*) had been the agent, not the omniscient and rational fathers of the couple. In such cases, *cupiditas* had overcome *caritas*; the flesh had overcome the spirit, which was seldom a good thing. Churchmen spoke sometimes of true love (*agape*) which bore no relation to the physical or spiritual love between men and women, but was the love of man for God and His love of mankind. *Agape* was beyond human experience and above the understanding of mortals.

In today's marriages, the bridal pair know each other in and out and have a child or two as often as not. They have often lived together for a while, so the wedding night brings few surprises. In Saga times, the couple were often just getting to know each other in the drunken noise of the wedding reception. Add the fact that sometimes they were in their teens and one can imagine clumsy approaches and unhappy wedding nights when the young couple finally shared a bed. The first intercourse of a married couple put the seal on the legality of the union, so it was important that it go well.

Grágás (the Grey Goose Laws), marriages and inheritance

The laws of the Commonwealth established the ownership of men over women. It was as well for a woman to accept the fact that she had very little control over her own life. Men had historical and divine rights over their women within the family and elsewhere. It is not surprising that many an oppressed husband in our day should look with regret to those times when the word of the husband was law which women were bound to obey.

Patriarchy is dominant in *Grágás* along with an emphasis on family ties. Many legal provisions protect men's right of possession over women, especially over their fertility. Women were not to be trusted and could ascribe to their husbands a child that some young idiot had popped into their womb.

A father's ownership of his daughter was absolute, and men appeared to look on daughters as property like any other, which could accrue interest through an auspicious marriage. The rule was that the closest male relative (usually the father) betrothed them to a man. Women had little say as to whom they married and were not expected to meddle in it. Men's right to choose a spouse, negotiate a betrothal and control family finances was a good deal greater than that of women.

Hallgerdur and Gudrún

The fathers of Hallgerdur *langbrók* (long pants) in *Brennu-Njáls saga* (the Saga of Burnt Njáll) and Gudrún Ísvífursdóttir in *Laxdæla* both gave them in marriage at the age of 14, to men the girls despised and had no interest in. By a strange coincidence, both these men were named Thorvaldur. Hallgerdur was very annoyed when her father gave her to this man she felt was not worthy of her. In the wedding feast, her *fóstri* (foster father), Thjóstólfur, and she had many private conversations, with much noisy laughter. She was utterly contemptuous of the groom in her own wedding and paid much more attention to her *fóstri*, Thjóstólfur, who had at that time, already begun abusing her sexually in spite of her youth. Hallgerdur and Thorvald's short marriage was stormy. Her husband considered Hallgerdur extravagant and scolded her for it. She answered him back and he hit her. Hallgerdur showed Thjóstólfur the mark of it and he immediately went to her husband and, after a short conversation, killed him. The male community is here confounded by Hallgerdur, who is using their tactics.

Instead of withdrawing, weeping and accepting Thorvaldur's domestic violence, she looks to Thjóstólfur, who avenges her wrongs in a fitting manner. He will, of course, have received appropriate payment.

Gudrún was very unhappy with her Thorvaldur and felt they were in no way equals. He, on the other hand, was prepared to do anything to gain the lady and accepted unusually harsh conditions to ensure the marriage. She was to be in charge of their money and he was to buy for her any such treasures as she wanted and pointed out. This is a marriage agreement that most modern women could well accept. Gudrún immediately became very demanding and made poor Thorvaldur buy all kinds of objects he could ill afford. After one such buying spree he slapped her face as if she were a naughty child. She then got out of the relationship with the aid of her lover, Thórdur Ingunnarson, who encouraged her to divorce Thorvaldur on the grounds that he wore a woman's shirt. They divorced and she ran straight into the arms of Thórdur, who was waiting for his beauty like a knight in shining armour. This is similar to many affairs today, where the participants make plans about and aid each other's divorces. Nothing is known about the sex life of Gudrún and Hallgerdur with the two Thorvaldurs, but both relationships were childless. We will look again at these two in the chapters about *Laxdæla* and *Brennu-Njáls saga*, but neither girl will have been compliant towards her husband. In fact, they both show strong symptoms of personality disorder and immaturity, and behave accordingly. One neglected her household duties and the other spent every penny her husband had. Both had lovers they treated better than they treated their husbands, Hallgerdur sleeping with Thjóstólfur and Gudrún with Thórdur Ingunnarson (who was actually also married). Both of these marriages end with a bang: Hallgerdur's with a murder and Gudrún's with a divorce. Both could be taking place today with the accompanying drama, fornication and childishness. The girls are, in fact, so young that people nowadays would not hesitate to call both the Thorvaldurs child abusers. The attitude toward teen marriage was very different then, being more like what we now see in many Eastern countries where child brides are numerous. The authors of the Sagas had full sympathy with these unfortunate husbands who thought they had gained happiness but both came to a tragic end.

The sons of Njáll

Brennu-Njáls saga tells how the farmer and lawyer Njáll Thorgeirsson of Bergthórshvol chooses a wife for each and every one of his sons. The sons had no say in the matter and knew little about their wives-to-be. Njáll made the decisions in consultation with the boys' prospective fathers-in-law, building up his sphere of influence.

The brief story of the marriage of Njáll's son Skarphédinn, the greatest hero among the brothers, is interesting. He is described as insolent, humourless and unwilling to take advice. When Njáll suggested Skarphédinn should marry, his son asked him to take care of it. Njáll then suggested to Thórhildur Hrafnsdóttir that she marry Skarphédinn and this was agreed on. There is no sign that Skarphédinn had his eye on any other young woman in the county, nor that he had any opinion about his prospective wife.

In fact, little is known about this Thórhildur or about the marriage itself, but Skarphédinn can hardly have been the easiest man to live with. This choice of a wife was considered insignificant since the girl came from a small farm, not an important one. They had no children, for whatever reason. Skarphédinn was obsessed with his arch-enemy at Hlídarendi, Hallgerdur. He was green with envy because of her influence and sex appeal, hated her while also admiring her beauty and elegance. This may have troubled his and Thórhildur's sex life, as so often happens in such cases.

The other sons' marriages were arranged in the same way. From Njáll's point of view, all these lads were pretty much dependent. Two of the sons remained with their father even after marriage. One can't help wondering what their sex lives were like under their parent's watchful eye; they had few children. The same was true of Njáll's three daughters who also remained at Bergthórshvoll as married women. Actually, the author of *Brennu-Njáls saga* has so little regard for them that they are only mentioned in passing and have very minor roles in the Saga. Marriage in those days was just like a lottery where you could be lucky with a prize or especially unlucky like the two Thorvaldurs who married Gudrún and Hallgerdur.

The catch word for this time could be "Father knows best". When marriages were arranged, the groom was hardly adult and the bride completely dependent. Today's fathers are envious and jealous when they look to that period: fatherly advice and decisions were treated with respect. Now they feel grateful if they are invited to the wedding, but they do not make decisions. The bride and groom have taken over these matters and want no advice. Njáll and other adult men of the Saga period would have thought today's father's influence over his children's lives pretty sparse. The existential crisis of many men probably comes from this lack of influence over their own families, where everyone goes his or her own way, taking advice from their cell phones rather than their wise fathers.

Yet a girl's consent was sometimes sought

In spite of their undisputed power over their young daughters, there are a few examples of fathers who consulted their daughters when a young man asked for their hands in marriage. When Bolli Bollason, in *Laxdæla*, proposed to marry Thórdís Snorradóttir, the proposal was put to her father, who wanted to get his daughter's agreement.

She had no objection and said she would marry Bolli. It would have been hard for her to reject him, since he was the most elegant of men, dressed like a fashion model. He came riding up dressed in furs, presented to him by the king of Russia or the emperor of Constantinople with a golden helmet on his head and a sword in his hand. Wherever he

went, women stared longingly at this splendid specimen. However, the descriptions in the Sagas of a vain peacock such as Bolli barely disguise their tone of mockery. It is clear that men did everything they could to impress the chosen woman and their prospective parents-in-law.

When Höskuldur Dala-Kollsson proposed to marry Jórunn Bjarnardóttir from Bjarnarfjördur in *Laxdæla,* she was asked what she thought of the match. She said she had nothing against it, but her father should decide. She is described in the Saga as a determined, strong-willed woman, so the reader accepts that her father wanted her agreement. It would have been difficult, though, for the father and daughter to reject Höskuldur. He rode north to make his proposal dressed in his colourful best, with a ten-man retinue, so it would be clear to all that there went a great leader with a gleam in his eye. This led to their engagement and a delightful wedding. The marriage itself had ups and downs, and Höskuldur was far from faithful. He bought himself a mute slave and mistress, Melkorka. He brought her into the home and had a son by her, all of which caused a lot of jealousy, conflict and drama.

Eiríks saga rauda (the Saga of Eric the Red) tells of another marriage proposal. The freed slave Thorgeir at Thorgeirsfell had a son, Einar. The father and son had plenty of money. Einar was very handsome and always well-dressed. He proposed to Gudrídur Thorbjarnardóttir at Laugabrekka on the Snæfellsnes peninsula. Her father rejected it immediately because Einar was the son of a former slave. There is no mention of Gudrídur's reaction, which was irrelevant anyway. Her father was himself the son of Vífill, one of the slaves freed by Audur *djúpúdga* (the deep), so he was not all that highly bred himself. Shortly thereafter she went with her father to Greenland, where she married the son of Eiríkur *raudi*, Thorsteinn. He died from a debilitating fever and came back to haunt his wife. Eventually, she rid herself of this irritating ghost and found a new partner. Her second husband was the explorer, Thorfinnur karlsefni from Skagafjördur. Gudrídur became a traveller, sailing to North America with her husband, where she gave birth to a son, Snorri.

In her old age she went all the way to Rome and became a nun, or recluse, on the farm Glaumbær during the last years of her life. This adventurous woman has been much acclaimed, and is indeed the most travelled woman of the Saga period. Her story would have been quite different and less eventful had her father been less prejudiced and given his daughter to the handsome Einar, even though he was born of a slave. Statues have been erected in honour of both husband and wife, Gudrídur's at Laugarbrekka on Snæfellsnes and Thorfinnur's next to the retirement home *Hrafnista* in Reykjavík. Gudrídur is the only woman in the Sagas to have been honoured with her own monument.

An odd engagement

The rule was that fathers and other male guardians controlled the gift of a young woman's hand and there were few exceptions. The following account from *Finnboga sögu ramma* (the Saga of Finnbogi the strong) is unusually dramatic.

Finnbogi *rammi* Ásbjarnarson was only 17 when he went abroad to seek fame and fortune. He was one of those children of an important father who had been exposed at birth but rescued by a poor couple. They brought him up as their own son, naming him Urdarköttur. Gradually the truth emerged. The boy was so precocious and handsome that he could not be the son of these humble people. Urdarköttur's name and parentage were changed in one fell swoop, he moved away from his foster parents and was named Finnbogi Ásbjarnarson from then on. The Saga is silent about the separation anxiety and other mental distress that accompany such upheavals.

Finnbogi was very young when he went to Norway and met a certain Álfur, farmer and chieftain of Sandey Island. Álfur's wife was the niece of an Earl, so he was a man of some consequence. Their daughter was the maiden Ragnhildur. Álfur and Finnbogi were on their way out to Sandey when they got in an argument. Álfur tried to kill Finnbogi, but

51

lost his own life, Finnbogi being a strapping fellow despite his youth. What led to this conflict is uncertain and it's difficult to work out the course of events. Finnbogi rowed to Sandey on his own and said that Álfur had sent him to fetch Ragnhildur and bring her to the Earl. On the way there he told the girl he had killed her father and lied to her and her mother. She wept bitterly, but by the time they reached the Earl she had regained her good spirits. The Earl forgave him for the slaying once Finnbogi had completed some tasks he assigned him. He wrestled with a fearsome black man, competed with a bear in swimming and made a long journey to southern countries. He returned unscathed from these adventures and asked to have Ragnhildur Álfsdóttir for his wife. The Earl gave Finnbogi his niece, since with the death of Álfur he could bestow her without consulting others. Finnbogi was reconciled with her mother and he and his wife went to Iceland, where they had a happy marriage and two sons. The Saga mentions that they loved each other dearly. Both the sons were later killed by some evil thug whom Finnbogi then killed in revenge. After this, Ragnhildur took to her bed and died of grief. Finnbogi was devastated, having lost both his sons and his wife in a short period of time. It was said that nothing ever gave him peace of mind after that.

This is an odd story and it is hard to imagine how Ragnhildur felt. She named one of her sons Álfur in honour of her father, who had been killed by her husband. This was a complicated situation and no wonder that she retreated to her bed and left this vale of tears in the face of even greater tragedy. This psychiatrist wonders how a woman would feel, that sleeps with her father's killer. Of course it seems that women who lived after their fathers or guardians had died could be disposed of like any other spoils. Is there much missing from this story? What was the relationship between the father and daughter? Nothing is known of Finnbogi and Ragnhildur's sex life and it is hard to imagine that he would have courted her before it was all settled and the Earl had given Ragnhildur to her father's killer.

Finnbogi is one of those people who enter adulthood with severe attachment disorder. He was raised by strangers when his blood parents wanted nothing to do with him. They then suddenly decided to accept the boy and remove him from his foster parents. Finnbogi had difficulty showing emotional empathy or imagining himself in another's shoes. It is not unlikely that he found it hard to understand his wife's grief or despair at the loss of her father. After the death of Ragnhildur he remarried and had many children with a new wife.

Dallying

So-called *fiflingar* (dallying, lit. foolery) or the flirting of a young man with a young woman without the permission of father or guardian was strictly forbidden by *Grágás*. The father could give the young man a warning and ask him to desist. If he did not then stop his advances, he could legally be killed on sight. Thus the law protected the father's rights of property over his daughter, as well as his authority to decide to whom she spoke.

The Sagas warn young girls not to listen to the blandishments of the boys from nearby farms. It might cause them to lose their lives, because a vigilant father or brother was watching over the girl's virginity and reputation as a hawk watches over its young. The Sagas contain many examples of young men who are killed for repeated visits to a single girl living at home.

There are no detailed descriptions in the Sagas of young people's interactions. They mostly mention chatting and other innocent human contact in the monotony of their everyday lives. Young people must have been bored and wanted to get to know more than their own household. Hormones were in control and young folks enjoyed feeling the mysterious tension that accompanies contact with peers of the opposite sex. Probably there were occasions when they let passion take over in an isolated out building or elsewhere. Today, it is considered barbarous to condemn a lad to death for chatting, strolling or flirting, but for them it was a question of protecting their legal property from trespassers.

Gísli and the suitors

The opening chapters of *Gísla saga Súrssonar* (the Saga of Gísli Súrsson) describe a little family in Norway, a couple with their three sons and one daughter. One of the sons has left home and has no role in the story. There was a lot of tension around the daughter, Thórdís, who was beautiful and charming. The book tells of the visits of a young man named Bárdur to Thórdís. The siblings' father, Thorbjörn Súr, was highly displeased and in the spirit of the age, insisted that Bárdur stop these visits. Gísli, the hero of this Saga, discussed this with the lad, who said their father's anger was of no concern to him and continued visiting. There is no indication that Thórdís was other than happy with these visits. Thorbjörn remained foul-tempered about this and felt he was being dishonoured. He urged Gísli to punish Bárdur, which ended with him being killed. This slaying was not particularly heroic since Gísli surprised him when he was off guard.

Gísli had carried out the death sentence his father had pronounced. Thórdís, bless her heart, had no say in the matter and was never asked her opinion of the father and son's plan to kill the boy who visited her in the boredom of her days. Another suitor, Kolbjörn, turned up, but Gísli killed him also, after quite a struggle.

These explorations by Bárdur and Kolbjörn had serious consequences in this society of revenge. Many young men lost their lives in the conflicts that followed, until the Súr family left Norway and settled in Dyrafjördur in the north-west of Iceland. The plot of the whole Saga rests on these events, when young folks began to find each other attractive against the will of the girl's father and brothers. This triggered the dramatic course of events the Saga describes.

The beguiling Ingólfur Thorsteinnsson

Vatnsdæla saga tells of a renowned womaniser, Ingólfur Thorsteinnsson Ingimundarsonar from the farm Hof in the Vatnsdalur valley in Húnavatn County. His family was the richest and most powerful in the valley at the time. Once, Ingólfur was playing a ball game with his friends. Among those watching was the strikingly beautiful Valgerdur Óttarsdóttir, the sister of Hallgerdur *vandrædaskáld* (the problem poet). Their family was not as eminent as the family at Hof. Ingólfur threw the ball towards Valgerdur. She caught it, stuck it under her cloak and said that whoever had thrown it should come and get it. Ingólfur went to her, paid her compliments and flirted with her. In his opinion, she had been hitting on him when she played that trick with the ball. After this, he made frequent visits to Valgerdur, totally against the wishes of her father, Óttar, who feared Ingólfur would seduce his daughter and reduce her value on the marriage market. He went to discuss this with Thorsteinn, Ingólfur's father, saying he would rather give him the girl honourably than to have him entice her that way. When they spoke to Ingólfur, he reacted badly saying he would go on meeting Valgerdur no matter what anybody said. The two of them continued meet and enjoy each others company despite this opposition. Óttar then returned to Thorsteinn, who admonished Ingólfur and asked him to behave himself. His answer to this request was to compose a serenade, or love song to Valgerdur. Love songs to young girls were strictly forbidden in that society, so Óttar was angered by this lack of respect, visited Thorsteinn yet again and complained. Thorsteinn said he had done what he could, but in vain. Óttar demanded financial compensation because of the serenade as he had the right to do, and threatened to prosecute. Thorsteinn's brother, Jökull, reacted very badly to this and felt Óttar was taking a liberty, litigating against the powerful farmer at Hof. This Jökull was a bully, always prepared for conflict and trouble, and never conciliatory. The case was taken to court but Jökull and his nephew Ingólfur caused so much trouble in the court that they destroyed Óttar's case.

Óttar realised he could not cope with the situation and moved, with all his family, south to Borgarfjördur. He simply gave up when faced with the power of the farmer at Hof. Besides, he wanted to move his daughter away from Ingólfur so that he need not fear a premature pregnancy or worse.

Ingólfur was a beguiling womaniser about whom verses were composed:

> All maids would like
> to walk with Ingólfur,
> those who are fully grown.
> Poor me, still so small.

The second reference is somewhat more comic:

> I, said the crone
> will walk with Ingólfur,
> while still remain two
> teeth in my gums.

When Valgerdur had moved south, Ingólfur married a certain Ásdís Ólafsdóttir from Haukagil, a very young girl. This made little difference. Every time he rode to the Althing, Ingólfur would stop by in Borgarfjördur and visit Valgerdur, in spite of Óttar's displeasure. Valgerdur was a particularly skillful needlewoman and made all kinds of fancy garments for Ingólfur. Óttar was so fed up with these visits that he sent a man north to kill Ingólfur, but he failed. Óttar had to pay a fine for this false step, but Ingólfur did promise to leave Valgerdur alone. This was not the end of it though, because Ingólfur went right on visiting Valgerdur and Óttar sent another man north to kill him. This attempt also failed so Óttar was especially unlucky in his choice of assassins.

In the end, Ingólfur was killed in a struggle with outlaws who had nothing to do with this love story. Shortly before he died he asked to be buried away from his family plot, "because it would be better for the maids of Vatnsdalur if his grave was near the road". Only a true ladies' man talks like that, one who has no intention of being forgotten after his death. His grave must be on the beaten track. After Ingólfur's death, Valgerdur was married to someone from the Stafholtstunga district, and left the stage.

On examining her story, we find a beautiful girl who falls in love with this heart-throb Ingólfur who does not want to marry her, but chose an illicit love affair instead. Ingólfur was a bold hero who enjoyed defying fate. He clearly had no respect for Óttar and his concerns, nor for Valgerdur and her feelings; he just had his own way. They had an intimate relationship even though he didn't want to marry her. She even made clothes for him, so she was clearly in love. Valgerdur was between a rock and a hard place. Her father was angry and highly censorious of their behaviour but she couldn't sever her relationship with the man she loved. It's easy to imagine her distress and discomfort at home. She knew of her father's hatred and attempts to kill Ingólfur. She had no option but to wait for whatever was going to happen and relish her few hours with Ingólfur. He, however, treated her with utter contempt, married another woman but couldn't put an end to his relationship with Valgerdur. Once Ingólfur was dead, she was able to marry someone else and look forward to a humdrum existence or a happy relationship.

Society was ruled by strong clans that decided who was punished and who got away with things. In this instance, the powerful folk at Hof were the most influential family in Vatnsdalur and had things their way. Obviously, in this atmosphere, the sons of notables got away with doing whatever they liked, secure in the wealth and influence of their families. They could go around getting farmers' daughters and hired girls to sleep with them. No one dared complain because the perpetrator had the upper hand in this closed society that had no official executive power.

A disobedient daughter

Ljósvetninga saga (the Saga of the Ljosvetnings) tells of the disobedient daughter, Fridgerdur Ísólfsdóttir from Tjörnes. She was a pretty and self-confident girl. A certain man from Grímsey Island made such hearty advances to her that her father decided to send the girl to a friend's farm. Ísólfur was a peaceful man, so he chose to send the girl away rather than kill the islander. She and an attendant set off in bad weather. By the time they got to the farm Fornastadir in Fnjóskadalur valley, the wind had increased so it was no longer possible to continue their journey. Fridgerdur decided to stay at the nearby farm Draflastadir, though some thought it a bad idea. Her father's intention with this trip had been quite different. He meant for her to be safely looked after by his friend Eyjólfur Gudmundsson at the farm Mödruvellir, but she decided to spend the winter elsewhere.

Young men from the area were frequent visitors to the farm that winter, bringing much revelry. Fridgerdur was lively, behaved like the lads, partied and worked on the farm. By the spring her waistband was getting too tight as sometimes happens where people make merry. She named the father as a certain Brandur Gunnsteinsson, son of the farmer at Ljósavatn. People were doubtful as to the paternity, though, because they felt she had been so promiscuous during the winter that there were other possibilities. Fridgerdur was made to carry a red-hot iron to prove the child's paternity. This was in accordance with the custom of the time. Guilt or innocence was to be determined by higher powers. The girl was made to handle a red-hot iron and then her hand was examined. If the hand was uninjured she was telling the truth but if there were burns on the hand she was lying. A churchman examined her hand and declared it to be unscathed with no sign of blisters. Wicked tongues said, in fact, that he had been bribed to say so. Brandur denied he was the father and lengthy disputes ensued.

The moral of the tale is pretty clear. Fridgerdur allowed the islander to seduce her. She agreed to leave home so she need not be under the same roof as him. She was clearly, however, also interested in getting out from under her father's watchful eye. Because of the weather, she decided to stay at Draflastadir for a while, instead of with her father's friend, thus altering the original plan. Fridgerdur was very young, innocent and simple and let the lads on the farm take advantage of her childishness. From the wording of the story it is clear that there were many who might have fathered her child so there must have been quite some activity in Fridgerdur's bed. She was left with the pregnancy and the shame and had to endure the humiliation of a long-drawn-out paternity dispute. The author points out to young girls that it is best to follow the advice of their fathers, who know best. Brandur, the alleged father, was driven out of the country and died along with King Haraldur III, *hardráda* (stern counsel), in a campaign in England. The Saga says nothing of the fate of the fatherless child and its mother, who both fade into history like other faceless extras.

Svala and Óspakur

In *Bandamanna Saga,* Svala, mistress of the farm Svalastadir in Hunathing, got engaged to Óspakur Glúmsson, quite against the wishes of her relatives. He was Svala's farm manager and wanted a wife. Her relatives refused absolutely to give him Svala, so she made her own decision. He turned out to be a total brute, and was in fact closely related to Grettir Ásmundsson, so Svala's family had been right. The girl should not have followed her own emotions, but been guided by her relatives. Óspakur got into serious trouble and had to go into hiding for a while. He and Svala divorced and she married another man, Már Hildisson. Not long after, Óspakur returned and visited his former wife at Svalastadir, where she lay in bed with her husband. Óspakur crept into the common room and stabbed her husband with his knife, killing him under cover of darkness. Then he recited a poem which ended:

I will not grant
the son of Hildir
the fair inviting
embrace of Svala.

This is easy to understand. Óspakur would not allow any man to rest in the embrace of the curvaceous Svala. Here we have a combination of strong emotion, jealousy and revenge, which caused the husband's death. This could be a modern drama where the deadly sins of lust, greed and envy have free rein in the relationships. There is no mention of Svala's reactions or feelings.

The story ended well because the husband's brother managed to stab Óspakur as he was leaving the common room. He was found shortly thereafter, dead from loss of blood. Svala lost two husbands at once and disappeared from the Saga after that fateful night. This is one of many instances in the *Íslendingasögur* where men are killed in their beds, lying beside their wives. There is a rather obvious sexual significance to this action. Jealousy is in control and the murderer stabs his rival repeatedly with his sword, thus nailing him to the bed like a woman. Freud would probably have asked Óspakur whether he had had an erection while committing the murder, the better to understand his feelings. Again, the moral of the tale is clear. Young girls should defer to the will of their fathers and relatives. If they disobey and follow their hearts, everything goes wrong.

What about older women?

There is a long section in *Grágás* how men can get a wife. It begins with the famous sentence: "A son of 16 or more years determines his mother's betrothal." Here we see that a 16-year-old youth is to see to his mother's marriage. If there was no son, the son-in-law took on the responsibility. After that, her father, then her brother and finally her mother. This legal paragraph bears clear witness to the weak position of women in that society. They are referring to an adult, mature woman and mother who has no say in her future, but must depend on her teenage son. As to her feelings, no one asks.

A sorry tale of second marriage

The Saga of Droplaug's sons tells the story of their mother, Droplaug Thorgrímsdóttir. She married a man named Thorvaldur Thithrandson and had two sons by him, Helgi and Grímur. They are the main characters in the Saga. This Thovaldur dies early on in the Saga, so the sons are always referred to by their matronymic. Hallsteinn from Breithdalur, a widower, proposed to Droplaug and she married him. However, her son Helgi declared that this had not been his advice. Hallstein's sons were also very much against the marriage and they totally stopped visiting their father. Droplaug and Hallsteinn tried to live a reasonable life and they had a son, Herjólfur. Little by little their marriage went sour, though there is no mention of why.

After some time, Helgi came to visit his mother and Hallstein at Víðivellir in Fljótsdalur Valley and asked to stay. Hallsteinn reacted rather coolly, saying he would rather give him oxen or horses than put him up. Droplaug had her way, though, and Helgi lived with his mother and step father for a while. Two weeks later, three people sat talking for a long time one morning; Helgi, Droplaug and the slave Thorgils, who was part of the household at Víðivellir. Meanwhile, Hallsteinn was working on the farm. Later that day, he and Thorgils met in the barn and suddenly Thorgils ran at Hallsteinn and killed him with an ax. There were serious repercussions to this killing, because the sons of Hallsteinn thought the mother and son had got the slave to kill the husband. Thorgils was not there to say anything, because Helgi Droplaugarson had been quick to kill him when he saw Thorgils had murdered Hallsteinn. Soon after, Droplaug moved to the Faroe Islands with her son Herjólfur, and nothing was heard of them again. Helgi was sentenced for his part in the murder and the killings continued to the end of the Saga.

That marriage, with all its problems, could just as well have belonged to our time. Families like that are sometimes called typical Icelandic combination families, where they all mix together, his children, her children and their children. Everyone glowering at everyone else. Droplaug's sons were angry at their mother and Hallstein's sons were angry at their father. The boys joined forces to oppose the new spouses. The story ended badly because Droplaug conspired with her son to kill her husband. Helgi could not bear being in the common room along with his mother and her new husband, seeing them get in the same bed at night. He lay awake, imagining what is going on under their duvet. Jealousy grew like a monster in the depth of his soul and became uncontrollable. Hallsteinn realised this, and didn´t want Helgi in their home anyway. Helgi got the slave Thorgils to kill Hallstein, promising him freedom and a better life. When the slave had done his part and Hallsteinn was dead, Helgi betrayed him and immediately killed him. Thorgils had little time to appreciate his freedom as he understood Helgi's infamy as he was dying.

The Saga says nothing abut the actual reason for the murder. This is one of the many secrets of the Sagas when it comes to people's private lives. Droplaug's impotence was total, and she seems to have had no way of coping with her son's jealousy and rage. He didn´t hesitate to make his mother a widow and his brother fatherless to satisfy some compulsion that the book never explains. Automatically, one's mind turns to the teachings of Sigmund Freud. He deals at length with the Oedipus complex in young boys who desire their mothers sexually and are dismayed by anyone who shows an interest in them. The crowded conditions in the old common rooms was an important factor. Young boys saw their mothers naked and watched their sexual activity in the next bed. Helgi will have been seriously afflicted with jealousy and hatred, leading him into the Greek tragedy of killing the man who received his mother's caresses.

A dispute between mother and son

In the Sagas, widows often have a lot of trouble establishing a new relationship, especially if they have sons, who tend to watch their mothers like hawks and be suspicious of their every undertaking. The balance of power inside the home changes with the death of the father. The sons take control and the mother has to get used to a new head of the household.

Flóamanna Saga tells of Thorgrímur örrabeinn (scarred legs) Thor-móðsson, so-called because he was covered in scars after a life of battles, hardships and danger. Thorgrímur went to the farm Tradarholt, near Stokkseyri, where he met the widow Thórunn. They were attracted to one another and he moved in. Home life, however, did not run smooth-ly. Thórunn's son Thorgils was still a child, and took it upon himself to

A psychiatrist's opinion

Once again the woman has no control over her own life. Helgi objected so strongly to his mother's affair with Thorgrímur that he did everything possible to prevent their happiness. The woman herself had no say in this, but had to defer to his notions. This story is a good illustration of the pro-blems facing women who lost their husbands in battles or accidents and were left on their own. Their lusty, controlling sons could prevent a new relationship or marriage. The young Thorgils might do anything so he was sent away to be fostered. Thorgrímur *orrabeinn* deserved to be admired for his fortitude and courage. He didn´t hesitate but took on his fanatical step-son despite his advanced age and failing health. Their combat was sad, since Thorgrímur could hardly defend himself, weak and breathless as he was. Helgi didn´t let that deter him, killed the old man and went home triumphant to give his mother the news.

This situation had a serious and detrimental effect on the mental health of these women. Áshildur was clearly fond of Thorgrímur and wanted him to be her husband. Helgi did not want this, and it ended with the death of both men. It is easy to imagine Áshildur's mental state, guilt, regret, self-reproach and depression. The Saga says nothing about her fate after the deaths of her son and lover. What was driving Helgi? Selfishness, arrogance, jealousy? Was he unable to allow any man to share moments of pleasure with her? Freud would undoubtedly have asked Helgi whether he had illi-cit feelings towards his mother. The Oedipus complex peers out from its hidey-hole in the soul like a curious country bumpkin visiting the city.

kill Thorgrímur's horse, Illingur, with a spear, in order to be allowed to play with some other boys. They had told the youngster he couldn´t play unless he killed some living thing. Thorgrímur responded by sending him away to be fostered, having a bad feeling about the future of this young horse-murderer. Even so, Thorgils was always known by his stepfather's name and called Thorgils *orrabein*'s foster son, and he lived a life of adventure. Thórunn died, so Thorgrímur was left on his own.

He started meeting up with the widow Áshildur of Ólafsvellir. Her son, Helgi, was unhappy with these visits and went to his mother to rebuke her. He said that Thorgrímur's approaches dishonoured not only Áshildur but all her relatives. She asked him not to be angry and warned him against Thorgrímur. Helgi answered that it was obvious the man admired her and he himself was not going to put up with this insult. Thorgrímur continued to sleep with Áshildur and Helgi visited again to criticise the relationship. She asked him to give it a rest, but was worried about her lover's safety. Once, when Thorgrímur was leaving, she asked him to go very carefully because she was afraid she might never see him again. She gave him a gold ring at parting to protect him against all evil. But all was in vain. Helgi waylaid him and asked him to leave his mother alone. Thorgrímur answered that he could not be bothered with this childishness. Helgi attacked him. Thorgrímur was old and short of breath and the upshot was that Helgi killed his mother's lover. He then went to Ólafsvellir and told his mother what had happened. She said he thought he was quite the man after this killing, but it would lead to his own death. This came true, as Hæringur, the son of Thorgrímur, killed Helgi in revenge.

Age and marriage

People were allowed to marry a good deal younger than is now customary. There is nothing in *Grágás* about the minimum age of a bride and groom, but in the 13th century Church laws of Árni Thorlaksson there is provision that the girl should be 12 and the boy 14. This young married couple were allowed to divorce if they had not had sex, so it could be pretty complicated.

A sad teen wedding

Gissur Thorvaldsson of the Haukdælar family, later titled Earl, and Sturla Thórdarson of the Sturlung family, decided to bring the hostilities in the country to an end and reconcile the two families. They wished to seal the peace through the marriage of their children, Hallur Gissuarson and Ingibjörg Sturludóttir. She was virtually a child when this betrothal was decided, 13 years old, while Hallur was just under twenty. There is no sign of the young folk having agreed to this, or of how they liked the idea of the marriage. It is unlikely that they would have known each other before they were led to their marriage bed. Their homes were far apart and they belonged to different arms of Iceland's internal conflicts in the 13th century.

The wedding feast, at Flugumýri in Skagafjördur in 1253, was lavish and accounted one of the greatest feasts to have been held in the country. The Saga describes the celebration and the speeches that were made and all the oaths men swore. The young bride and groom went together to their bed, but there is no account of their interaction there. Their bed was beside the bed of Gissur and his wife. The wedding feast came to a sudden end, as Eyjólfur *ofsi* (fury) Thorsteinnsson had planned to betray Gissur. Eyjólfur was married to Thurídur, the daughter of Sturla Sighvatsson and his concubine Vigdís. Eyjólfur decided to take revenge for his father-in-law and attacked Gissur under cover of night. He set fire to the Flugumýri buildings which were soon in flames. The young bridal couple awoke and Ingibjörg managed to escape with the help of her cousin, Svarthöfdi Dufgusson. She was led weeping from the fire, dressed only in a nightgown. The marriage thus came to a sudden and miserable end. Not much is said about Ingibjörg after this event, but one can just imagine what a shock this must have been. She was made to marry a young man she didn't know. Their marriage was first and foremost for reconciliation between two families so the young folk are powerless pawns in their fathers' game of chess. Ingibjörg is suddenly in bed with the seven-year-older Hallur. Shortly thereafter the arsonists arrived and set fire to the house. The marriage was over before it started. The groom who had just then deflowered her was no longer among the living. She herself was outside in the night, clad only in a nightdress, surrounded by the slayers of her in-laws, her own relatives, the passion of the wedding night still surging in her blood.

In our day, such a series of events would have called for sessions with a psychologist and crisis counselling, whereas in *Sturlungaöld* (the time described in *Sturlunga*) people had to accept the cruelty of fate without complaint. The girl Ingibjörg had to live her life with the memory of the one night she rested in the arms of Hallur before the flames ate him alive. Gissur escaped, but his wife and children burned to death. Bystanders said that when Gissur was shown the ravaged bodies of his wife and sons, hailstones burst from his face. This is a close as it comes to saying Gissur wept, yet it was not then customary for men to cry.

Thorgils *orrabein's* foster son; his women and his fate

Returning to *Flóamanna Saga* and Thorgils the horse-killer *orrabein's* foster son, we see him growing up and becoming a great hero and warrior. He went to Norway and there encountered Gunnhildur, the king's mother. Their relations ended when they quarreled and Gunnhildur kicked the Icelander and pushed him away from her throne. He set off raiding as young men would and in Norway got to know Hákon *jarl* (Earl) of Hladir and a courtier of his, Thorsteinn *hvíti* (the white). Hákon sent the friends to collect taxes in the Isles of the Hebrides off Scotland. They were far from successful; got lost at sea, wrecked their ships and lost all their money. They made their way to Caithness and met a certain Earl Ólafur, who had a gorgeous sister, named Gudrún. The berserker Surtur *járnhaus* (iron-head), a criminal and the worst of men, had his eye on Gudrún and demanded she be given to him in marriage or as his concubine. Earl Ólafur would not go along with this so the berserker challenged him to single combat as was the habit of such violent men. Surtur wanted to sleep with Gudrún and chose the viking way; to fight for beautiful women against elderly men who had little experience of armed combat.

Thorgils decided to take on the single combat with the brute, and Ólafur had in fact promised his sister to anyone who managed to kill Surtur *járnhaus*. After a tough battle, Thorgils succeeded in both slicing his leg off from under him and slicing his head off his shoulders, so the berserker no longer posed a danger. Thorgils got the first prize for this deed, Gudrún, sister of the Earl. Not long after, the couple went to visit Earl Hákon who greeted them warmly. Gudrún gave birth to their son, Thorleifur, and life was good. Later Thorgils decided to go to Iceland to check on his property there. He asked his friend Thorsteinn *hvíti* to look after his property in Norway and retain it for his son Thorleifur. He said that Thorsteinn had always served him well and he meant to reward him with a good gift. "I will give you my wife, Gudrún, because I have noticed that you are enamoured of her." Thorsteinn thanked his friend for this princely gift and with that they parted. Gudrún is never again mentioned in the Saga, but her son by Thorgils, Thorleifur, turns up many years later in Greenland. Thorgils had then moved there and Thorleifur came to visit his father and be of service to him.

Just imagine the Earl's sister Gudrún's state of mind in all this. She was nothing but a bone of contention between strange men who fought over her and passed her around as they liked. The berserker Surtur insisted on getting her into his bed, which cost him his life. She was married to the hero Thorgils and has a baby by him. Then he gave her to his friend and foster brother like any other possession. She herself is never asked her opinion and she disappears from history when, with his friend Thorsteinn, she leaves Thorgils' life. Her lack of control over her own life is total.

In Greenland, Thorgils lost his second wife, with whom he had had the son Thorfinnur. According to the Saga, Thorgils suckled the child, providing either milk or blood from his nipples. In later years people have speculated that Thorgils might have had a tumor in his pituitary gland that caused him to produce milk. Thorfinnur was breastfed by his father for several years. His household marvelled at this and wondered whether Thorgils was a man or a woman. Such tumors being very rare, people must have gaped when they saw the boy sucking at his father's nipple with such success.

Thorgils returned to Iceland and proposed to a certain Helga Thóroddsdóttir from Hjalli in the Ölfus district. He was now in his mid-fifties and Helga was very much against this marriage. Her relatives, however, did not dare to oppose this elderly, well-travelled champion, so they were married. Helga's unhappiness with the marriage grew day by day. Once, when Thorgils was away, she fled to her parents' house, but he came after her fully armed and took her back. Her people dared not hinder him or rescue Helga so he forced his unwilling wife to come home. They remained together and it was said that she became resigned to her destiny and they had three sons together. Thorgils threatened Helga with continued violence if she showed any tendency towards independence and that was that.

In reality, Helga had no options in this situation. She had to accept her fate and hope time could be on her side, that Thorgils would die really soon. Nowadays we find it hard to understand the oppression some women had to live with. Helga was forced to marry this old man and couldn't get out of the marriage for fear of violence and revenge.

Thorgils himself was seriously disabled emotionally. He lost his father as a child, and his foster father sent him away to strangers when he killed his horse. It is clearly very difficult for him to form relationships. His interactions with women were superficial and pitiful. He gave away his first wife and son with no sign of regret. His relationship with Helga was built on violence and oppression. Thorgils was a self-centred man who thrashed his way through life with no regard for the feelings of those around him. Perhaps the only one he makes a connection with is the boy Thorfinnur, whom he suckled for so long. That is yet another part of the tragedy, that Thorfinnurr died young, and Thorgils in his mourning starved himself for four days. He said then that he understood how mothers loved their sucklings more than anyone. It seems that only a benign tumor of the pituitary gland enabled him to show any emotion.

Another bestowed woman

Egils saga tells of a certain Bárdur Brynjolfsson whose wife was Sigrídur. He was the comrade-in-arms of Egill's uncle, Thórólfur Kveld-Úlfsson. In one savage battle, Bárdur was mortally wounded. As he lay dying, he

---

Reflections

It is not surprising that many of our contemporaries look to those days with regret and longing. Men had their way and women weren't asked what they thought of the men they were to marry. Nowadays the greatest worry of some men when they are dying is what will happen to their wives. They think with horror of some blockhead climbing into bed with their wife moments after the funeral service. It would be better for all concerned to be able to give his wife away from his deathbed, deciding whom she should lie beside the following years. In this case Sigrídur was given away after her husband's death, just like any other bequest, and had to accept it. Men seem not to have had the least curiosity as to how she felt about these suitors, and indeed, it was irrelevant.

In modern grief theory, it is usually argued that people need a long time to recover from the loss of a spouse and should not replace the deceased right away. Obviously, this insight had not caught on in the merciless, harsh world of the *Íslendingasögur*, where survival was of the essence. A great many women had entered a new relationship before their late husband's body was quite cold.

---

not only bequeathed all his property to his friend Thórólfur but even gave him his wife and young son. King Haraldur *hárfagri* (fair-hair), who stood nearby, confirmed Bárdur's decision. Thrólfur went to meet Sigrídur and gave her the news that her husband was dead and had given her to him before he died.

The widow Sigrídur received this well since she rather liked Thórólfur. Her father was of the same mind, not least in view of the fact that King Haraldur had declared himself responsible for this act. They were married and Thórólfur remained in the service of the king. Their friendship went sour over time and the upshot was that the king had Thórlfur killed, after serious disputes. Sigrídur was yet again a widow, but the king did not leave it at that. He gave her to a member of his company and friend of Thórólfur's, Eyvindur *lambi*. They married and shared a bed, producing two promising children. Eyvindur and the king always remained friends, and in fact Eyvindur's brother was one of the king's courtiers.

Magic, strong women and bondwomen

In the *Íslendingasögur*, magic plays a big role where sex is concerned. There are many references to wizards and witches putting spells on men and making them impotent or spoiling their love lives. Magic was seen as a woman's practice and any men who practiced magic were feminised, called homosexual or queer. Such magicians could control both weather and terrain so that people got lost on familiar paths and couldn't find the way home.

In *Hávamál* (sayings of the high one), there is frequent mention of men's magic for getting into women's beds, so-called love spells. This kind of magic was later attributed to women. This knowledge is said to be spoken by Óðinn himself and he claims to be able to turn a woman's mind to make himself the focus of all her thoughts and pleasure.

Egils saga tells of a young girl who had the bad luck to have a neighbour who would do anything to get to sleep with her. He carved her so-called *manrúnir* (love spells) on whalebone, but was so inept at it that his efforts made her ill. Luckily the rune-master himself, Egill Skalla-Grímsson, came along, inspected the bed she had been lying in and found the runes. He said there were ten secret signs there that caused the girl's illness.

Egill burned the runes and had her bed-clothes aired, since he had seen through the lad's attempts at magic.

During the Saga age, sorcery was often sexual. Men would perform magic to geld their enemies and make them impotent or tried to lure women and make them willing. Throughout the ages, people have wondered how to win the love of another. No one has an infallible answer to that riddle, any more than to other mysteries of love. One can see why people looked to wizards and witches for help in winning the heart of the girl or boy they wanted for themselves.

Two women fight over a young man

Eyrbyggja saga tells of the clash between two older women over a young man, Gunnlaugur Thorbjarnarson. He was from an important and powerful family, closely related to the chieftain Snorri *godi* (priest-chieftain) Thorgrímsson. While still quite young, Gunnlaugur started going regularly to Mávahlíd to visit Geirríður Thórólfsdóttir, apparently to study magic. The observant reader, however, soon realises that Gunnlaugur was the lover of Geirríður, who was a grown woman, a good deal older than Gunnlaugur. Nearby lived another magical woman, the widow Katla. She was tormented by the relationship between Gunnlaugur and Geirríður and said he went there to smooth the granny's groin. It is all too easy to understand her meaning. Katla was a good-looking woman and thus dangerous, as Geirríður said, you often find a wolf in sheep's clothing. Realising that Katla was jealous and full of hatred, Geirríður warned Gunnlaugur against her. He paid no attention and went where he wished as is the habit of horny young men.

Once when Gunnlaugur had visited Geirríður, he stopped by Katla's place on his way home. She invited him to stay the night but he turned her down and set off into the night. He was found the following morning, more dead than alive and utterly mad. He was all bruised and bloody and extremely weak. People said Geirríður had done this by magic and Gunnlaugur had been ridden by her in the way of witches. She fended off the accusations and managed to direct attention towards the witch Katla, who admitted she had caused Gunnlaugur's illness and was executed.

Various things are hinted at in this story, some fairly openly. It is clear that Gunnlaugur and Geirríður were having an affair and that Katla hated it and tried to put a stop to it. Love life on the farms was of course a lot more lively than people felt they could report. In this case we have a healthy young man who satisfied an older woman so well that other women on nearby farms were consumed with jealousy and envy, leading to his destruction.

In this story, as in fact elsewhere, sex is connected to magic and other dangerous phenomena. Saying that Gunnlaugur's mistress had powerful magic emphasises his vulnerability in the face of such a woman. Lust is no longer a natural state; it is caused by the sorcery and supernatural abilities of this dangerous woman. Gunnlaugur shames his relatives by sneaking into the bed of an older widow at night. The author tries to justify this behaviour by painting the picture of an innocent youth driven mad by the tricks of a sorceress. In this case, the woman was active and the man passive in the relationship. Everything went wrong and the promising young man Gunnlaugur went insane long before the days of psychiatric medicine. Today's doctors have argued that what the lad suffered from was epilepsy rather than the tricks of Geirríður and Katla. Little is known of Gunnlaugur after these events. He is basically remembered only as the lover of these two older women on nearby farms, not for any other achievements.

Haraldur *hárfagri* and magic

One of the most famous kings of Norway was Haraldur hárfagri, about whom Snorri Sturluson writes in *Heimskringla*. He conquered all of Norway and turned the country into one kingdom. He swore an oath not to cut his hair until he had completed this mission and kept to it.

Many of the first settlers in Iceland fled Haraldur's tyranny and sailed north. He was a vigorous man on the battlefield and in bed, had many wives and numerous children.

In the Saga of Haraldur *hárfagri*, there is an account of his acquaintance with the Sami woman Snæfrídur Svásadóttir. She mixed a vessel full of mead for the king which he drank and afterwards touched her hand. A fiery heat spread through his skin (read: penis) and he longed to have intercourse with her that same night. Her father, Svási, said there could be no question of that unless they married, which they did. Their passion was so great that Haraldur neglected his kingdom in order to fulfill all of Snæfrídur's needs. The king and she had four named and promising sons. Snæfrídur died but did not change in spite of this, retaining her youthful bloom and colour. The king sat by her day and night, waiting for her to come back to life. Three winters passed in this way, the king mourned his queen and his people mourned his madness. Then a learned man came along, Thorleifur spaki (the wise), and asked the king to let him change the queens clothes. He said it dishonoured her to have to lie there always in the same clothes. When they moved her in the bed a great stink of putrefaction gushed up. They burned her body on a bonfire and worms, lizards and bugs burst from her body. She was turned to ash, and the king came to his senses and returned to running his kingdom as he should.

Snorri Sturluson here tells a quite remarkable story. He speaks of the great womaniser Haraldur *hárfagri*, who became so enchanted by Snæfrídur that he neglected his royal duties. Snorri clearly implies that Snæfrídur bewitched Haraldur, and indeed, after her death it is clear she is nothing but a sorceress. She entraps the mind of the king and manages to geld him so completely after her death that he sits by her death-bed neglecting all else. It is only when the doctor, Thorleifur, succeeds in tearing him away from the power of the spell that the king escapes the enchantment.

Troll women

Throughout the sagas, there are stories of encounters between men and troll women, who lived on the outer edges of society. In the story of Jökull Búason, his ship got stranded and he went ashore along with his companions. They all fell asleep but Jökull stayed awake and wandered down to the shore, where he saw two young sisters, 12 and 14 years old, who were troll women or troll-teens. They both wanted Jökull for a husband and he heard them extolling his fame as a hero. They offered Jökull the choice of marrying one of them or dying. The story goes on to describe their appearance and how repugnant they were. They were very mannish with their lower lip hanging down to their chests, clad in fur smocks that were long in the front but barely covered their bottoms in the back. When it became apparent that Jökull would choose neither of them, they attacked him.

Jökull fought them valiantly, killed the younger one immediately, wrestled with the elder and managed to bring her down. Then she said, "Enjoy the fall, fellow!" Jökull took pity on the teenager and spared her life on the condition that she would remain loyal to him at all times. She then informed her parents and other trolls, all of whom Jökull killed with great vigour. He did, however, spare one promising troll lad who later married the troll girl he had spared. The story clearly illustrates the options for a troll woman in that society, she would either be killed or accept the rule of a man. There is a rather amusing sexual undercurrent to the story when the troll girl falls in the wrestling match and tells Jökull to enjoy the fall. She might as well have said: "And now bang me, fellow!" But this could not be written due to the etiquette of the times. The author appeals to the fantasies of many men as to the ultimate test of virility, where he either has to sexually satisfy two young troll women or die trying.

A man-like woman

Freydís Eiríksdóttir was the daughter of Eiríkur *raudi*. She appears in the *Grænlendinga saga* among others. She was considered very domineering,

but her husband, Thorvardur, was no hero. He was very well-built, reminiscent of a giant, but she had been married to him for money. This description of a couple in the Sagas never bodes well. Freydís was the daughter of Eiríkur's concubine but he had two sons by his wife, Thjódhildur. Freydís' upbringing will probably have reflected this, that she will have been left out and grown up in the shadow of her promising brothers. They were Leifur *heppni* (the lucky) and Thorsteinn Eiriksson who later married Gudrídur Thorbjarnardóttir.

Freydís is particularly remembered for two incidents. One time in Vínland a group of *Skrælingjar* (natives) attacked the Icelanders who were there. The latter ran off and Freydís, who was slowed down by pregnancy, lost touch with the group. She fled into the woods where she found one of her companions lying dead. His sword lay by his side and she picked it up. When the *Skrælingjar* noticed her they ran at her, shouting and screaming. She swung her breasts out from under her smock, bared them in the face of the attackers and slapped the flat of the sword across them. The *Skrælingjar* were astonished, turned tail and ran off. Her companions crowded back around her, praising her ingenuity and courage.

The other incident also took place in Vínland. There were two brothers who had joined Freydís and her husband on the trip west from Greenland. When they got there, Freydís broke her word and provoked a dispute with the brothers and their companions. She had her eye on the brothers' ship and other possessions and wanted the men out of the way. One morning she got up early, walked across to the other camp and spoke with the brothers and their companions. When she returned to her camp she woke her husband and lied that she had been beaten and injured by those men. She exhorted him to go take revenge. This he did, gathered his men and went to the brothers' camp, where everyone was fast asleep. The men were woken, tied up, led out and killed. No one wanted to kill their women except Freydís, who killed all five with an ax. These killings were seen as an odious deed, and in fact Freydís asked her men to keep quiet about it. The did not do as she asked so her brother Leifur heard about it and rebuked her severely.

This has given Freydís a bad reputation ever since. Yet what she did is comparable to many killings in the *Íslendingasögur* and *Sturlunga*, where defenseless people were taken from their beds to be killed. The only difference is that she had the women killed, which was unusual. In fact, the Vikings killed men, women and children in their raids but the Sagas keep quiet about many of their violent deeds. In the society of that time all kinds of character flaws had free rein and psychopathic behaviour flourished. Freydís was at home in this atmosphere. She decided to get rid of the brothers in a masculine way, but with a feminine touch, lied to her husband, made out she was a victim and martyr and exhorted her husband to attack people who had no reason to expect such a thing. The male dominated society was frightened by women who behaved like that. Freydís was determined and resourceful and did not hesitate to go against societal norms. Freydís presented a strong and frightening picture standing there pregnant and half-naked with her breasts bare, swinging a sword and striking it against her breasts with a clang of metal. The *Skrælingjar* must have thought she was a god-like creature and naturally feared her.

Freydís is one of those slave-born children who grow up feeling inferior and needing to constantly prove themselves to their father and his family. In this case, she wished to show behaviour that would waken the admiration of the patriarchy and be seen as evidence of determination and valour. However, her plans backfired and all she gained was condemnation and dislike. In comparison, her brother Leifur became even more of a hero, and in fact statues have been raised to honour him, both in the United States and in front of Hallgrímskirkja in Reykjavík.

Bondwomen and slaves

Bondwomen are a group of women that the Sagas do not deal with at length. There were quite a few of them, since settlers on their way to Iceland would sometimes go first to Ireland and the Shetlands to get hold of slaves and bondwomen. There is no doubt that some portion of these bondwomen were some kind of sex-slaves or concubines who were meant to serve their masters at table and in bed. This was in no way wrong in a society where people were born into a certain class and to do certain jobs. In *Grágás* there is a provision for punishment by fine for lying with a bondwoman, but we have no knowledge of how often it was used. *Grágás* also provide for exceptions to the maximum price for a bondwoman if she was being bought specifically for "*karnadur*". People do not agree on the meaning of "*karnadur*", but there is every indication that it implies love or sex. Some bondwomen are named in the Sagas, the most famous being Melkorka in *Laxdæla*.

Melkorka

It was very common for settlers on their way to Iceland to make raids in Ireland, Orkney or the Shetland Islands for plunder and slaves. These slaves were part of the young Icelandic society, though not much is said about them. *Laxdæla saga* tells about Höskuldur Dala-Kollsson going abroad to buy himself timber to build his farm. On one occasion, somewhere in Denmark, he saw a colourful tent standing away from the others in a camp. He approached the tent and there he met a Russian merchant, named Gilli. Inside the tent he saw 12 women Gilli had put

---

A psychiatrist's reflections

This story reveals a great contempt for women and the view that it is best for women to keep quiet and not speak unless necessary. Höskuldur obviously found the girl's handicap of being mute attractive, considered it a pleasurable asset. We have already seen that his wife, Jorúnn, was a strong-willed woman who had an opinion on all subjects. Höskuldur seems to have been tired of his wife's constant fuss so he jumped at the chance to own a mute concubine. The Russian merchant Gilli was unhappy when Höskuldur bought the girl, because he had intended her for his own pleasure. A mute woman was clearly considered a valuable item. This fits with the view that women should keep in the background and absolutely not speak unless necessary. This admonition is constantly repeated in religious works which tend to emphasise how much evil can result from the careless speech of women.

---

up for sale. He examined all the women carefully but paid special attention to a poorly dressed woman who sat by the entrance to the tent. He had his eye on her as a great beauty and asked the price.

Gilli replied that she was for sale for three marks of silver, which was usually enough for three bondwomen. Höskuldur, without hesitation, handed over all his money for the girl. Before they completed the purchase, Gilli told him the woman could not speak, which was undeniably a flaw. Höskuldur did not let that deter him, since this made the woman even more desirable from his point of view. The bondwoman was a gorgeous, mute woman he could have for his pleasure. Höskuldur went back to his camp and it is said that he bedded her that same night, so his intentions in making the purchase were clear from the outset. In the morning, he dressed her in costly garments that he had in his chest. It was important that the mute bondwoman be as splendid as possible and a credit to her owner.

At home at Höskuldsstadir, his relationship with the concubine produced a strong reaction on the part of his wife, Jórunn, and eventually the two women actually brawled in mutual jealousy. Jórunn protested surprisingly little to begin with, when Höskuldur brought a stunning young girl into the home, with whom he obviously had close relations, since she soon started to show. It was as if she thought it perfectly natural that he should bring home a concubine after travelling abroad. The bondwoman bore Höskuldur a son who became the forefather of a great many people of the Dalir region. When the son, Ólafur, was very young, Höskuldur discovered that the bondwoman could speak fluently and had been feigning her lack of speech. She said she was Melkorka, daughter of Mýrkjartan (Muirchertach mac Néill), king of Ireland. In spite of this royal connection, Höskuldur sent the bondwoman away once she started speaking. His wife, Jorúnn, was not impressed by this news of the concubine's heritage. Shortly after the discovery, the women brawled yet again and Melkorka punched Jórunn in the nose until it bled. This was a jealousy drama equal to any modern play where hurt and angry women get violent. The husband stood by grinning and watched the women show their admiration for him using fists, screams and oaths. Melkorka will not have been the only bondwoman who was bought and sold. Farmers bought slaves for sexual use.

Marriage and Divorce

With marriage, husbands took on the role that fathers or male relatives had had, and became the legal guardians of their women. Within marriage, a woman's rights of ownership were strictly limited, and she was allowed to spend only a specified amount of money each year. Marriage confirmed the husband's ownership of his wife.

Love in a harmonious marriage

Once the courtship and wedding were over, the couple was faced with every day life with all its monotony. The *Íslendingasögur* often speak briefly of these marriages and married life. In a single sentence it is said that the married couple managed to love each other well, or that their intercourse was good. The reader senses that they got on together and had made a good choice of partner. The couple got to know each other and realised that they were well suited. The principle was that love grows out of marriage, not that marriage grows out of love. This principle is in accordance with the teachings of patriarchy. The belief was simply that two individuals who had a similar position in the community and were fairly equal as to maturity and intelligence would have a good marriage. The bride and groom would grow together and start to love each other naturally. Sometimes the relationship between the couple is said to have been bad from the start, as in the case of Gudrún and Hallgerdur and the two Thorvalds.

The Sagas often describe relations between young people, saying that they chat together, or sit talking. Gunnlaugur *ormstunga* (worm-tongue) and Helga the fair played chess. This was clearly a way of intimating close relations, and in fact this chat sometimes led to the woman becoming pregnant. The author was describing what he knew and saw. He had evidence showing that people would sit talking, or playing chess. Then woman became pregnant and the reader can envisage what happened when the actual conversation ended. The Sagas are respectable and have to appeal to the reader's imagination, since nothing must be said that would violate the church's teachings.

Divorces

Couples could demand a divorce with the permission of the bishop. A woman could get a divorce if her husband intended to move her out of the country against her will or had been violent towards her. If a husband did not sleep in the same bed as his wife for three years she could demand her money and probably petition for a divorce. There was no comparable provision regarding a wife's inability or unwillingness to have intercourse, unless it involved her leaving the home.

Women could get a divorce if the marriage was difficult, but this was usually subject to the approval of the bishop. Probably divorces were a source of income for the bishoprics, so rich people who could offer the bishop greater amounts could more easily get out of their marriages. *Grágás* has very detailed provisions regarding how divorced couples are to divide their property so perhaps divorce was more common than we realise. The Sagas describe a number of divorces where the woman chose to leave the marriage because of her husband's violence, among other reasons.

A heartless divorce

Kormáks saga tells how the hero's beloved, Steingerdur Thorkellsdóttir, was married to *Hólmgöngu*-Bersi (challenger-Bersi), a rich man and worthy. He was a champion and often fought in single combat, as evidenced by his by-name. The poet Kormákur had decided to marry Steingerdur but got cold feet at the last moment and did not turn up for his own wedding. Her father wished to save her from the shame and loss of reputation caused by Kormákur's behaviour, which discredited the girl, in his opinion. He got Bersi to propose to Steingerdur and when he did, the father accepted the arrangement. She herself did not get to know what was planned until in the wedding itself, and she did not, in fact, wish to marry Bersi. She tried to get a message to Kormákur to come rescue her, but it came too late. Kormákur rode after Bersi and his bride and wanted Bersi to give him back his former love. Bersi refused, but offered Kormákur his sister Helga, a fine woman, in marriage instead. Kormákur took the offer very badly and they parted in enmity.

In medieval medicine they spoke of love-sickness as one kind of obsessive-compulsive behaviour of young men. The object of their love, the young woman, was always on their minds and made them melancholy and apprehensive. The cause was said to be black bile (*melan choler*) and the accumulation of semen in the body of the love-sick. The treatment was complicated, advising intercourse in order to take the mind off the beloved. Perhaps *Hólmgöngu*-Bersi knew this when he offered his sister to the love-sick Kormákur for marriage and intercourse. Kormákur himself tried to get Steingerdur off his mind by travelling widely and composing defamatory verses about her.

Not much is said about the marriage, but Bersi continued doing battle in single combat. In one fight he received a serious blow on his buttocks

and down to the backs of his knees. He was bed-ridden for a long time with this injury, but he did finally recover. While he lay ill, Steingerdur was even more spiteful to him than usual and eventually decided to divorce him. When she was ready to leave, she went to Bersi saying that he had hitherto been called *Hólmg*öngu-Bersi but from now on he would be known as *Rassa*-Bersi (Back-side Bersi). With this, she left.

The tale of Steingerdur's wedding is sad, leaving her with a deep sense of rejection. The man she loved and intended to marry didn't turn up for his own wedding. With no warning, she was married off to another man she knew nothing about and taken away to another county as if she were a pauper on public assistance. Steingerdur took advantage of Bersi's weakness as he lay ill, divorced him and took revenge on this male dominated society that pushed her around. She transferred her rage against Kormákur onto Bersi and relished the opportunity to humiliate the hero who had to lie there on his stomach with a putrid, suppurating wound on his backside. Steingerdur jumped at the chance, divorced Bersi when he was totally helpless and not likely to chase after her.

A caring husband

Vopnfirdinga saga tells the story of the marriage between Brodd-Helgi Thorgilsson and Halla Lýtingsdóttir. Brodd-Helgi lost his father while still a boy and was brought up by his grandfather. He soon got a reputation for recklessness but was rather slow to speak. He got his by-name after a competition in which farmers' sons pitted their steers against each other in a butting contest. Helgi's steer was performing so badly in the fight that Helgi tied a spike onto the beast's forehead so it could harm its opponent. This spike is a clear phallic symbol.

Halla became sickly and warned her husband that she would be unable to run their household as she had up to then. Helgi answered that he considered himself very well married and intended to remain in the relationship while they both lived. Shortly thereafter, unfortunately, Helgi visited a gorgeous woman, the widow Thorgerdur *silfra* (rich in silver). She placed Helgi in the high seat and made much of him. Helgi was so taken with this woman that he got engaged to her before he returned home. When he got home he told his wife and divorced her. He refused to divide their property as he was obliged to do, which resulted in a long and complex legal battle. This story is particularly disgraceful in light of Helgi's declarations about the marriage before he set off on this fateful journey and got to know Mrs. *Silfra*.

In fact, Helgi and Halla remained in touch as her illness grew worse. She appears to have suffered from some kind of tapeworm and it is said that Helgi drained the cyst for her. That must have been the first abdominal perforation procedure to have been performed in Iceland, so Helgi was not all bad. Halla was very weak after the procedure and asked Helgi to stay by her overnight but he was in a hurry, as doctors so often are. Then Halla said that not many men would leave their wives in such a state as he was doing. Helgi did not let this affect him, said good-bye to his patient and ex-wife and went on his way. She died later that same night. This we must see as a reminder to doctors not to treat their own families and especially not their ex-wives.

A dramatic divorce in *Landnáma*

Difficulties in marriage have dogged humanity through the ages. Usually people tried to solve their problems peacefully but that did not always work. *Landnáma* tells the story of the difficult marriage of Hallbjörn Oddsson and Hallgerdur Tungu-Oddsdóttir. The author says straight out that things were "unaffectionate" between the two of them. They lived with Hallgerdur's father but were about to move. Her father did not want to be around when they left, since he suspected that Hallgerdur didn't want to move away with Hallbjörn. So he went to look after his sheep.

The book then recounts how Hallbjörn came into the farmhouse where Hallgerdur sat and asked her to accompany him, but she gave no answer. He then tried to take her with him by force but to no avail. Hallbjörn composed a verse about how stubborn she was and what disrespect he felt she was showing him. Then he grabbed her hair, which was long and thick and tried to pull her down off the platform but she did not move in spite of this violent assault. After this he drew his sword and cut off her head.

Thereupon Hallbjörn rode away with his companions. Soon after Odd's people set off in pursuit under the command of a certain Snæbjörn *galti* (boar). A fight broke out and Snæbjörn slew the evil husband. It may be that there is an underlying suggestion that Snæbjörn was the lover of the unhappy and unfortunate housewife.

This is an example of the disobedient wife who was not prepared to quietly follow her husband. She had no right at all to refuse to accompany Hallbjörn and her father was not in a position to protect her. Thus the price for her independence was her life.

A double divorce

Bardi Gudmundsson in *Heidarvíga saga* divorced two wives. The first time he broke it off with Gudrún Bjarnardóttir because he couldn't get on with his father-in-law, and said he was doing what would show Björn the greatest disrespect. Bardi had asked his father-in-law for help and been refused. The daughter, Gudrún, had also done everything she could to get her father to help Bardi, but to no avail. Bardi was angry, called Björn every nasty name he could think of and said it was now beneath his dignity to have such a father-in-law any longer. At which he divorced Gudrún, who thus left the story.

Later Bardi married Audur, daughter of Snorr *godi* and the two of them went to Norway. In the end of the story they get divorced after an event that it's difficult to interpret. They were in an outbuilding. Bardi wanted to sleep but Audur was going to wake him and threw a little pillow at him. He threw it back at her, and she again at him. They continued throwing it back and forth until Bardi let his hand go along and hit her. She was angry and threw a stone at him. Later that day Bardi stood up and declared himself divorced from Audur. They divided up their goods and Bardi went to *Gardaríki* (Russia) to be a soldier. In this case it's a little difficult to determine which of them was violent to the other.

Obviously, Bardi's marriages can't have been particularly happy and he looked for a chance to get away. Both of these reasons for divorce are minimal and there must be more to it. Bardi was an impetuous, ill-tempered man with attachment disorder, who let his temper lead him astray. He was killed in battle in a distant land, mourned by very few.

Women as property

A woman continued to belong to her family after marriage. If a husband violated his wife's rights he was violating her family. The marriage was first of all a contract between two families and it was important that the families be equal. Adultery was seldom a reason for divorce, rather a reason to pay reparation to the injured party, and the fee was the same for men and women.

Sex in *Grágás*

There were strict penalties for any sex outside of marriage. A woman could be prosecuted for lying with a man of her own free will. The plaintiff could be her husband if she was married, or some other relative. According to *Grágás* it was possible to demand she pay a fine for such conduct. When a man had an affair with a married woman, the victim was above all her husband, and whether the woman had agreed or not had no bearing on the case. If a man secretly kissed a woman at her instigation he would have to pay a fine if he was charged. The social standing of the woman and her family, and who the man was, were mostly the determining factors as to whether a charge was laid in such cases. The sons of powerful farmers could get away with a lot more that the sons of ordinary people, which is nothing new. A man who got into a woman's bed, even if it was her idea, could legally be killed by close relatives of the woman.

The Sagas contain a number of stories where fathers had young men, who made advances to their daughters, killed, even though nothing is said of kisses or other blandishments between them. Close consideration of these legal provisions makes it clear how lame the law is if there is no executive available to carry it out. The laws were of course broken at will by those who considered themselves in a position to do so, i.e. men of higher status who felt the laws did not apply to them. The fact that these laws existed suggests that some people will have been charged with such crimes, even though it did not reach the pages of the *Íslendingasögur*.

Uni the Dane and Thórunn

Gardar Svavarsson, the Swede who first found Iceland and gave it the name Gardarshólmi (Gardar's Island) had a son, Uni the Dane. Gardar did not return to Iceland but Uni came to the Eastern Fjörds and attempted to conquer the country for King Haraldur *hárfagri*. When the folk in the east found out about his plans, they drove him away. He went to the Skógarhverfi district, to the Leidólfur *kappi* (warrior) at Sída and spent the winter there. He was attracted to Thórunn, Leidólfur's daughter, slept with her and by spring she was pregnant. Uni decided to say good bye forever to Leidólfur and his family and fled. Leidólfur rode after him and, after a fight in which several of Uni's men fell, forced him to return.

Leidólfur wanted Uni to marry Thórunn and be his heir. Shortly thereafter, when Leidólfur was away from home, Uni took to his feet again. Again, he was not very successful, because Leidólfur found out about it and rode after his son-in-law and fought him and his companions. This time it ended with Leidólfur and his men killing Uni and those who followed him. Thórunn and Uni's son was the hero Hráar Tungugodi who would later be a man of consequence. He married the sister of *Brennu-Njáls saga's* Gunnar Hámundarson at Hlídarendi. This whole story is in many ways a sad one. Uni wanted nothing more to do with Thórunn than sleep with her. He decided to flee from Leidólfur and his daughter when she was carrying his child. Everything went wrong for Uni and he was eventually killed by his prospective father-in-law. One can not help wondering about Thórunn's state of mind. The father of her child wanted nothing to do with her and ran away. He was killed by her father. What kind of relationship would they have, the young son and his grandfather who was also his father's killer? In that society of absolute punishments, death was ever-present. Uni had to pay with his life for not wanting to marry Thórunn, because she had a powerful father who protected his property. He would of course have got away with things had he chosen a different farm to stay at, where sexual relations with the farmer's daughter would have been less dangerous. Uni has never had any standing in the Sagas. He was the first to attempt to subjugate Iceland under the king of Norway but got no further with his project than to subjugate Thórunn Leidólfursdóttir under himself, to this mournful end.

Love tragedies

People didn't have much faith in love in relationships and saw it as a liability. Lust and love were two sides of the same coin, so people were wary of such emotions. Lust was among the greatest enemies of true Christians, and love was its dangerous confederate. The most important saints of early Christianity fought bitterly against lust, which they considered the devil's work. The Apostle Paul, one of the most forceful theologians of the early church, compared lust to a pregnant woman: "Then the lust, when it has conceived, bears sin; and the sin, when it is full grown, brings forth death." It is easy to see why people were afraid of lust and its companion, love.

In spite of this, some of the *Íslendingasögur* speak quite a lot about love and intense emotions. What these accounts have in common is that they all end badly, as though the aim was to emphasise the harmfulness of intense emotions.

The best known such Sagas are about the relationship between famous poets and their special sweethearts. Their plots are all similar. A young poet, usually a real dreamer, is entranced by a young woman in the first few chapters. They usually do not join up, but have some sort of strange spiritual relationship over a long period, against the wishes of all their friends and relations. The poets are primarily in love with love itself, somewhat less than of the woman in question. The poets under discussion are Hallfredur *vandrædaskáld* (the problem poet), Kormákur Ögmundarson, Gunnlaugur *ormstunga* (worm-tongue) Illugason and Björn *Hítdælakappi* (Warrior of Hítardalur) Arngeirsson. There is a separate story for each of them, but they have a lot in common. These accounts are the closest thing to love-stories as we understand them today, but it would perhaps be better to call them love tragedies.

Hallfredur *vandrædaskáld* Óttarsson

One of the most famous of these Sagas is that of Hallfredur *vandrædaskáld*, the two-part biography of a poet. It deals on the one hand with his loves and predicaments in Iceland and on the other hand with his relationships with his Norwegian wife and the king, Ólafur Tryggvason. These two parts are pretty dissimilar and seem at times not to be in agreement, as though they were two different stories. Hallfredur's love story starts when he became enamoured with Kolfinna Ávaldadóttir. In accordance with the spirit of the times, her father did not want him to seduce her but marry her. Hallfredur, however, did not wish to marry Kolfinna despite all his protestations of love, but be on friendly terms with her without commitment. Her father had control over her so he sought the advice of a good friend about what to do. His friend told him to get a widely travelled Viking, Grís Sæmingsson, to ask for the girls hand, and that went well. When Grís came to meet his bride-to-be, Hallfredur was there already, with Kolfinna on his lap, kissing her repeatedly. Grís was surprised and asked whether this was a habit of theirs. He decided to deal with Hallfredur in such a way as to be rid of this competition. Grís took Hallfredur prisoner, tied him up and handed him over to his father, Óttar. This was most derisive treatment for a young poet in love. After this Grís married Kolfinna and took her home with him. Kolfinna was not asked her opinion of these arrangements, since it was none of her business.

Hallfredur could not tolerate this, went abroad, had all kinds of adventures and got to know the spiritual leader of his life, King Ólafur Tryggvason. He gave Hallfredur the by-name *vandrædaskáld* because of how resistant he was to becoming a Christian. Hallfredur married a certain Ingibjörg Thórisdóttir and they had two sons. His wife died after a short marriage and Hallfredur mourned her deeply. Not long after her death he turned back to his home in Iceland. In this account there is no mention of Hallfredur missing Kolfinna while he was in another country looking after his wife and sons.

No sooner was Hallfredur back in Iceland than he went to visit her, defied her husband and insulted him in many ways. His aim seems to have been to win back Kolfinna and come to a lasting agreement. They met in a mountain dairy and had a happy romantic time. While there he composed some verses containing "dishonourable words" about Grís, which the scribe of one version of the Saga says there is no reason to record. Kofinna appears to have had a very guilty conscience after that love play, as married women often do after a night's pleasure with an irresponsible lover. The conflict hardened until Hallfredur was about to challenge the husband to single combat, but then he had a vision of King Ólafur Tryggvason who prevented the fight. So that was the end of Kofinna as far as Hallfredur was concerned, and he later died at sea. This Saga is in part a legend of King Ólafur, describing some of his miracles and how he appeared to Hallfredur several times at critical moments. Thus Ólafur watched over his followers in both life and death.

The relationship between Hallfredur and Kolfinna was characterised by love or longing that is hopeless, since Hallfredur was more in love with love than with the woman herself. He was resigned to the unhappiness that became a part of him. Kolfinna became the anguish that is central to his whole life. In the end of the book, Hallfredur appears to have given up the conflict with her husband for Kolfinna's favour. He decided to move to Sweden but on the voyage he has an accident and dies. As he lay dying, he composed a poem saying that the woman he has hurt (Kolfinna) will mourn his death. Ólafur's final intervention in Hallfredur's business was to appear, after his death, to a certain abbot to tell him that malicious boys had stolen valuable objects from the poet's coffin. The dead king's information was acted upon and the rogues made to return the stolen goods.

The moral of this Saga appears to be that hopelessly chasing after married women will not bring men luck. In *Hávamál* it says: Be you with ale most wary/ and with another's wife (woman). Throughout *Hávamál* and indeed in the *Book of Sirach* in the *Apocrypha* men are warned against married women. The author of this Saga uses the sanctity of Ólafur Tryggvason to persuade Hallfredur of this truth. His love of Kolfinna gave Hallfredur strength. When he decided to stop chasing after her and move to another country he breathed his last. His life had lost all meaning when Kolfinna had turned to the arms of her husband and King Ólafur had died. There are no explicit sexual descriptions in the Saga but the author implies some wild love play in the mountain dairy when her husband was nowhere near. In fact, there is mention of all Hallfredur's companions having got themselves a woman that night, there being plenty of these little dairy huts. The author intimates that travellers from afar will sometimes have received particularly good hospitality in a hut or farm. The book vividly describes Hallfredur's grief at the death of King Ólafur. The description is so mournful and even harrowing that the sensitive reader feels as if a close loved one has died. Hallfredur took to his bed and could find no comfort when his majesty was dead. The question arises whether Hallfredur was in love with the king, whether his hesitation and awkward behaviour towards Kolfinna were the result of his having been homosexual and tightly locked in the closet. As a theory this is, however, probably taking rather a liberty.

Kormákur Ögmundarson

Another love-sick poet was Kormákur Ögmundarson. His Saga describes his meeting with Steingerdur Thorkellsdóttir, who after that was mistress of his heart and mind. Love struck him like lightning when he first set eyes on the girl, and he knew from that moment that she would bring them sorrow and misfortune. He composed renowned love poems about the beauty of her eyes and general elegance. The attraction was mutual as she could not take her eyes off the poet, and her father had to lock her in a storehouse to prevent her from being with Kormákur. They were betrothed and the date was set for the wedding but Kormákur did not turn up, disabled by either supernatural or psychological powers. He left his bride to wed another. At this point in the story we see that Kormákur appeared to find it easier to admire Steingerdur and compose love poetry to her than to take action. He is the most prolific of all Icelandic love poets and half of all the love poems in the *Íslendingasögur* were composed by him.

Steingerdur then married *Hólmgöngu*-Bersi Véleifsson on her father's advice, when it was clear there would be no marrying Kormak. She was far from happy about this match, in fact, she had no idea what was about to happen until the wedding guests came riding up to the house. She later divorced Bersi most dramatically and was then given to a man named Thorvaldur, who was called *tinteinn* (tinker). She made no objection to this marriage.

Kormákur became a problem for Steingerdur and did everything he could to dishonour her husband. Three times he entered single combat because of her and he wandered across land and sea but she was never out of his thoughts. When he entered battles with his companions, her name was on his lips. They met often. They stayed together in a little mountain dairy in Iceland but lay on either side of a plank, and there is no sign that they crossed over that obstruction. This scenario is described as particularly awkward. Kormákur was virtually paralised with Steingerdur resting beside him on the pallet. He started composing incomprehensible poems about Steingerdur and her husband and recited them endlessly in the dim of night, to her chagrin. This must be one of the most embarrassing lovers' meetings ever recorded. He saved her from the clutches of raiders, and then brought her to her husband. It's as though he lost interest when she was nearby. In the end of the book, he wrestled with a giant in Scotland, killed him with his sword, but was fatally injured himself. In his battle of arms with the giant he thought of Steingerdur's arms and the delight he found in her embrace. Here the book ended and they never got to make love.

Kormákur's poems about Steingerdur are unique in Icelandic love poetry. In one he equates the various parts of her body to all sorts of treasures, in another he considers her comparable to scores of kingdoms. Major rivers would run uphill before he would abandon her. Elsewhere he writes that boulders will float on water and mountains sink into the sea before another woman of such beauty is born. The poetry is full of pain and passionate feeling. Kormákur was a man of words rather than action.

The story is abut the hopeless love of a man for a married woman and is thus a close relative of chivalric romances. Kormákur was a bohemian of his time, went his own way, free of the duties and demands of the family-dominated society. Love gave his life meaning. He was above all in love with love itself and lived with the torment this can bring. The poet was not prepared to exchange his freedom for the banality of marriage. He didn't attend his own wedding, though he well knew what the consequences would be, considering what a brutal insult this was to Steingerdur and her family. He chose to love her from afar, feeding his love on endless love poetry and his own unhappiness.

When I was a teenager, I was enthralled by the life and fate of Kormákur. He was young, in love and unhappy, all of which was popular in my college years, when poets were meant to dress in black and have eyes full of pain. Poetry was no joke but bloody, miserable and earnest. Kormákur is described as an impetuous dreamer who could neither have

Steingerdur nor live without her. There is no sign that they ever had physical relations. In the mountain dairy they rested on either side of the plank and Kormákur decided to keep her awake all night with endless, unintelligible poetry rather than jump into her side of the bed and let lust take control. Perhaps he was homosexual and all this mega-love of Steingerdur was just to hide it. The course of the story is very much in the spirit of Christianity in that age. Kormákur managed to reign in his lust, never let it take control but triumphed over it.

Björn *Hítdælakappi* Arngeirsson

Yet another love-sick hero of the Sagas was Björn *Hítdælakappi* (champion of Hítardalur) Arngeirsson. He was brought up by his relative Skúli at Borg in the Mýrar district, because his neighbour Thórdur Kolbeinsson in Hítarnes bullied, derided and mocked him. Björn fell in love with a certain Oddný Thorkellsdóttir, who was called Oddný *eykyndill* (island candle – i.e. very beautiful). They were betrothed before Björn went raiding, and she was to remain plighted for three years. Björn's enemy, Thórdur, played Björn false, telling people he had died in one of his battles, and thus won the hand of Oddný with trickery and lies. They married and had a good life together, producing five sons and three daughters. Björn heard this news but continued his warfare in distant lands. Björn and Thórdur ran into each other abroad and Björn got the upper hand. He threatened to kill Thórdur but let him go, and made this mercy as derisive as possible. After many years abroad, Björn returned to Iceland and decided, after some deliberation, to live with Thórdur and Oddný. This was a pretty strange choice, considering all that had happened, but sometimes it seems people choose to dance with the Devil even when there are plenty of other, less dangerous, partners available.

His stay with the couple did not bring them any happiness. Thórdur and Björn were like two cocks on the same walk, constantly doing what they could to impress Oddný. They composed insulting verses and pro-

voked each other with sexual innuendos. One verse suggested that Björn shagged cows and he answered by implying that Thórdur was homosexual and shagged other men. Björn carved a little figure that he put in Thórdur's landing place. It showed two men where one had a blue hat on his head and was standing behind the other. This was supposed to mean that the men were gay. As the story progressed, it reflected the close quarters on the farm, because from his bed, Björn would observe all the relations between the couple, filled with jealousy and lust. One evening he witnessed Thórdur forbidding Oddný to get into bed because they had had an argument. Björn then recited yet another verse to provoke Thórdur. In those common rooms everything was a live broadcast, so to speak, even the sex life of the married couple. Björn soon moved away from Hítarnes, where he had hardly been a welcome guest.

Their feud continued, fighting each other with verses and weapons, and Björn usually won. After great struggle and strife, Thórdur succeeded in beating Björn with the help of his neighbours. Thórdur was so delighted by this that he chopped his enemies head off and took it to show Björn's mother. He also took a necklace that Björn had worn around his neck and gave it to Oddný. But pride goeth before a fall. The end of the book describes Oddný's inconsolable grief at Björn's death. She was so sad and morose that Thórdur had to seat her on a horse and lead it back and forth, this being the only way to give her the slightest relief from her depression. Thórdur said his greatest wish was that Björn was alive, as he had never imagined that his death would affect Oddný so deeply as to rob her of all happiness and even sanity. But by this time there was no going back.

The story of Björn *Hítdælakappi* and Oddný *eykyndill* is in many ways a strange love story. It does not look as if they ever consummated their love and Oddný had many children with Thórdur. Björn did, however, compose a famous verse in which he implies that Kolli, son of Thórdur and Oddný, was actually his son. Yet again the author keeps to the narrow path between what may be implied and what must not be spoken.

Nothing was done about Björn's claim to Kolli. Björn did, in fact, marry another woman who played little or no part in the story. The youthful conflict between Thórdur and Björn almost certainly rankled with Björn. He felt deeply that he was inferior to his torturer, as is so common in the victims of bullying. He saw his beloved in the arms of his worst enemy and his soul writhed in anguish. The Saga is primarily about the struggle between Thórdur and Björn over Oddný, where they fought with insulting verses, backbiting and eventually, weapons. Clearly Thórdur loved Oddný and would have done anything to maintain his relationship with her. He betrayed Björn to gain Oddný's love and had a good life with her until Björn returned to Iceland. Björn and Oddný both lost, he his life, she her mind. Thórdur won the combat with Björn but is left in the end of the book a lonely man, who risked all and lost everything.

The Saga is reminiscent of a Greek tragedy or the love stories of the troubadours, where everyone loses in the end. Perhaps the author is emphasising the message of *Hávamál*: "Another's wife/never reach for/ to whisper in her ear" (Never beguile the wife of another to be your confidante). The only direct reference to sex is the verses they composed about each other, with implications of homosexuality. Probably these were simply pretty successful insults, since they would stop at nothing to vilify one another.

Gunnlaugur *ormstunga* Illugason

The most famous love story of the *Íslendingasögur* is that of Gunnlaugur *ormstunga* (worm-tongue). It tells of the love of Gunnlaugur and his competitor, Hrafn Önundarson, for Helga *hin fagra* (the fair) Thorsteinsdóttir of Borg in the Mýrar district. In the beginning of the story, before Helga's birth, her father Thorsteinn had a disturbing symbolic dream about his daughter and some suitors. It upset him so much that he ordered that his daughter should be exposed and killed as soon as she was born. She was rescued, as was so often the case in the Sagas with exposed children of prosperous families, and the Saga then follows her story to the end of her life. She was brought up by non-relatives to the age of six, when she went home to her parents.

Helga was said to be the most beautiful woman in Iceland. She had a glorious head of golden hair with which she could cover her whole body. When Gunnlaugur was a youth, he started visiting Helga regularly, the distance being short between Gilsbakki in the Hvítársida district to Borg. They started to get close and would sit chatting or playing chess as young folk did. Helga was betrothed to Gunnlaugur with her father's blessing and she was to be bound for three years while Gunnlaugur went abroad raiding, as was the custom of young men. Gunnlaugur did not get home within the time allotted and Helga was given as wife to Hrafn Önundarson, Gunnlaugur's sworn enemy. Yet again, we see the patriarchy at work. Helga's father decided that Hrafn should get Helga despite her objections and clear wish to wait for Gunnlaugur. Thorsteinn was fully within his rights, legally, and Helga did not blame him, she mostly blamed Gunnlaugur, who messed up his return and their relationship, carelessly prancing poncing around in foreign lands. Thorsteinn went directly against his daughters wishes and ignored her protests and depression on the wedding day. He felt that Gunnlaugur had humiliated him and his family by not respecting the time limit they had agreed on. The pride and honour of the family were most important. This was in total accord with the provisions of *Grágás*.

Everything worked against Gunnlaugur on his return. He came ashore on Melrakkaslétta in the north, was injured in a pointless wrestling match when he landed and had many days' ride ahead of him. He came too late and Helga and Hrafn were married. The bride discovered that the lover she had been waiting for had finally come home safely. Hrafn faced the fact that his bride loved another man and had no interest in him.

Their marriage was dreadful. Helga wanted nothing to do with her husband and yearned for Gunnlaugur. Once when they met at some feast she gazed at him with loving eyes and the Saga quotes the old saying: "The eyes will not hide it if a woman loves a man." This saying is in fact quite often quoted in modern weddings. Old Illugi, Gunnlaugur's father, was completely baffled by this ardour of love. He rebuked his son for investing so much love in one girl, saying there were plenty of other beautiful women.

Events eventually let to Gunnlaugur and Hrafn fighting over Helga. Hrafn challenged his rival to single combat, saying he would get no use of his wife while Gunnlaugur lived, which means that she had refused him any and all sex in this loveless marriage.

The winner was to get Helga, so the prize was a rich one, but neither won it since both died in the fight. Gunnlaugur won the fight, but Hrafn managed to give him a severe head injury after Gunnlaugur had laid down his weapons to bring Hrafn a drink of water. As he lay dying, Hrafn could not bear the thought of Gunnlaugur sharing the bed of Helga.

In the conflict between Gunnlaugur and Hrafn, Helga was a passive victim of whatever fate the men's love would determine for her. The Saga highlights how powerless women were in the dance of life, as Helga had

A psychiatrist's opinion

All these love stories are actually teaching the same lesson. Love crazes and maddens young men, who lose all sense and judgment and behave at odds with the rules and customs of society. Of course it would have been best for these young men to take their fathers' advice and let them decide whom they should marry. They choose to follow their emotions and end up in accordance with that. Love brings men nothing but unhappiness. Women are all victims in these romances and have control over neither their progress nor their end. Descriptions of close relations or sex acts of the protagonists are nowhere to be found, as that would have been improper at the time. Thus the stories are, among other things, words of warning to the readers, that blindly following one's emotions will be a blessing to no man.

no defence against the hate and fury of both her suitors. The plot we are familiar with: young lovers swear loyalty to each other, the young man gets delayed abroad and loses the girl to another suitor. Helga's pain was great, since for all her beauty she was an insecure and dependent young lady. She knew her father wanted her exposed at birth and she owed her life to people who disobeyed his orders. She had rejection issues and was full of self-doubt. When Gunnlaugur didn't return at the agreed time all these feelings came to the fore again, and she felt she had yet again been betrayed by the patriarchy. Her father gave her to Hrafn against her will, so the betrayal was manifold. She could trust no one.

Somewhat later, Helga was married to another man, Thorkell Hallkelsson, with whom she had children. The Saga ends on a charming description of Helga's mourning for Gunnlaugur. Many years had passed, circumstances were totally different. Some disease had come up on their farm and many of the household were ill. Helga caught the disease but did not take to her bed. Once she was sitting in the kitchen and laid her head on her husband, Thorsteinn's, knee. Then she sent for a mantle that Gunnlaugur had given her and died holding it in her arms. Nothing else mattered to her at that moment, not her husband, her children or her life after Gunnlaugur's death. She was again the young farmer's daughter at Borg, waiting anxiously for a visit from the young man from Hvítársida. This most famous love story of the *Íslendingasögur* has gained its status in part due to the heartbreaking ending which has moved Icelanders through the ages.

The dream of Helga's father Thorsteinn came true. He dreamt that two eagles were fighting over a beautiful swan. They both died, but a gyrfalcon that came from another direction got the swan. These cruel birds fought over the swan which could do nothing in its impotence but watch how things turned out.

The moral of the story is that lusty young men are endangered by the beauty of women. This fits with the sayings in *Hávamál*: "Fool out of hardy/ makes the son of men/ the powerful love" (The power of love makes wise men's healthy sons foolish). Another moral is that no man should ever trust his enemy.

Freud and the poets

A long time later, Sigmund Freud developed a concept he called the "Madonna-whore complex". The theory applies to the man who does not desire the woman he loves and does not love the woman he desires. The poets in the *Íslendingasögur*, such as Hallfredur and Kormákur, seem unable to desire the women they love. They long for them from a distance all their lives but never put these powerful emotions to the test in a physical relationship. There is no evidence that Kormákur and Steingerdur ever shared a bed, let alone Björn *Hítdælakappi* and Oddný *eykyndill*. It is difficult to tell whether Gunnlaugur and Helga ever caressed one another.

Freud claimed that men put the woman they loved on a pedestal alongside their mother or the Virgin Mary, and it would be impossible to lust after such sacred women. Had Kormákur, Hallfredur or Björn had a session on Freud's couch he would doubtless have asked searching questions about their relationship with their mother and attempted to explain their mental paralysis on those grounds. Actually, Freud explained most human weaknesses in connection with the relationship with the mother, so that would not have been anything new. Many people have, in fact, speculated on Kormákur's paralysis regarding Steingerdur. It looks as if he totally despaired when the woman he loved was within reach. The 20th century poet David Stafánsson from Fagriskógur said he had never properly tried to gain the woman he loved because his "Kormákur's nature" overpowered his will.

Young men fight over the same woman

Asperger in the foothills of Mount Esja

Kjalnesinga saga tells of the fight between three young men, Búi, Örn and Kolfinnur, over the girl Ólöf, who was deemed the most elegant of women. Their attempts to win the girl's admiration are described, and how they eventually took to their weapons to rid themselves of the competition. Örn tried to kill Kolfinnur, which ended with Kolfinnur killing him. Búi wounded Kolfinnur and took Ólöf away with him to the cave where he dwelt. Because he had killed others and burned down a holy place Búi was forced to flee the country, but Ólöf was left in Iceland. In the fullness of time she gave birth to a little girl who had been conceived in the cave. Búi became a soldier in the service of the King of Norway. He went on a mission from the king to the land of the giants, to meet King Dofri and try to buy a chess set he owned and the King of Norway coveted. While there he met the daughter of Dofri, Frídur the giant maiden, and slept with her. She had received Búi particularly well and immediately directed him to her bed where he more or less stayed all winter, high in her favour.

Búi decided to go to Iceland and leave the giants behind. As he was

saying goodbye to her, Frídur announced that she was with child. Búi decided to return home despite this news. Frídur's goodbye to her lover was generous, as she got her father to give him the fine golden chess set that the king of Norway coveted so. This trip of Búi's to the land of the giants was a total success, he got not only the chess set but also a good woman to pleasure himself with. The pregnancy was an unexpected bonus that he soon forgot.

In Iceland things got heated. Kolfinnur had recovered from his wound and kidnapped Ólöf and taken her away. Búi could not tolerate that and fought with Kolfinnur. The upshot of this was that Búi chopped his rival in two down the middle, so that the parts fell one to each side. He considered Ólöf tainted by her time with Kolfinnur and sent her off along with the daughter who had been conceived in the cave. The characteristics of this society show up clearly in this account. Men do not hesitate to kill their competitor for a woman with total disregard for the value of life. The woman herself has no say about anything and really does not matter once the competitor is dead.

Búi married again after this and had several children with his wife. The end of the book is especially dramatic. Twelve years after all this, a young boy, named Jökull, turns up from abroad and says he is the son of Búi and the troll maiden. Búi wanted nothing to do with the boy and offered him the chance to prove himself in a wrestling match. He had forgotten all about his gratifying time in the bed of the giantess and how helpful she had been to him. The wrestling match ended with Jökull killing Búi, his father the womaniser. After this, Jökull disappeared from the story. Búi got his just desserts for his treachery. The fruits of illicit love were his bane. His fate is reminiscent of Greek tragedy, where killing of fathers is fairly popular. Jökull killed his father in the wrestling match, thus proving his paternity, so it was all in vain. This dramatic story also speaks of Búi's nurse, named Esja, whose name was given to Mount Esja, the pride of Reykjavík. She was of course highly skilled in magic and her relationship with Búi was close and sexual, as was often the case between female wizards and young hot-heads.

This is a Saga that teeters on the edge of fantasy. Búi is the real hero, who competed for his beloved with two other suitors. In the story he is described as introverted and idiosyncratic. He was a master at shooting rocks with sling-shots or some sort of catapult.

A modern person would probably have called him square, on some autistic spectrum. It is clear that Búi and Ólöf were in love, had a child together, but then everything went as wrong as can be. Ólöf had absolutely no effect on these clashes and lovers came and went like migrating birds. In the end, Búi threw her out like a faulty purchase that had passed its sell-by date. He was so uncompromising that he couldn´t accept that she had lain with another man. In his relations with Frídur the giantess, she was active and he passive. She directed him to get in her bed and he obeyed. He was not at all in touch with his feelings in that case, rather thought he had a better chance of getting the chess set for his king if he had sex with the giant maiden. When Jökull turns up, Búi's limitations become very obvious. He had not registered that Frídur was pregnant, and Jökull was not at all welcome into the four-sided world of this strangely constructed personality. Today, he would probably be diagnosed as having Asberger disorder or something like that.

In this Saga everyone loses, but it would have been interesting to be able to keep track of Jökull Búason, who caused his father's death when only 12 years old. He disappeared into the dark like so many others so there are no stories about any complexes he might have developed. Nowadays, this young man would have ended up with chronic problems in the Children's Mental Hospital. This is yet another love tragedy with numerous victims and variations.

A love story with a happy ending

Víglundar saga tells a story of two young people in love that has a happy ending. The lovers get together in the end after weathering incredible storms. It is abut Víglundur Thorgrímsson and Ketilrídur Hólmkelsdóttir, two teenagers on the Snæfellsnes peninsula, who fell in love. Both their fathers were big-name powerful farmers. The situation was complicated by the fact that Ketilrídur's brothers, Einar and Jökull, had a bone to pick with Víglundur and would do anything to prevent them from getting together. On Víglundur's side was his brother, Trausti. There are many other aspects to this situation but the focal point is the developing love between Víglundur and Ketilrídur. Víglundur suffered from the fact that Hólmkell, the girl's father, was in charge, and the feelings of a couple of teenagers was of no significance in those days.

They did actually get engaged with rings and ceremony but all in vain. Her brothers slandered Víglundur and managed to get Hólmkell to marry her to a young steersman from Norway, named Hákon. The brothers had offered her to Hákon, either for marriage or as a concubine. But they were not satisfied, and ambushed Víglundur in order to get rid of him permanently. Things don't always go according to plan, and he killed both the brothers and the newly-married steersman. Víglundur and Trausti were severely wounded in the battle and it took them a year to recover. Ketilrídur felt bad and spent sleepless nights, having just been made a widow and lost both her brothers. She knew, of course, that her engagement to Víglundur was the indirect cause of her husband's and brothers' deaths, so she was overcome with guilt and sorrow.

The brothers Trausti and Víglundur set off for travels and raids, but before they embarked, Víglundur went to say good bye to Ketilrídur. She combed his hair and he declared that no one would be allowed to cut his hair but Ketilrídur herself. While they were away raiding and killing people, Ketilrídur was married off again, to an old, impotent man from the Eastern Fjörds . She never had a day's happiness while in this relationship. Víglundur came back and went to visit his fiancée. The old man let him have her without a fight, saying he had just been keeping her for him. He assured our hero that he never touched her in an inappropriate way, nor had any other man, so she was back to being a virgin, despite two marriages. Víglundur would not need to worry about the paternity of any children they might have. The young people ended up together in a happy marriage, which was really unusual.

Víglundur was a poet, like the tragic quartet of Kormákur, Hallfredur, Gunnlaugur and Björn, and he composed many lovely poems to Ketilrídur. This love story is unusual, though there are many familiar aspects. The father's absolute power over the girl is like a refrain throughout the story. He twice gave her to men against her will, so her feelings mattered not a bit to him, any more than to their fathers. This changed, in fact, as the story progressed and the fathers of the lovers started speaking together about the dire straits things had come to. Hólmkell had by then lost two sons and a son-in-law due to the strong feelings of the young folk. One can't help doubting that his satisfaction with his new-old son-in-law was genuine. This was a complex situation of conflicting emotions.

The story ends on a Christian note, with a prayer. The ending is not, however, in any way consistent with the church's views on love or lust or the power of a father. Víglundur and Ketilríður actually violate her father's rulings. This Saga was clearly written under the influence of chivalric romances or other romantic literature.

Even more problems

Víglundar saga is first and foremost about the love between the hero and Ketilríður, the farmer's daughter. They are like love-sick teenagers in an American movie and get together in the end after many an adventure. This is the only one of the *Íslendingasögur* that ends more or less well. Víglundur's parents, Ólöf and Thorgrímur, had to go through rather more for their marriage. Ólöf was the daughter of Earl Thórir of Norway. Her beauty was so great that she was always called Ólöf *geisli* (sunbeam). The Earl was terrified for his daughter and built an especially strong lodge for her and her handmaidens where they were to sit and learn womanly skills. Myriad young men came to court Ólöf but the Earl refused them all.

King Haraldur once came to visit Thórir bringing also his courtiers. Among them was a young man, son of a powerful man and his concubine, named Thorgrímur. His father was a womanising notable who had a number of children with his wife and concubines. Thorgrímur's and Ólöf's eyes met and it was love at first sight. Thorgrímur was a hasty lad and immediately asked for the girl's hand but Thórir refused without a second thought. Shortly thereafter an elderly widower named Ketill, filthy rich, asked for her hand and got it. The rumour was that Ólöf objected strongly to this marriage, and was in fact secretly engaged to Thorgrímur. But all to no avail. Daddy would decide this like everything else. Thorgrímur was distraught at the news and asked his master, King Haraldur, for advice. His majesty advised against taking Ketill on because he was a renowned fighter. He told Thorgrímur to ask for the hand of Ketill's daughter but Thorgrímur had no interest in a solution of that kind. Yet again, men negotiate about women as if they were cattle. The king's insight into the secrets of love and the maze of the mind must have been very little and shallow. Thorgrímur attended the wedding and kidnapped the bride in a fantastic manner. He asked Ketill whether he had bought Ólöf, which Ketill admitted. Then he asked whether this had been according to Ólöf's wishes which she denied. Earl Thórir said that this was his decision and told the lover Thorgrímur to leave. At that moment all the lights in the hall went out causing great confusion. When they managed to light the hall again both the bride and Thorgrímur were gone. They sailed to Iceland where they were married. This is an amusing tale and the discerning reader will be wondering how it was possible to put out all the lights at once in a time of candles and long-fires. The flight of the couple might have been cut out of a Hollywood thriller. A valiant young man rescues his girl from the clutches of evil men with a frequently used Hollywood trick, darken the house and use the ensuing confusion to get away. Discerning readers will also be surprised at the assurance of the old men, letting the disappointed suitor into the feast where his girl was being married to another. *Víglundar saga* is again the Saga with happy endings, lovers manage to join in a marriage bed and have a good life. Thorgrímur and Ólöf *geisli* got together after a fantastic sequence of events that could have come from one of today's thrillers.

Hazardous love

Thórdar saga hreda (hostile) tells of the married couple Thórhallur and Ólöf Hrolleifsdóttir at Miklibær in the Óslandshlíd district. People thought her a fine woman, enterprising and good company. Thórhallur, on the other hand, they considered both cowardly and base. He was boastful and professed to be able to handle any situation. She had been married to him for money and he was a good deal older. This is never a promising combination. The Saga describes their constant bickering, with Ólöf listing his faults, saying how uninteresting he is, total scum. Not so very different from unhappy marriages in modern times.

Thórhallur allowed the hero of the Saga, Thórdur *hreda*, to hide in his house. He and the unhappy housewife got along swimmingly from the start. She bedded the fugitive right away in the close quarters of the common room, so the belittled husband could not have helped noticing their love games. Thórhallur decided to get rid of his wife's lover and disclosed Thórdur's whereabouts to his enemies. Midfjördur-Skeggi himself, armed with his sword *Sköfnungur* (shiny metal), turned up to slay Thórdur. That went wrong and Skeggi decided not to kill Thórdur after all, but to kill Thórhallur instead. Why he did this is unclear, but he went to the marriage bed, where the man and wife were lying. She asked him to spare her husband, but to no avail, and Skeggi chopped off his head with his trusty sword, right there at the bedside. Before felling the blow he said that this scum had lived long enough! It's obvious that the wife was not very convincing when she asked Skeggi to spare her husband. The story ends well because Thórdur *hreda* married Ólöf, she won the lottery and the churl got his just desserts. This is yet another instance of an unlucky husband being killed in his bed with his wife looking on.

Mutual love

Ljósvetninga saga tells of Gudmundur *ríki* (the rich) at Mödruvellir. His daughter Thórdís was a woman of great beauty. On Gudmundur's farm

there was a certain Sörli Brodd-Helgason, a fine young man. Sörli and Thórdís start making friends. Gudmundur did not like this and made her move for a while to his brother's, Einar at Thverá. Sörli continued to visit her there. One morning Thórdís was outside on a lovely day, attending to the laundry. She saw a man ride up to the farm and said, "Now we have sunshine and southerly breezes, and Sörli rides into the yard." This is said to be the most famous declaration of love by a woman in the Sagas. Sörli proposed marriage to Thórdís but Gudmundur was reluctant. Everyone in the district did what they could to help these young lovers get together and in the end they were married. This is one of very few instances in the *Íslendingasögur* where the voice of a young woman in love is heard.

Gudmundur at Mödruvellir is one of the few powerful men in the Sagas who is obviously homosexual. There are a number of signs that his reluctance in this case was because he himself was in love with Sörli and could not accept the idea that this beautiful youth was heterosexual and about to spend his life in the arms of a woman.

Sex in Specific Sagas

Gísla saga Súrssonar

The idle talk of women and its consequences

According to the Old Testament, a woman should be submissive to her husband. Eve allowed herself to be tempted by the serpent's flattery and took an apple or other fruit from the tree of the knowledge of good and evil, which grew in the middle of the garden of Eden. Adam took part in the crime at her instigation. God punished them both severely and the fall of man came to be. From that moment, the holy scriptures advised men not to listen to their wives. Wives should remain silent and unnoticed.

There are numerous places in the *Íslendingasögur* which maintain that only evil can come from the idle talk or chattering of women. In *Hávamál*, there are many verses that warn of the dangers of loose talk. The 73rd verse declares that "the tongue is the bane of the head", and in *Grettis saga* we find: "No one is totally stupid if he can keep quiet." This fits neatly with the misogynistic attitudes we so often see in the Sagas.

No Saga is so influenced by the idle talk of women as *The Saga of Gísli Súrsson*. There a great web is woven of the fates of promising young men, and the weavers are women whose idle talk brings about nothing but evil. This Saga is a good example of how a minor incident and thoughtless word can lead to an appalling series of events where vengeance takes on a life of its own and the protagonists become victims of fate and turn against each other.

Gísli's family moved to Iceland, and the story goes on to tell the tale of four friends, promising young men, in the Western Fjörds: the brothers Gísli and Thorkell, and their brothers-in-law, Vésteinn and Thorgrímur. They decided to swear themselves blood brothers to strengthen their friendship but at the last moment, they changed their minds and parted somewhat coldly.

There was a great contrast between the brothers, Gísli and Thorkell. Gísli was hard-working but Thorkell lazy. He did not work on his farm like other men, but was happiest at home, lying down and napping. Once he snuck up on the women of the house who sat sewing and chatting about former lovers and old infatuations. He heard that his wife might once have been involved with another man, Vésteinn, who was the brother of Gísli's wife, Audur. She understands the dangers of such careless talk and tries to silence the women. But her silencing came too late because Thorkell had heard what they were saying. Then Audur said: "Oft comes evil from women's talk, and it may be that here will come the worst." This could have come directly from the Old Testament, and Adam would have agreed strongly with the sentiment. No one suffered as much from a woman's talk as he did. Audur knew that in their society of honour and revenge it was dangerous to awaken jealousy in vain men. A husband owned his wife lock, stock and barrel and assumed that she had had no friendships with other men. Information and hints of this kind were thus an attack on a man's masculinity and ownership of his wife.

And the result is yet another fall of man. Old friends and brothers-in-law turn against each other and the blood brothers' bond, which had actually never been sworn, is drowned in blood.

Reflections of a psychiatrist

Gísla saga is first and foremost a tragedy about a talented hero who has no control over his own life but drifts like an rudderless boat on the high seas of fate and coincidence. There is not much mention of the protagonists' sex lives, though the author does draw a poignant picture of a young couple that are thinking about love-play just moments before the husband's death. The relationship between Gísli and his sister is more than a little odd and the discerning reader might suspect they had perhaps had a love relationship, which could explain the ill will Gísli bears towards her suitors and husband. Such sibling love was, of course, utterly forbidden, so the writer of the story would have have found it difficult to write it down. He does, however, make some implications. Why did Gísli choose to feel his sister's breast as she lay in bed next to her husband? Gísli left it up to Thórdís to decide whether he would be punished for murdering her husband. He composed and recited an enigmatic poem when he confessed the killing to his sister. She did not hesitate to tell on him, which is when the real tragedy of his life started.

Thórdís' second husband, Börkur *digri*, vengefully pursued Gísli for decades, which might have been fuelled by jealousy. He suspected that the relationship between Gísli and Thórdís was not your normal sibling relationship, that she both loved and hated her brother, as is common with the victims of incest. Gísli and Audur's marriage is described as very solid but there is little in the way of lust or sexual tension.

Gísli is described as a rather depressed intellectual and poet, pursued by misfortune and no hedonist. Many of his poems were about two dream women who came to him in sleep in his exile. They were different, one bright and the other dark, and brought him contradictory messages of life and happiness on the one hand and death and destruction on the other. The women appear to reflect the double morality in Gísli's soul, so full of conflicting ideas. The dreams are sexual. One woman threatens bloody mutilation while the other offers gentle comfort. Was one of these dream women Thórdís herself, accusing him of some crime against her? Does that explain all the blood in his poetry? Is the author covertly referring to some case of incest that some people will have known about? In his exile, Gísli was plagued by sexual dreams and fantasies that Freud would have wished to study more closely.

In the course of the story, it becomes abundantly clear that Gísli lacked independence and confidence and needed the approbation of others. He longed for praise and reward from his father, so for his sake he killed the two youths in Norway who were chatting with his sister, Thórdís. He was himself enamoured of his sister and envied these lads who could so casually chat with her. His inferiority complex and his own jealousy lay behind the deaths of those young men and of his brother-in-law, Thorgrímur. Gísli was a gifted young man but amazingly managed to wreck everything he touched. At the end of the book we see him as an ill-fated, grief-stricken hero who welcomes death like a long-lost friend.

Following that incident, Vésteinn was killed. The women's talk being the underlying cause of the killing, either Thorgrímur or Thorkell sneaked over to Vésteinn's in the night and killed him. This killing was no heroic deed but a base savagery. A man snuck up to Vésteinn's bed under cover of the dark and killed him. The Saga does not say who the murderer was, but the natural assumption was that this was Thorkell's work. It was his wife, Ásgerdur, who had talked about having been close to Vésteinn.

Gísli chose to kill his brother-in-law Thorgrímur in revenge. He also snuck around in the night into the hall where people were sleeping and went to the bed of his sister Thórdís and Thorgrímur. She was pregnant at the time. He placed his hand on her breast to wake her. She thought it was Thorgrímur touching her, wanting some loving. They exchanged meaningless whispers, then fell asleep again. Gísli stood there with his spear raised like a giant phallus, waiting for the chance to shove it into his brother-in-law and former friend. Then he did it, and Thórdís awoke startled to find her husband covered in blood and dying beside her in the

From Haukadalur.

bed. Her pregnancy and nakedness make the murder even more barbarous and dramatic. Those with an interest in sex and death manage to connect the two and say that Thorgrímur died with his penis erect, but of course there are no actual witnesses. Gísli snuck back to his house, trying to hide his tracks like a petty criminal, and indeed, he had intentionally broken the law.

This killing had horrifying consequences and is the climax of the story. The murder was unsolved for a while but Gísli decided to tell his sister Thórdís, in confidence, that he had done the deed. She was by this time married to her dead husband's brother, Börkur *digri* (broad or boastful), as was often the way with widows in those days. According to customs at that time, it was Börkur who should take revenge for his brother, Thorgrímur. Thórdís told him about Gísli's confession and all hell broke loose. In court, Börkur got Gísli sentenced to exile from the country, but Gísli chose to remain in Iceland, making himself an outlaw and legal target for killing. Börkur was in charge of the pursuit which went on for years. Gísli had to traipse all over the Western Fjörds and Breidafjördur, in constant flight from Börkur and his men. Gísli's wife, Audur, stayed with him throughout, sacrificing her chance of a normal life on the bonfire of hostilities that had been lit the night Thorgrímur was murdered. The longer their exile lasted, the more Gísli became dependent on Audur, entering a kind of mother-son relationship with her. She comforted and encouraged him as she would an unhappy child, as he was very frightened of the dark and could not abide the loneliness of exile. He and Audur had no children but took on one foster daughter, Gudrídur.

Thórdís and Börkur's marriage was loveless and sad. She was always between the Devil and the deep blue sea, between the husband she slept with at night and the brother her husband tormented. It can't have been easy to have peaceful family gatherings in these circumstances. When they had finally killed Gísli, Eyjólfur *grái* (the grey) and his men came to Helgafell to give Börkur the news. He was delighted when he heard his arch enemy Gísli had fallen and thought that now his brother Thorgrímur had been fully avenged. He decided to hold a feast for these killer guests. As housewife at Helgafell, Thórdís brought her brother's killers porridge while they sat and boasted about their feat. She appears to have decided to avenge her brother because she got hold of a sword and lunged at Eyjolfur. Her attempt failed miserably, Eyjolfur suffered a scratch but Börkur was furious and struck his wife. This was the decisive moment leading to their divorce, though of course there had been a long history of dissatisfaction.

It is easy to deduce Thórdís' feelings. All the years of Gísli's exile she had lived in a constant state of tension, guilt and doubt. Did I do the right thing or not? Should I have given him away? She saw the miserable life her brother and sister-in-law were leading and got in bed every night with the man who wanted to kill them. She felt cursed. Gísli killed the man she loved and sent her into the arms of a man she did not love. Gísli's death freed her from her chains, gave her the strength to use a sword, challenge her husband and then divorce him. Thórdís is one of the stronger characters in this Saga and by far the most dramatic, a mover of destinies.

More night-time killings

There are more accounts in the Íslendingasögur of men who were slain in their beds, lying beside their wives. The Droplaugarsonar saga contains an account of the killing of the well-born Helgi Ásbjarnarson as he lay beside his wife, Thórdís. Grímur Droplaugarson came to avenge his brother. The course of events is reminiscent of Gísli's slaying of Thorgrímur except that Grímur laid his hand on Helgi himself, not on the victim's wife as Gísli had done. Helgi woke up thinking his wife had been stroking him and was surprised at how cold her hand was. They fell back asleep but Grímur brandished his sword and told Helgi to wake up because he had had all the sleep he needed. He feminised Helgi, ordered him to wake up, lie on his back and accept the phallic symbol, the sword. Here the authors are toying with the forbidden, connecting death, nakedness and the closeness of married couples. It is an amusing irony to tell a man who is about to enter the final sleep that he has had enough sleep.

Grettis saga

The lusty Grettir Ásmundarson

Grettir Ásmundarson from Bjarg in Midfjördur is one of the most celebrated heroes of the *Íslendingasögur*. He was strong as an ox, intelligent and a fine poet. Grettir often spoke in brief aphorisms which are still in use today, especially when people have a speech to make. He is described as seclusive, cantankerous and sullen in his daily conduct. Grettir clearly had a serious personality disorder, was amoral and a real brute. He appears to have slept with a number of women during his exile, so we can see that women fell for criminals at the time of the Sagas, just as they do today.

In his youth, Grettir was so disobedient and troublesome that this father was prepared to do anything to get him out of the country. Today's psychiatrists would have diagnosed him as having oppositional-defiance disorder, ADHD and PDD-NOS (atypical autism). Ásmundur at Bjarg got the merchant Haflidi to take his son with him when he sailed to Norway. The steersman on the ship was Bárdur, whose beautiful young wife was travelling with them. The ship sailed into storms, lost its way and took in seawater and they were all in grave danger. The crew was bailing night and day, but Grettir was just carrying on with the steersman's wife, "patting her stomach". The men didn't like this and rebuked Grettir, but he just bad-mouthed them and recited couplets about Haflidi. The steersman's wife seemed quite content in the arms of Grettir the strong and the story mentions that she attended to his hands, or gave him a manicure. Finally, Grettir stood up and went to help the crew bail out the ship and after quite a struggle they reached land.

This story is incredible when you think of how small the ships were with little or no enclosed spaces for people to play love games. The activities of Grettir and the woman will have been obvious to everyone on board. One can just imagine the atmosphere. The ship rolling, the wind howling, waves splashing everywhere and everyone struggling to row or bail. While all this was going on, Grettir was lying there, having sex with the woman, complete with the accompanying moaning, groaning and general commotion. But nobody dared take on Grettir, with his big muscles and bad temper. That must have been an astonishing voyage. What was the steersman's wife thinking of? Had she fallen for the strong man? Was she bored with her husband? Did Grettir use force? There is no further mention of this foolish girl after the voyage, but it is hard to imagine that she and Bárdur the steersman had a happy marriage after this disgrace. It would not have been easy for him to forget the love play and sensual noises that his wife and Grettir provided to the accompaniment of sea and storm.

There are more stories in *Grettis saga* of his sexual exploits. There was the time he came cold, wet and exhausted after swimming from Drangey and asked to rest at the farm Reykir. This was years after he lay with the steers-man's wife out at sea. By this time, he had been outlawed and lived on Drangey with his brother and one slave. A great many people were constantly hunting him, wanting to kill him. The fire on the island had gone out and Grettir swam ashore to get fire. When he came to shore he warmed himself in a hot spring, then went to the farm and went to bed. While he lay sleeping, the farmer's daughter and a maidservant come in

Drangey.

to have a look at the hero. The maidservant peeked under the blanket and said she was surprised he was not better hung, considering his size and build. The farmer's daughter peeked as well and shouted with laughter at what she saw. This woke Grettir and he heard what they are saying. He recited two very bawdy verses. Then, according to the story, he pulled the maid into his bed and she did not criticise him after that. She shouted loudly when he took her into bed but went quiet when he had his way.

This section in the book is hard to understand. The author has drawn a pretty consistent picture of Grettir, the superman and hero who speaks in epigrams and verses. He is a most unfortunate man, but that is to some extent due to enchantments and magic. Everything that happens to him is actually someone else's fault, never his own. Suddenly, we find Grettir naked in bed with young women examining his nether parts and making fun of him. They both found his penis incredibly small. In the first verse he recited, Grettir admitted this, but said on the other hand that he had really big balls. Then he recited the second verse, which is full of sexual promises, and pulled the girl into bed. The verse opens thus:

> Seamstress sweet you can't afford
> To think that mine's a little sword.

Was one of Grettir's problems that he was so big and strong, yet had a small penis? Did he have to prove himself in other ways as men do today by owning big cars, motor bikes or other phallic symbols? Grettir brandished his sword and killed many a good man with it. Was the sword an extension of the little penis that he was ashamed of?

At the time of the Sagas, a large, erect penis was a fertility symbol. Statues of Freyr with his member sticking out were very common. Grettir discovered early on that he was not well-endowed and that probably had some effect on his temperament and attitude towards the world. It is difficult to see why the author included this joke or tall tale unless it was to lighten the story at a point when things were getting heavy. But the picture he draws is undeniable laughable. The strong man and superhero lying naked on a bed and two silly girls make fun of his small penis. The author derides the hero and shows him in a completely different, more comic light than elsewhere in the book.

Rape

According to *Grágás*, rape was a serious offence against the family and owners of the woman, but not so much against herself. If a woman was raped, it was pretty certain that the perpetrator would be punished according to the marital and social standing of the woman. If a married woman was raped, it was first and foremost an offence against the husband, who had a duty to take revenge. Raping an unmarried woman was an offence against her family, her father and brothers. The amount of the compensation was dependent on her social class. The daughters of powerful farmers could receive very considerable compensation but less well-connected women would get a good deal less.

Grettir clearly took the girl against her will, so it was a case of rape. There were no consequences, however, despite the clear provisions in

Grágás. Grettir was an oft-sentenced outlaw, so there was not much point in adding to his punishments. The girl had no family so there was no one to stand up for her honour or their property. She had no rights in her dealings with the hero. Great champions were allowed to grab slaves and women of no family and use them sexually whether they liked it or not. Here as elsewhere, the author is completely on Grettir's side. The girl was asking to be raped by making fun of the hero's little penis. Grettir had no choice but to pull the girl into his bed to defend himself. She had no voice in the matter.

Sex with giants

The authors of the *Íslendingasögur* avoid describing sexual relationships between people. But they long to tell about such adventures too, and sometimes they do tell about absurd encounters between men and giantesses. In fact, there is such a story in *Grettis saga* where he comes as a guest to the farm Sandhaugar in Bárdradalur. Two men had recently disappeared from the farm and people suspected that giants had been at work. Grettir offered to stay there over Christmas Eve and did so. Towards midnight, a huge giantess came into the room, carrying a trough and other kitchen implements. She clearly intended to chop to pieces any men she found and take them home in the trough. When she saw Grettir, she grabbed at him and they wrestled all night long. The struggle between her and Grettir was obviously sexual, as if the author had allowed his imagination to carry him into the darkest depths of sex. He imagines a hag with huge breasts who presses Grettir to her in a wild game of lust and death. This brawl ended when Grettir managed to use his sword, chopped off one of her arms and threw her into a nearby waterfall. The giantess died, either from her wound or because she turned to stone when the sun hit the cliff side, where some say she stands to this day.

After slaying the giantess, Grettir went into the gorge under the waterfall and found a huge giant who was probably her son. Grettir killed him too, and threw him in the river. It's interesting that the son made his mother go out into the community to get supplies, contrary to the way things are done among humans, where the woman's place is by the fire while the man goes out to find food for the family. The story points out the terrible fate of women who think they can take over the traditional role of men. They come to a sticky end.

After this, Grettir returned to the farm where he found Steinvör, the mistress of the house, and stayed with her for a time. The story says that their relationship was close. Grettir had defeated the giantess after a long, hard battle by using his sword, undeniably a phallic symbol. He proved his manhood and was rewarded with the housewife's caresses. This is typical for Grettir's relations with women, where we are given to understand that he occasionally could break off killing people to attend to other, more pleasurable things. In the fullness of time, Steinvör of Sandhaugar bore a son who was named Skeggi. He was attributed to Kjartan, the son of the priest, but he was very different from his siblings in strength and size. When Skeggi was fifteen years old, he was counted the strongest of all men in the North of Iceland, and once that was clear he was attributed to Grettir. They had high hopes for this promising youth, but he died in his eighteenth year, so there were no achievements to tell tales about.

Thorsteinn *drómundur* (battle ship) and Spes

At the end of *Grettis saga* there is a short episode about Thorsteinn *drómundur*, who was Grettir's half-brother and avenged him in Constantinople in Turkey. Grettir was killed in Drangey after a long battle against overwhelming odds. His brother Illugi, who was with him on the island, was executed as they thought he would avenge his brother if they let him live. The man who killed the brothers, Thorbjörn *öngull* (fishhook), fled the country after the slaying because people were saying that he would not have brought Grettir down had he not sought the aid of a witch. She had used magic to cause Grettir to injure his leg so he became sick and couldn't defend himself.

Thorbjörn joined the Varangian Guard of the emperor in Constantinople. Thorsteinn followed him there and slew him when he was bragging about having killed Grettir. The rules of the Guard stated that it was unlawful to kill a man inside their living quarters so Thorsteinn was guilty of a serious crime. He was arrested and locked in a dungeon where he would have to stay until someone paid to free him. Thorsteinn had no friends or relatives so far from home, so such a rescue was unlikely.

Thorsteinn is described as being very self-confident and sure of himself though he was slender and in no way the muscle-man Grettir had been. Thus he did not lose heart in that situation but started chanting and singing loudly in his prison.

His singing could be heard for some distance, and eventually a certain high-born woman, named Spes, heard him and wished to speak with the singer. She liked Thorsteinn so well that she bailed him out of prison and took him home. The story points out that Spes lived in a loveless and cold relationship with her husband, Sigurdur. She had been married to him for money and was aware that he was of lesser kin. Thorsteinn lived alternately with Spes or the Varangian Guard, with whom he took part in military operations and was considered an excellent soldier. Little by little, the relationship between him and Spes grew closer and she provided him with money. Her husband, Sigurdur, marvelled at the speed with which his riches dwindled and asked Spes about it, but she answered evasively and denied the relationship with Thorsteinn. Her husband was not inclined to believe his wife and took to spying on her. He surprised them twice but she managed to hide Thorsteinn at the last moment, so Sigurdur never got proof of their relationship. The book describes various tricks Spes and Thorsteinn used to fool the jealous husband, who did everything he could think of to catch his wife in her infidelity but never managed to do so. All their plots were successful. She falsely swore that her husband's accusations were untrue. The story is like a modern film script in which the hero barely manages to escape his pursuers. Thorsteinn hid once in a large chest while the husband searched all over for him. This is reminiscent of farcical adulteries of our day where the lover hides in the wardrobe while the jealous husband interrogates his wife at the bedside.

Spes divorced Sigurdur and the cuckolded husband was driven from the country. He lost everything and disappeared from the story. Thorsteinn and Spes married and went to Norway to claim Thorsteinn's property. The relationship began with sinful adultery but ended in happiness. Lady Luck never abandoned Thorsteinn and he got a wife, money and promising children. When they had both grown old, they sold everything and went south to Rome, where they confessed their sins. They paid the fines that were set and then ended their secular relationship, joined holy orders and lived the rest of their lives there.

The author of the book wishes to emphasise the fact that the church does not condone adultery, so the couple travel all the way to Rome to gain absolution for their transgressions towards the Lord and Sigurdur. The message is clear: what matters is remorse and penance, they gain forgiveness for even the most serious offences.

Svarfdæla saga

Yngvildur *fagurkinn* (fair-of-face)

One of the greatest tragedies in the *Íslendingasögur* is the story of Yngvildur *fagurkinn* in *Svarfdæla saga*. Ingvildur was an exceptionally beautiful woman as her by-name suggests. She also had a will of her own and would not be intimidated. Her father, Ásgeir *raudfeldur* (red vest), wished to consolidate his friendship with the chieftain Ljótólfur, so Yngvildur became the latter's mistress at her father's behest. Later, she was forced against her will to take a certain Klaufi who was an utter boor. He was as ugly as she was beautiful. There is no sign that her father or her lover, Ljotólfur, interfered in any way with this marriage. She managed, with her brothers' support, to slay Klaufi. We are told how she employed her

A psychiatrist's opinion

This story can be seen as a parable. Men should beware of the beauty of women and women are supposed to avoid arrogance and recognise their position in society. Which yet again fits in with so much in the Bible that also warns against beauty. In the Song of Solomon we read: "Favour is deceitful, and beauty is vain."

Yngvildur's beauty is described in detail. Everyone fell for her, berserkers, slaves and chieftains, all were defenseless when faced with her body. The berserker Klaufi lost his strength when she sat on his knee.

The young Karl Karlsson has Yngvildur beaten and tortured until she gives up and stops quarreling with the men. He has this beautiful woman disfigured physically and mentally and leaves her in a state where she will accept any old lout. At the end of the story, Yngvildur is utterly defeated while the society of men claim victory. The story of Yngvildur fagurkinn is the tragedy of a woman who challenged the patriarchy and got her just desserts. Her beauty was dangerous and the men were justified in doing whatever they wanted.

In *Sólarljóð* (Songs of the Sun) we see it yet again:

> The force of pleasure
> has many a one bewailed.
> Cares are often caused by women;
> pernicious they become,
> although the mighty God
> them pure created.
>
> *(Benjamin Thorpe, Translation 1866)*

The story of Yngvildur fagurkinn is very sexual. She became the mistress of a powerful man in the district on the advice of her father, who thought it would increase his influence and get him into Ljótólfur's good books. It was probably quite common at the time for fathers to agree to their daughters becoming the mistresses of important men. Against her will she was given to the violent Ljótólfur and then to Skídi with whom she had her three sons. Karl *ómáli* hated Yngvildur and was allowed to treat her as he wished, kill her sons and sell her into bondage.

The writer has no sympathy for this tormented woman, showing a great deal more understanding of Karl and his problems. Once again, we are seeing the misogynistic attitude that pervades the *Íslendingasögur*. The moral of this story is that Yngvildur got what she deserved for her beauty and independence. She stood up to the men, had her say in their discussions and was cruelly punished for it. Her beauty was not an asset but a liability.

feminine wiles to prevent Klaufi from using his weapons. She returned to Ljótólfur, who married her to a freedman of his, named Skídi. His face had been mutilated in a fight with Karl Thorsteinnsson, leaving him with a cleft lip. This Karl was related to Klaufi, Yngvildur's former husband, which complicated matters. Yngvildur was not keen on this marriage and would not agree to marry Skídi unless he had the scar in his lip filled every five years so it would look full to her. In this description there is the insinuation that she doubted Skídi's masculinity, as he had the picture of a woman's vulva on his face.

Skídi and Karl were brought to a mediation meeting, but Yngvildur spoiled it and there was no reconciliation. The men at the meeting made her the scapegoat and all turned against her. Even Skídi said she was of all women the most wretched. The men agreed that only evil result-ed from women's talk, a view seen elsewhere, both in the Sagas and in holy books. Skídi then slew Karl whose son, Karl *ómáli* (not speaking) Karlsson, sought revenge for his father. Interestingly, the vengefulness was directed primarily at Yngvildur, not Skídi. This Karl *ómáli*, who was twelve to thirteen years old, was considered a great fool, since he spoke seldom.

After some time, Karl the younger came to the home of Yngvildur early one morning and took Skídi and their three sons prisoner. Karl chopped the heads off all the boys in front of Yngveldur but allowed her husband to live. He then made Yngvildur his mistress and constantly taunted her with the sword he had used to kill her sons. The story focuses on Karl's youth, he being hardly of confirmation age when these events took place, barely into puberty. This made Yngvildur's humiliation all the greater, to have to admit to having been defeated by a psychopathic teen-aged boy. But Karl did not manage to subdue Yngvildur fully. She continued to defy him and would not give in despite his threats and all kinds of violence.

But Karl felt he had not done enough so he sailed with her to Denmark and sold her to two men who were both brawny and evil-looking. They walked away with the woman, one pulling her by her hair and the other beating her with a whip.

A few years later, these gentlemen returned Yngvildur to Karl as damaged goods. They said she had never wanted to work for them no matter how hard they beat her. Karl took her with him back to Iceland and continued taunting her with the sword and threatening her, but she did not change or become deferential. He was older by this time and more practiced in violence and malevolence, so Yngvildur's ordeal was not over. Karl went to Sweden and sold her as a prostitute to an exceptionally evil man. Three years later, he ran across her in Norway and now things had changed. Yngvildur had become pinched and ugly and now she finally asked Karl for mercy. He took her from her tormentors though they did not want to sell her, having planned to torture her to death. Karl had a pool made for her and gave her good clothes and she admitted total defeat.

He tried after that to get her into the care of her husband Skídi or her former lover Ljotólfur, but neither of them wanted anything to do with her. Yngvildur was rejected by all the men who had in their time enjoyed her beauty and grace. It looks as if they all felt they had finally triumphed and subdued her and made her obey them. At the end of the story, she is said to have either married again or destroyed herself in desperation.

Brennu-Njáls saga

Hrútur and Gunnhildur

Brennu-Njáls saga is the longest of all the *Íslendingasögur*. It traces the destinies of a number of families that are teeming with heroes, beautiful women and mischief-makers. Clearly, in such a dramatic story, mention of sex and other relations between the sexes will be frequent.

We are first introduced to Hallgerdur *langbrók* (long-pants) and her father, Höskuldur Dala-Kollsson and his half-brother Hrútur Herjólfsson. Höskuldur brought his daughter, while still a child, to Hrútur, so he could see and appreciate her beauty and allure. She actually failed this test because Hrútur was more concerned with her eyes than her graces. He thought she had a thief's eyes, which was a portent for what was to come in the story. Hallgerdur strongly affects the destinies of the people in her life.

Hrútur was engaged to Unnur Mardardóttir when he set off for Norway to attend to his property there. He and her father, Mördur, had arranged the engagement without consulting Unnur. At the court of King Haraldur *gráfeld* (grey-skin), he met the king's mother, Queen Gunnhildur Össurardóttir. She was enchanted by this good-looking young man and asked Hrútur to come to her bed that very night. This he did and the story says that they stayed in the queen's bed more or less all winter. Gunnhildur looked after this Icelandic champion, slept with him, dressed him well and made certain that his situation in court was of the best. Hrútur was happy with this, as it brought him high status and a reputation as a fine courtier. When spring came, Hrútur wanted to go back to Iceland and asked the king's permission to leave. Gunnhildur asked him whether he had a fiancée in Iceland and he lied, saying he didn't. However, his engagement was common knowledge in the court, where gossip was rife. He was allowed to go and Gunnhildur walked him down to the ship. At parting she gave him a magnificent ring and also laid a spell on him. He would never be able to have intercourse with the woman who was waiting for him in Iceland but have excellent sex with other women. Hrútur laughed cheerfully at this curse, as one would expect from a great womaniser. He sailed home, turning the ring on his finger and thinking about the queen's final words. He knew well that Gunnhildur had the reputation of being not only beautiful and highly sexed but also skilled in magic. (These qualities often go together in the Sagas.)

Hrútur and Unnur were married and the guests noticed how sad the bride seemed at the wedding feast. Truly, the queen's curse had hit him where it hurt. He could not have intercourse with his bride. He was nicely erect, but could not get his penis into the woman. After some fuss and close consultation with her father, Unnur decided to divorce Hrútur because of this.

The divorce had quite an aftermath, as people all over the country made fun of Hrútur's supposed impotence. Hrútur, however, can't have been pleased that his and Unnur's relations in bed made him a laughing stock even among children. The author makes Hrútur's disgrace even worse by describing the gossip people were spreading about his impotence and other problems. Hrútur fell off the pedestal where he was Queen Gunnhildur's sex machine down to the depths of being a useless guy that people can make fun of. This story also tells us that people chatted more about sex and sexual prowess than conversations in the Sagas reveal.

Hrútur married twice after this and had many children with his wives. *Landnáma* mentions 20 children and *Laxdæla* says 16 sons and 10 daughters. Both the bad and the good predictions of Gunnhildur were fulfilled. He was potent with other women but the opposite with Unnur. Later in this Saga, there is an account of the interaction between Hrútur and Hallgerdur *langbrók*. In her he sees a she-devil who will bring bad luck and problems everywhere she goes. Surely Hrútur, badly burnt by the curse of Gunnhildur, sees her in Hallgerdur's beautiful eyes and transfers his anger and bitterness to his niece. Hrútur warns suitors against her, saying in no uncertain terms that she will bring them misfortune. Freud would have called this transfer from one woman to another.

In the short account of Hrútur and Gunnhildur, nothing is said explicitly, but the reader is in no doubt as to what happened. Gunnhildur was somewhat older and she was so enamoured of Hrútur that she got him into her bed. Hrútur was engaged to a girl in Iceland, so the love games of Hrútur and Gunnhildur were morally wrong. The Saga made Gunnhildur the leader in their love games and Hrútur a mere instrument of her pleasure. She ordered him into her bed and he obeyed without a word. He followed his erect penis into her bed and continued to let it control him. His engagement to Unnur didn't bother him, as it's clear that what he was after was not the girl but her father's money.

The story of Hrútur and Gunnhildur belongs to the category of myth or legend in which a powerful woman or female monster ensnares the hero of the story. This is what the Sirens in Homer's Odyssey were trying to do to Odysseus himself, and a great many purely Icelandic elven women tried to tempt good lads like Ólafur *liljurós* (lily-rose) into their hill to be their lovers. These seductresses or "*femmes fatales*" try every way they can to control the lives of men, but they don't always succeed. This story makes it clear that influential and strong women had the power to order men about. Hrútur became the queen's lover without thinking twice, as the relationship meant he would have more influence and power in the court. In this story, the woman was active in the love relationship with a man instead of being a powerless pawn in the complex power games of fathers. Actually, a number of Icelandic heroes are mentioned in other Sagas that also got into the queen's bed without a word. Perhaps that is why our author seems to hate this bold queen.

Hallgerdur and Thjóstólfur

Brennu-Njáls saga gives a detailed account of the dealings of Hallgerdur *langbrók* Höskuldsdóttir with *Thjóstólfur*, her slave and foster father. He was entrusted with Hallgerdur's upbringing by her father, something

Reflections of a psychiatrist

Brennu-Njáls saga's descriptions of the relations between Hallgerdur and Thjóstólfur are unusually explicit, and the discerning reader can easily sense what a tragedy Höskuldur staged when he charged Thjóstólfur with the protection and upbringing of his daughter. They had a love affair that subsequently had dire consequences for everyone involved. Their relationship was in direct opposition to all the customs and laws of the time. Thjóstólfur was a man who solved all his problems with weapons and killed his enemies. Hallgerdur has sadly been remembered with little affection. She is still blamed for the death not only of the great hero Gunnar from Hlídarendi but also of her other two husbands. She had three husbands and a number of lovers, but Icelanders have always maintained that she loved none of them, and for that she has never been forgiven. Hallgerdur never behaved like a submissive wife, but more like the men themselves. She entered restricted areas that women were not allowed to enter. She disappeared from the Saga around the middle of the book, and according to theory was buried at Laugarnes in Reykjavík.

The Saga contains no condemnation of Höskuldur for having failed his daughter. Instead, all the blame for the deaths of her husbands has been ascribed to Hallgerdur. Woman was yet again the instrument of fate for men who couldn't control their feelings when faced with beauty and deceit. Even the evil Thjóstólfur was blameless compared to Hallgerdur. The relations between Adam and Eve come to mind and the countless warnings of the wise, who exhorted men to be wary of women and their duplicity.

people have always found very strange. He is described as a thug and violent man who started abusing Hallgerdur sexually when she was still young. She grew up in the midst of great family dramas, since her father kept a mistress in the home with all the resultant tension, arguments and scenes. Her father felt incapable of bringing up his daughter in these circumstances, so he got the violent Thjóstólfur to take on the father's

role. The relationship between Hallgerdur and Thjóstólfur would not be classified as incest, but the effect on the girl´s psyche was the same. Thjóstólfur killed Hallgerdur's first two husbands. The first, Thorvaldur, slapped Hallgerdur's face and paid for that domestic violence with his life. Her second husband was Glúmur. She loved him, as they were more socially equal. She had her daughter Thorgerdur by him. Hrútur had warned Glúmur against Hallgerdur and told him that she had plotted to have her first husband killed. He made little of these warnings, saying it would probably not happen again. Thjóstófur was among the wedding guests and was very rude. He strode around the rooms scowling, with his ax raised while the guests pretended not to see him. This description is extraordinary, as if we nowadays read the account of an ill-tempered convicted murderer striding around in a wedding reception with a shotgun on his shoulder. Surely many people would feel anxious, not least the groom, who had been warned.

Thjóstólfur did kill Glúmur after a short argument up in the mountains. Saying that Glúmur was good for nothing but to wallow on Hallgerdur's stomach, he slew him with his ax. Hallgerdur laughed when he told her the news but sent Thjóstólfur to Hrútur, straight into the jaws of death, because Hrútur killed him without further ado. Thus, she got rid of Thjóstólfur when he got beyond her control. In this situation, Hallgerdur conformed to the rules and customs of the patriarchy.

The relationship between Hallgerdur and Thjóstólfur is is described as very close, though there is no mention of their sexual connection. It is, however, easy to read between the lines that their relations were extremely unnatural. Thjóstólfur seems to have been bewitched by Hallgerdur and was always ready to do whatever she wanted. He was insanely jealous when she married, and did, indeed, kill both her husbands. His sexual fantasies about Hallgerdur are clearly revealed in his conversations with the two men as he slew them, when he rejoiced in the fact that they would never again enjoy her embrace. Hallgerdur reacts in different ways to the news of the deaths. She was quite happy when he killed her first husband, but when he killed Glúmur he had gone too far and it cost him his life.

Most probably Hallgerdur and Thjóstólfur were lovers so that she was effectively the victim of incest as it is understood today. A close member of the household, whom she should have been able to trust, abused her sexually and thus betrayed her trust. Many of the flaws in her personality could be traced to this. She was considered temperamental and moody but behind these descriptions one detects an uncertain and sensitive woman who feels rejected and vulnerable. She was abused by the evil Thjóstólfur from childhood so she learned early on that men were not to be trusted. Her father didn't protect her and gave her in marriage to Thorvaldur, who was her social inferior. She felt most ashamed that her father should accept that proposal and turned to Thjóstólfur, who was always prepared to help her. The perpetrator and victim developed a sick pattern of behaviour where each was dependent on the other. Hallgerdur knew that Thjóstólfur had betrayed the trust of both her father and herself and blackmailed him to follow her instructions. Thjóstólfur was in love with the girl and gradually their roles changed until the foster father had become the slave. Hallgerdur recognised the power she had over men and how easy it was to control them with sex appeal, flirting and intimidation. She had learned that men were vain, weak and easily fooled.

Love at first sight

The most famous lovers meeting in Icelandic history was at Thingvellir by the Öxará River when Gunnar and Hallgerdur met for the first time in *Brennu-Njáls saga*. Gunnar was walking away from *Lögberg* (law rock) when he saw some very well-dressed women walking towards him. The one at the front was the most splendid. She greeted Gunnar cheerfully, he took her greeting well and asked who who she was. She introduced herself as Hallgerdur Höskuldsdóttir. They sat down and spoke together for a long time. Their clothing is described in detail. Hallgerdur was wearing

Reflections

The story of Gunnar and Hallgerdur describes gorgeous people who were so attracted to one another that they immediately become betrothed. Hallgerdur was famous and the same applied to Gunnar. Chances are that Gunnar recognised this splendid woman when he saw her. She took part in the game and pretended not to recognise Gunnar Hámundarson, the most talked about hero in the country. The two most famous people in Iceland met by chance in the most popular meeting-place in the country and pretended not to recognise one another. There were no stories of women in Gunnar's life up until this fateful meeting at Thingvellir. He is described as a hero, equally skilled in all sports, but he had little to do with women, lived alone at Hlídarendi and accumulated wealth. He had travelled for raiding and met Hákon *jarl* in Thrándheim where he showed an interest in Bergljót, a relative of the earl's. It was said Gunnar had only to mention it and the earl would have given her to him. However, our hero had no plans of that sort, but wished rather to return to Iceland. He was most likely a virgin, entranced by this famous, experienced widow he had heard so much about. So Gunnar was setting himself an ambitious task. It is common for young men inexperienced in sexual matters to be entranced by experienced women. He was anxious and feared he wouldn't meet Hallgerdur's expectations in bed.

She was also uncertain and stressed. Many years had passed since Thjóstólfur killed her husband Glúmur, and ever since she had lived alone with her daughter at Laugarnes. Men had not wooed this beautiful woman during that time, as everyone had heard what happened to her husbands. Finally a man came along who seemed to have the courage to propose to her and thus reestablish her femininity and beauty. She both desired him and feared him. They mirrored each other's insecurity and each feared the other's expectations.

This meeting had disastrous consequences. Gunnar's best friends, the couple at Bergthórshvoll, were hostile to Hallgerdur who, as usual, gave as good as she got. Gunnar couldn't cope at all with the situation and instead a red tunic with a scarlet cloak. Her hair was abundant and beautiful. Gunnar was dressed in a grand outfit that the king had given him. They chatted for a while until Gunnar asked whether she was unmarried. She said she was. Gunnar asked whether nobody was good enough for her. She said she was choosy when it came to suitors. Gunnar asked how she would answer if he proposed to her on the spot. She directed him to her father in accordance with the custom of the time. Even an adult, twice-married woman, a mother and widow, could not answer such a petition without referring it to her father. Gunnar went and spoke with Höskuldur and his brother, Hrútur.

They reacted positively but Hrútur did warn him against the woman, saying she was temperamental and dangerous. The hero was not daunted by this so the betrothal was confirmed. Hrútur and Höskuldur both considered that the betrothal was based on lust and that Gunnar and Hallgerdur were chasing their hormones instead of good sense. Gunnar's special friend, Njáll of Bergthórshvoll, said the same thing when he heard about the betrothal. Everyone foresaw bad things for the young couple, so it was an uphill climb. Njáll and Bergthóra appear to have wanted Gunnar as their own son-in-law, since they had unmarried daughters back at the farm. Gunnar was not interested in such a marriage and in fact it's likely that the daughters of Njáll (a man with no beard) and Bergthóra (with ram's-horn nails on every finger) were no beauty queens, unlike the beautiful Hallgerdur *langbrók*.

A horny man divorces his wife

In the wedding of Gunnar Hámundarson from Hlídarendi and Hall-gerdur *langbrók,* one of the guests, Gunnar's relative Thráinn Sigfússon, couldn't take his eyes off Hallgerdur's daughter, Thorgerdur, who was then 14 or 15 years old. Earlier in the Saga, his wife, Thórhildur, was described as garrulous and unpleasant and their marriage as loveless. Thórhildur disliked his behaviour and told him not to stare so at the girl. Thráinn was angry at this, divorced her on the spot and secured Thor-gerdur to be his wife despite the difference in their ages. He asked her grandfather, Höskuldur, for her hand, but he referred the question to Gunnar, now her stepfather. Gunnar sought advice from Njáll, as usual, and the two men decided that the teenager should marry Thráinn.

Her mother, Hallgerdur, was the last to be consulted. She agreed to the match, which she could hardly refuse to do once all the men had declared their approval. Thorgerdur had her mother's sex appeal and so enchanted this wedding guest that he was more than ready to divorce his wife on the spot and marry the girl. This was what they called a lust match since the marriage was not based on the prudence and good sense of the relatives, rather on Thráinn's lust and impulse. This story is a good example of the suspense that accompanied Hallgerdur and her daughter and their beauty. A few romantics have called it love at first sight but it looks as if lust alone was in control.

The story of this proposal and the lead-up to it is disturbing. Thráinn's wife, Thórhildur, went beyond the bounds of femininity by reciting part of a verse where she made fun of her husband's staring. The verse is obscure but implies that Thráinn pegs the girl down and on top of that, he's got an erection. It was not for women to compose such verses nor to recite them in company, and Thórhildur was indeed punished by being divorced and immediately excluded from the wedding feast. Her story is most humiliating and there is no sign that the author has any sympathy for this unlucky poetess.

Nothing is said about Thorgerdur's feelings or wishes. It is difficult nowadays to imagine how this young girl felt. She attended her mother's wedding in good faith. In the middle of the feast she noticed this middle-aged man staring at her lustfully. In the blink of an eye she was married to him and got into his bed that night instead of going home with her people. However, she didn't complain but lay on her back, lifted her nightdress and accepted her fate as women were meant to do at the time. Thráinn can hardly have believed his eyes and ears. He went to a feast with his tiresome wife and was suddenly in bed with a 14 year old beauty queen. This is many a middle-aged man's dream when he attends today's confirmation parties.

Thorgerdur was very young when her father, Glúmur, was killed by Thjóstólfur. She moved south to Laugarnes with her mother and lived there. There wasn't really any man in her life until Thráinn Sigfússon turned up at the wedding feast and became both her husband and father. She was nervous about moving east to Gunnar's home at Hlídarendi and afraid that her close relationship with her mother would suffer. This is probably one reason why she accepted this marriage without fuss. In one night she changed from a confused teenager to a woman with a role in life. She was forced to grow up in record time.

Thorgerdur and Thráinn had a son, Höskuldur, who was later called *Hvítanesgodi* (chieftain of Hvítanes) and became an important influence in the lives of Njáll's sons. They killed him and his father, so Thorgerdur had grievances to avenge, but there is no mention of her after that. She disappeared into the obscurity of history like so many other forlorn widows. Thorgerdur was a victim in this relentless revenge society, losing her father, her husband and her only son in pointless feuds. The same was true of her mother, Hallgerdur. The *Brennu-Njáls saga* names six men that she definitely slept with. All were slain in the Saga's conflicts as were her son-in-law and grandson. At the end of the day, mother and daughter were left alone and abandoned after these deplorable killings. They were not the only women to have this destiny.

Two friends

There are many stories of unnaturally close friendships between two men who neglect their wives, but it has never been considered good historical practice to insinuate that such men were homosexual. *Brennu-Njáls saga* describes the unbroken friendship between Gunnar Hámundarson of Hlídarendi and Njáll Thorgeirsson of Bergthórshvoll. Gunnar neglected his wife, Hallgerdur, and didn't stand by her in their relations with the people of Bergthórshvoll. He was a virgin when they married and the marriage was difficult from the start. Gunnar was dependent on Njáll and asked his advice on absolutely everything. This close relationship between Gunnar and Njáll was distasteful to Hallgerdur and must have surprised her. She thought she was marrying the most vigorous man in the country but into her marriage bed came a nervous man, totally inexperienced in sex and relations with women. He worshipped Njáll and would rather speak with him than his wife. The proud woman could not put up with this, quickly becoming alienated from the hero and turning to other, more entertaining men who knew about women. Gunnar was betrothed to his own misfortune and had a unique skill in making the wrong decisions in important matters. He had blind faith in Njáll but of course the time would come when he would have to take responsibility for his own life. That was when everything went wrong.

In the Saga, there is actually an implication that Njáll has some feminine characteristics and Hallgerdur and her followers were constantly going on about his lack of a beard and lack of manliness. Other enemies of Njáll follow her example. At the Althing, Flosi spoke of the beardless man. This constant talk of Njáll's smooth chin gives food for thought. Nobody else in the Saga is criticised for lack of a beard. Now, it is known that men's beards are of differing thickness. In my student years, as indeed today, young men grew long hair and beards. Many of my friends suffered deeply because of how thin and straggly their beards were. Some tried time and again to grow a beard but had to give up because they had little on no beard roots. The same must have been the case in the time of

the Sagas. Many men will have had thin beards without their opponents making an issue of it. Njáll, on the other hand, had to listen to this criticism repeatedly. Perhaps the sexual orientation of this great leader and legal mind was a well-hidden secret that was mentioned only *sub rosa*.

Thorkell and Ormhildur

The legal expert Mördur Valgardsson, a close relative of Gunnar's, was said to be envious, spiteful and slippery as an eel in his endless legal disputes. Once he decided to set Gunnar and a promising young man named Thorkell Otkelsson against each other. He advised Thorkell to make advances to Gunnar's cousin Ormhildur, to provoke him. Thorkell took the lawyer's advice and courted Ormhildur. This led to even worse enmity between Gunnar and Thorkell which ended when Gunnar pierced Thorkell with his spear and swung him on the weapon out into the River Rangá. With this manly feat, Gunnar had taken full revenge for Thorkell's womanising. The story goes that these bad relations all had their beginnings in Mördur the swindler and conspirator who simply wanted to aggravate Gunnar. I can't help wondering whether the youngsters hadn't been getting together due to mutual affection, which Gunnar used to increase his enmity towards Thorkell. He had earlier killed his father, Otkell, so he needed to get rid of the son because of the duty of revenge. Nothing more is said of Ormhildur after these events, so her part in the story was small. She just had pleasant romantic meetings with young Thorkell, but they led to his death.

Culpable sex

One of the best-known psychopaths in the *Brennu-Njáls saga* is Hrappur Örgumleidason. Because he had killed a man, he fled Iceland for Norway and went to visit Gudbrandur in Dalir who was a friend of Earl Hákon. Gudbrandur was a great chieftain and he had two children, Thrándur and Gudrún. To make a long story short, Hrappur spent hours talking to Gudrún, so her father was afraid he might seduce her. Gudbrandur asked his steward, Ásvardur, to keep an eye on Gudrún to prevent this. The request came too late, however, because Hrappur was already sleeping with her.

One time the couple managed to escape the watchful eye of Ásvardur and went to have sex in a nearby grove. He found them lying there in the midst of their love-making and tried to kill Hrappur. But Hrappur was quicker and killed Ásvardur, showing reflexes that any soccer goalkeeper could be proud of. He was in the middle of intercourse when Ásvardur approached with raised ax, but managed to jump to his feet and attack the attacker totally naked and kill him. This was, of course, a great sporting achievement. After this, Hrappur went to Gudbrandur, told him he had killed the steward and used the opportunity to mock him at the same time. Ásvardur had been complaining of back-ache, which Hrappur said he had now cured for good (which was true). Gudbrandur tried to seize the villain but he got away from him, fled and hid for a time. Even so, he was still around and met regularly with Gudrún, though the whole household was searching for him. Proof yet again of the old adage, that an erect penis will find its way home if there is will enough. The story ended with Hrappur escaping to Iceland, killing Gudrún's brother, Thrándur, before leaving Norway. Gudbrandur was totally defeated. His daughter had been seduced and left pregnant by a criminal, obviously worthless in the marriage market of the period, and his only son dead by the hand of this same, dreadful man. Hrappur had thoroughly emasculated Gudbrandur.

When he arrived in Iceland, Hallgerdur *langbrók* took Hrappur as her lover and thus the author closed the circle. He led the most hated woman in Iceland to the bed of the worst villain. Skarphédinn was so incensed by this that when he came to speak to Hrappur he called Hallgerdur a harlot. His story ends when the sons of Njáll kill him. They did allow him, though, to say some final words, as were found in the heroic world. When they had chopped off his right hand he called it a very necessary deed "for this hand has injured or slain many a man." He could as well have said that the hand had caressed many a woman and now got what it deserved.

This story shows yet again the patriarchy's attitude to daughters who allowed themselves to be seduced by young men with fire in their eyes and an erect penis. Lust was fatal and nothing came of it but trouble and betrayal. There was, though, a certain consolation in the fact that the stud and villain Hrappur got what he deserved in this story.

There is actually no further account of Gudrún Gudbrandsdóttir after Hrappur left, but one can assume that her life was tragic. She will have been constantly aware of her father's reproachful looks as long as they both lived. "Why the hell did you have to let that criminal have you, you slut? If only your brother, Thrándur, were alive!" Her child by Hrappur is never mentioned but Gudbrandur will hardly have been especially fond of this grandson.

Laxdæla saga

The dreams of Gudrún Ósvífursdóttir

Dreams have always been important in the cultural history of human beings. They have been seen as a doorway to the subconscious where each of us keeps our innermost desires and fears. In dreams these feelings force their way out and make people aware of hidden memories and longings. In *Laxdæla saga* there is a famous story of dreams and their interpretation. As a teenager, Gudrún Ósvífursdóttir met Gestur Oddleifsson the wise and asked him to interpret four dreams she had had.

In the first dream she wore a high woman's hat which she took off and threw into a stream. In the next she was wearing a silver ring which slipped off her finger in water and could not be found after that. In the third dream she was wearing a ring that fell off onto a stone so it broke, and blood came from the break. In the fourth she had a golden helmet on her head which fell off and into nearby Hvammsfjördur.

Gestur's interpretation of the dreams was that Gudrún would marry four times. Her first husband she would leave, the second would drown, the third would be killed by a weapon and the fourth would die in Hvammsfjördur. All of this came true and Gestur correctly forecast Gudrún's life. In the book it's as if she has read a screenplay of her own life and acted it out. The husbands come and die according to the screenwriter's plot.

Our friend Sigmund Freud would probably have interpreted the dream otherwise. He called dreams *via regia* or the royal way from the subconscious to the conscious. Dreams are full of complicated symbols and signs that are not easily interpreted. He would have looked to the original family, where Gudrún grew up with her five brothers.

The high hat in the first dream Freud would have construed as a phallic symbol. As she became sexually mature, Gudrún would start to dream of penises. Freud called this *Penisneid* or penis envy. The young girl envies the man for his penis which she feels she is lacking. Freud said that a girl would try to overcome this shortcoming by behaving like a man, which Gudrún undoubtedly does. She was as integral a part of the revenge and killing culture as any burly man. She threw the hat away which would be a sign of her fear of the organ. In the second dream, the ring would be a symbol of a woman's vulva and vagina. The dream was sexual, like the first, meaning that Gudrún was aware of her own genitalia and their value. The ring or genitals disappeared into water, meaning Gudrún wished to hide her femininity. Dream number three would point to her fear of menstruation and puberty, she wished to remain young and innocent, didn't want to grow up. She couldn't resign herself to not having a penis and was not comfortable in her role as a woman. The fourth dream would be a sign of her fear of losing her virginity and having a sex life. The golden helmet was valuable as was her own innocence. So all the dreams would be signs of this girl's insecurity in her gender role.

All these dreams, then, were sexual and symbolised the yearnings and desires of a young girl who still lived with her parents and had yet to learn about the world in all its glory and horror. Their predictive value was unquestionable. Gudrún would eventually conform to the patriarchy by living according to its values and thus make up for the penis which, somewhere in the depths of her soul, she felt the lack of. It was difficult, being the only girl out of six siblings and not unlikely that she envied

her brothers for all the opportunities they got but she was not given. She must have connected this disparity with the organ they, but not she, had hanging in front of them.

Fun in the hot pool

The most famous courtship of the *Íslendingasögur* is in the way Bolli, Kjartan and Gudrún Ósvífursdóttir came together in *Laxdæla saga*. After the death of her second husband, Thórdur Ingunnarson, the young widow continued to live in Sælingsdalur. There was geothermal water there and a hot-pool outside that people used for washing and socialising. Two young men from the Laxárdalur valley to the south, the friends and cousins Kjartan Ólafsson and Bolli Thorleiksson, started coming to the pool on a regular basis. Gudrún sat there with them and there was much good conversation. She was newly widowed, a mature, experienced woman who will have charmed these young men. They knew her history, that she had twice been married and had born Thórdur a son, so she would know all the secrets of sex. They were most likely naked in the pool and it's not unlikely that the men's flesh would have risen somewhat in the hot water.

The young widow would have sat bare-breasted across from them like temptation incarnate, making them stare their eyes out, to her amusement. The two youths were never the same after these visits to the pool and its sights. They both fell head over heels in love with the merry widow in the water and after that she controlled their whole lives. Gudrún chose Kjartan and they were betrothed. He went abroad, she wanted to accompany him but was not allowed to because she was a woman. She was to remain at home, promised, for a certain length of time. Kjartan stayed abroad and was said to be having an affair with Ingibjörg, the king's sister, who was said to be the Miss Norway of her day, she was so beautiful and elegant. Bolli was with his cousin in Norway. He went home and persuaded Gudrún to marry him, since Kjartan was not on his way home, but on a fast track into the Norwegian royal family. He

Sælingsdalslaug.

used half-truths and trickery to get her to accept him. The wedding was celebrated, Bolli was in high spirits but people thought Gudrún looked rather sad.

Kjartan came home to claim his Gudrún, being by now bored with the Norwegian Ingibjörg. He realised then how his foster brother had betrayed him. These events brought about major disputes, since Kjartan and Bolli were totally estranged. Kjartan proposed to another woman, Hrefna, and they were married. Gudrún could not accept this and instigated enormous enmity with her jealousy and childish behaviour. She loved Kjartan and could not bear the thought of another woman taking pleasure in him. Bolli loved Gudrún and quite understood how she felt about Kjartan. Hrefna loved Kjartan and was very fearful of her rival, Gudrún. Kjartan seems to have come to terms with having lost Gudrún, and was in fact in love with Hrefna. This Gudrún could not endure and did everything she could to destroy their happiness. Bolli was like putty in her hands and would do anything to prove himself to her. Tension built up, as so often happens. Gudrún had Kjartan's sword stolen, and a fine scarf of Hrefna's. Kjartan took revenge by humiliating his opponents deeply. Gudrún decided Kjartan must die and urged Bolli to do the deed. He killed his cousin Kjartan at his wife's insistence. When she heard about her former lover's death, what made her happiest was that Hrefna would not go laughing to bed that night. Bolli himself was later killed by Kjartan's brothers, among others. Hrefna died of a broken heart. Everyone lost in this drama which started when two innocent youths sat naked in the hot pool at Sælingsdalur and stared at the breasts of the lonely widow who sat across from them. Nobody should underestimate the delicious and sometimes deadly emotions that can be unleashed by love and lust.

Poop and piss

In their fight over Gudrún, Kjartan and Bolli used every trick they could think of to demean one another. After a joint feast, Gudrún and her brothers behaved like shabby small-time criminals, stealing both a sword and some scarves from Kjartan. They threw away the sword and burned the scarves. Kjartan was furious, since the king had given him these things. He just had to take revenge and not long after he called his men together and they all went to Laugar where Bolli and Gudrún lived. Kjartan closed up all the doors to the house to prevent people from getting to the outhouse. This meant that everyone in the house had to piss and poop in buckets or other containers inside the crowded house. This maneuver was known as "shitting people in" and had no other purpose than to humiliate them.

By doing this, Kjartan reveals the pervert in his heart. He enjoys thinking of Gudrún, his former love, in this situation. The smell in the house must have been dreadful, with people having to relieve themselves in front of everyone. The tension in the house would be at its height, with frustration and anger at these tormentors who prevented people from getting out of the house to the privy. Clearly, Kjartan felt powerful when he humiliated his former love in this way. No doubt he was erect the whole time he had Bolli and Gudrún locked in, when he imagined their discomfiture in the house. In the Saga period, this was erotic humiliation at its best.

A woman in trousers

Before he married Gudrún, Thórdur Ingunnarason divorced his wife, Audur, on the grounds that she wore men's clothing. When we first meet Thórdur, he is said to be both handsome and valiant. Of Audur, on the other hand, it is said that she was neither good looking nor gifted, and that Thórdur married her for money. This introduction is preparing us for their divorce. Audur is in no way worthy of her husband.

He started an affair with Gudrún Ósvífursdóttir, one of the most gorgeous teenagers in the country. She named her lover's wife Trousers-Audur and suggested he divorce her because she wore trousers, which was forbidden by law. This he did in order to share Gudrún's bed in marriage. Audur's brothers did not want to assist her, though she had been unjustly treated, so she had to hatch her own plan.

After Gudrún and Thórdur were married, Audur, dressed in men's clothing, attacked Thórdur in a mountain dairy, armed with a large knife. He was lying in bed when Audur wielded her weapon and received serious wounds on his nipples and a deep cut on his right hand, from which he never fully recovered. Thus she emasculated her former husband by feminising him, making his breasts bleed and disabling his sword hand. This reversal of roles was humiliating for Thórdur. Audur was armed with a long knife, a phallic symbol, and nailed Thórdur like a woman as he lay there on his back. He had accused her of being masculine but feminised himself at the same time. There were no repercussions of this event despite the absolute prohibition in *Grágás* against women misrepresenting themselves by dressing in men's clothing. His father-in-law, Ósvífur, was the first to come and helped Thórdur, offering to pursue Audur, but Thórdur did not want him to. Enough was enough.

The *Íslendingasögur* were preserved orally for some centuries. Storytellers travelled from farm to farm and told the stories from memory. No doubt women will have enjoyed the description of Audur's attack on Thórdur and expressed their pleasure when she got away and Thórdur was left with bleeding nipples and a useless right hand. An unfaithful man finally got what he deserved in this story, which in fact is very rare. This is one of very few instances where a woman takes up arms and deals with things in the way of men. She failed to kill Thórdur, but succeeded in shaming him greatly. Audur disappears from the story like so many minor characters so no one knows whether she continued to wear men's clothing or adopted more feminine customs.

Fleeting love for a wizard

The wizard Stígandi was the son of the shiftless couple in *Laxdæla saga*, Kotkell and Gríma. It was they who had used sorcery to create the storm that caused the death of Gudrún's second husband, Thórdur Ingunnarson. They were killed for this deed along with one of their two sons, but Stígandi managed to escape. He became an outlaw, stole sheep and was a dangerous man to run across. Thórdur, the farmer at Hundadalur, found he was missing some sheep and heard of this guest who was hiding in the district. He discovered that many of the sheep went missing on the days one particular girl was watching over the sheep. He found this suspicious and made her tell him everything. She said she was afraid of the outlaw that turned up when she was with the sheep. The girl was clearly an accomplice to the sheep stealer.

When asked where he lived the girl refused to give him away. Then her master, Ólafur *pá* (peacock) Höskuldsson, offered to pay her to betray Stígandi. She agreed. The next day she went to watch over the sheep. After a while, Stígandi came to her. She greeted him warmly and he laid his head on her knee. She started searching his hair for lice, as young women would often do with their lovers. The outlaw fell asleep on the maiden's knee with her soft hands in his hair. After a while she crawled away so the local farmers could get to Stígandi and kill him. Her master, Ólafur *pá,* kept all his promises to the girl, freed her and paid her well for the betrayal.

This is a sad story about the vicissitudes of a woman whom a man trusts blindly. Perhaps Stígandi was no wizard but just a frightened youth on the run. He hadn't actually done anything wrong other than be the son of his parents. He ran across the bondwoman who looked after the sheep and felt as if she understood him. She was a slave who must obey her master whatever his whims. He fell in love and allowed himself to dream that they could run away and have a good life away from these ignorant, boorish, prejudiced farmers.

Stígandi laid his head in her lap and drifted off. All of a sudden he was dead and the woman had profited greatly. In this case, it's clear that Stígandi and the nameless slave girl became lovers when she was watching over the sheep. They had made a pact about sex, love and sheep stealing. He died and his death bought her a new life.

A weird marriage

Ólafur *pá* Höskuldsson had a daughter named Thurídur with his wife, Thorgerdur, daughter of Egill Skalla-Grímsson. On one of his trips to Norway, Ólafur met a man named Geirmundur. He was very rich and a mighty Viking so Ólafur was captivated by this seemingly talented man. In the end, he took Geirmundur along to Iceland and let him stay in his house at Hjardarholt. Geirmundur is described as aloof and unpleasant to most people. He was usually very well dressed in a scarlet tunic with a bearskin hat on his head and his sword, which was known to be of high quality, at his side. The sword was extremely sharp and no rust ever touched the blade. He called this prize possession *Fótbítur* (foot-biter). This guest was not good company even though he was always dressed up. The household was wary of such a bad-tempered man who stayed armed in the house, and wished he would return to Norway.

Geirmundur became enamoured of Thurídur, Ólafur's daughter,

and spoke to her father of marriage. Ólafur responded rather coolly and didn't like the look of this suitor, he was clearly tired of the Norwegian and just wanted rid of him. Geirmundur didn't give up, but spoke to the girl's mother and offered her a lot of money. He knew she was the daughter of Egill Skalla-Grímsson, the legendary miser and money-grubber. When she saw the money she agreed, and so did Ólafur in response to his wife's constant pleading. He held a great wedding feast where the poet Úlfur Uggason recited a long poem in Ólafur's honour, referring among other things to the illustrations from Old Norse mythology that decorated the kitchen in Hjardarholt. It's remarkable that the entertainment in the wedding feast should celebrate Ólafur, his wife and their home rather than the bridal couple.

The marriage was unstable and after three years Geirmundur wanted to go abroad and leave his wife and year-old daughter, Gróa, in Iceland. It turned out that he didn't want to leave them any money to live off of, so the general opinion was that he was leaving for good. Thurídur's family felt he was humiliating them by leaving in this fashion. Ólafur mocked his wife for her gullibility and avarice when she had been so very keen to get Geirmundur for a son-in-law. Geirmundur would not change his mind, so it was decided he would go. Ólafur seems to have been ready to do anything to get rid of Geirmundur, because he gave him a ship with full tackle as a good-bye present, a royal gift.

Geirmundur prepared to sail but there was no wind so he anchored near Öxney Island in Breidafjördur for a few days. Then Thurídur got her father's men to take her and little Gróa out to the ship in the night when Geirmundur and the crew were fast asleep. She took the child to Geirmundur's bed, left it beside him sleeping, and took his fancy sword Fótbítur away with her. Then she left the ship. Geirmundur woke up, saw the child in his bed, but not his sword. He was going to send his men after Thurídur but she had destroyed his dinghy so there was no chase after all. Geirmundur then shouted after her that the sword would be a curse on her family. These words came true: later in the Saga, it was Fót-

An Opinion

This is a rather unusual story in that a young mother left her child with its father, who was himself leaving the country. She took from him the sword which was his pride and joy. By doing this, Thurídur feminised Geirmundur, taking his phallic symbol away and leaving him in the role of mother with a year-old child. They were both lost at sea, so Thurídur never saw her daughter again. She was later married again, to a fine man and well off Gudmundur Sólmundarson from Vídidalur, and had five children with him. The Saga describes Thurídur as wise and spirited. It also shows how strong the thirst for revenge was at the time. Thurídur felt humiliated by Geirmundur so she decided to punish his betrayal in this way. She was a very vengeful person as would later become clear.

It has occurred to me that perhaps little Gróa was somehow ill or deformed, and that this made all the difference when her mother decided to leave her behind. The story of the proposal is strange. Neither Thorgerdur nor Ólafur liked the Norwegian, yet they decided to give him their daughter because he offered his prospective mother-in-law money. They sucked up to Geirmundur's money even though the man himself was extremely unpleasant and tiresome. Ólafur tried to make up for his offence and helped Geirmundur leave the country by giving him a ship. It would be comparable to a modern father getting rid of an undesirable son-in-law by giving him an airline ticket, or even a plane. As ever, there was no mention of Thurídur's wishes regarding this marriage. She was like something on a shelf in a shop and had no say in her own fate. She was cruelly punished for stealing the sword, which she gave to Bolli Tholeiksson, with unforeseen consequences. The Saga indirectly blames her for the eventual slaying of Kjartan Ólafsson with the sword, rather than blaming her parents, who got her into this situation by giving her to that hopeless Norwegian. The message of the story is first that women should not handle swords and secondly that money can buy anything.

A Typical Female Paragon

This same Thurídur Ólafsdóttir is a character in *Heidarvíga saga*, which is mostly about avenging her son, Hallur Gudmundsson, who was killed in a mysterious conflict. Those who should avenge his death were his brothers, but it was complicated, since most of Hallur's killers were dead, so it was difficult to get a firm grasp on who should be killed in revenge. Thurídur was dissatisfied with how the revenge was going and once, when her sons were having breakfast at her house, she was exhorting them to get on with it. She served them with such huge portions of beef that they were astonished, and asked why she did that. She said it was meant to remind them that their brother, Hallur, had been chopped to pieces like a slab of meat. She also gave each of them a stone with their food. They asked what that was about. She said that the brothers had swallowed worse than the stones, since Hallur had not yet been avenged. Here Thurídur fits well into the spirit of the age, egging her sons on to take revenge for Hallur. The Saga ends in numerous killings and unhappiness, so Thurídur must have been satisfied.

bítur that Bolli Thorleiksson used to kill his friend and cousin Kjartan Ólafsson. Geirmundur sailed on towards Norway with his daughter. The ship went down in its virgin voyage and the father and daughter were never heard of again.

A strong woman

The story of Gudrún Ósvífursdóttir is first and foremost the story of her husbands and lover. It is they who are active in her life and shape the story. She is like a character in a script that someone else wrote. Kjartan and Bolli compete for her favour and both die in the struggle. They both focus on her, but she dominates a good part of the chain of events. Gudrún stops at nothing to defy her lover, Kjartan, and even descends to petty thieving in the process. She is jealous, vain and childish and fits well into the revenge society. Gudrún sent her son at the age of twelve to kill Helgi Hardbeinsson in revenge for the slaying of her third husband, Bolli. Icelanders have always persuaded themselves that she loved her three husbands, not to mention her lover Kjartan. In fact, she had that same Kjartan killed, but Icelanders have made Gudrún a holy woman who rests at the base of Mount Helgafell. Her rival, Hrefna, was a much sounder person, but she met her match in the personality-disordered Gudrún. Hrefna behaved as a woman should in the patriarchy, and conformed to the morality of her period. Gudrún will have been a beautiful, charming woman who soon learned to wrap men around her little finger. She realised that men are sensitive and would do anything to get the recognition and admiration of an elegant woman. She uncovered their weaknesses and made great heroes look and act like reprobates.

Fóstbrædra saga

Thormódur

The greatest lady's man of the *Íslendingasögur*, was Thormódur Bersason *Kolbrúnarskáld* (Kolbrún's poet) from Laugarból in *Fóstbrædra saga*. It tells of the life and times of two young men, foster brothers but as different as chalk and cheese. Thormódur was a high-spirited poet, welcome wherever he went, a stealer of women's hearts. His friend Thorgeir Hávarsson was a sullen, seclusive, amoral killer. Thormódur had one girlfriend after another but Thorgeir lived and died a virgin. Both were only sons but their backgrounds were very dissimilar. Thormódur's father was an exemplary farmer in the Western Fjörds but Thorgeir's father was a petty criminal and violent.

In the beginning, we hear that Thormódur had regularly been visiting the farm Ögur, home of Thórdís and her mother Gríma, who was accounted highly skilled in magic. His visits became very frequent and he would sit talking for hours with the daughter. Rumour had it that he had seduced Thórdís, which was probably true. Gríma was unhappy with this, since it would give Thórdís a bad reputation and scare away other suitors. She wanted Thormódur to marry her daughter but he refused, saying he wasn't the marrying kind. He would stop these visits for a while, but the time came when lust got the upper hand and back he would go. Gríma asked him to stop coming to spare Thórdís from criticism, but he ignored her. They argued for a while about these visits, but Thormódur would not give in and continued to visit the girl's bed.

Gríma then turned to magic and sent the slave Kolbakur after Thormódur, having first protected before and behind by magic. She tied a magic band around him which would prevent Thormódur's weapons from harming him. Kolbakur attacked him and slashed his right hand, leaving a gaping wound. They fought for some time but Thormódur's sword could not pierce Kolbakur's protective magic. After a while, Kolbakur felt he had done enough, stopped fighting and returned home. Thormódur bound his wound with his underpants and stumbled home, bare-bottomed and bloody. It took him a long time to recover, the wound healed badly and he was left-handed from then on. Kolbakur managed to destroy his sword hand, symbolically castrated him.

Later on, when his wounds were healed, Thormódur met another mother and daughter, the widow Katla and her daughter, Thorbjörg *kolbrún* (dark brow), in Arnardalur. He was travelling with his companions but left them to visit with the ladies for a while. They made him very welcome in their isolation, and and they sat all day chatting and laughing. Thormódur made up poems and verses for the amusement of the mother and daughter, and they had never met a more amusing man, nor one so handsome. Katla invited Thormódur to stay with them for a fortnight while his companions went to Bolungarvík to fetch dried fish. He composed a poem or love song in praise of Thorbjörg *kolbrún* and recited it to the mother and daughter. Katla thanked him for the poem, gave him a ring as his skaldic prize and called him Kolbrúnarskáld, a name which stuck.

Poems of this kind were declarations of love to a girl and were forbidden by law, as being a great insult to her family. Thormódur was lucky in that Katla was a widow so there was no man on the farm to protect the two ladies. They probably hoped that Thormódur would take the girl to wife. He stayed there in comfort for a while and the implication is that he slept with both of them. In modern sexology, the wish to sleep with both a mother and her daughter would be called a fetish, and is a popular subject in today's pornographic films and stories. It is obvious that Thormódur sought out man-less mother-daughter pairs with whom he could have some fun.

Thormódur was a great opportunist as ladies' men so often are. He left the ladies in Arnadalur with regret when he went home. Not long after, he renewed his acquaintance with the mother and daughter at Ögur, but things had changed. Thórdís was very angry and said she had heard of his stay with the women in Arnardalur, and the poem. Thormódur admitted he had visited them, but said he had composed the poem in praise of Thórdís, not Thorbjörg *kolbrun*. He recited the poem for her with necessary changes and Thórdís was overjoyed and particularly obliging to the poet. Thus he used the same poem twice to get into bed with the two women.

But he was found out, and Katla in Arnadalur set a dreadful spell on him in revenge. Thormódur got an unbearable headache, so his eyes felt as if they were popping out of his head. He lay moaning in bed and could hardly move. Then his father, Bersi, spoke the immortal words: "Superfluous girlfriends you've got!" There are probably many fathers today who could say the same to their womanising sons. Now the ladies' man had finally been gelded. He could neither see nor fight with his sword. Thormódur then returned the poem to the original girl and admitted his fault. With that his headache was cured, but his hand remained useless.

Thormódur was a very handsome man and a good poet, so he had easy access to the beds and secrets of the women on the farms. The book describes more of his adventures, since he was always on the lookout for soft female flesh to play with. In Greenland, he started sleeping with a housemaid named Sigrídur. She was the girlfriend of a work slave named Lodinn. He was most displeased to see his girlfriend disappear into the bed of the poet Thormódur. He was said to have been reminded of an old verse about promiscuous women, when he noticed what the two of them were up to:

> on a potters spinning wheel
> their hearts were shaped,
> fickleness placed in their breast.

These lines are from *Hávamál*, and warn against the treachery of women.

Once, when Sigrídur was on her way to the shed with Thormódur, Lodinn grabbed her arm and tried to hold her back. Thormódur grabbed her other arm and they pulled her back and forth like sailors competing in a tug-of-war. Another man stopped this, promising Lodinn that he would look after Sigrídur's honour and maintaining that there was nothing sinister about the time she spent in the shed on late evenings. This was a bizarre statement in view of Thormódur's reputation. The slave Lodinn wasn't happy with this solution and once took hold of Thormódur's feet when he was sleeping and pulled him onto the floor. Their disputes came to an end when Thormódur killed Lodinn when he was working, unloading the cargo of a ship. Thormódur suddenly pulled his hand ax out from under his cloak and sank it in the slave's head when he wasn't looking. After this ignominious killing, the poet went on his way. There is no record of Sigrídur after this, but it is likely she was reduced to begging when her partner was dead and her lover gone. Lodinn will have had strong feelings for Sigrídur and suffered from jealousy when she disappeared into the arms of the poet. The story is in many ways a sad one. Thormódur slept with Sigrídur a few times, damaging her relationship with her boyfriend. Then, simply to show his manfulness, he killed the slave Lodinn whose only fault was being in love.

Like many ladies' men, Thormódur was sensitive about his reputation. He killed two men in Greenland that had said he acted with men as a mare with a stallion, thus feminising him. Our champion could not put up with that so the men paid with their lives for their indiscretion. No further explanation is given for this rumour, but one can only wonder whether Thormódur was also interested in lads. His foster brother, Thorgeir, was probably homosexual. Was it the general opinion that the ladies' man also lay with men on occasion, or was this slander the voice of envy?

Thormódur fell alongside King Haraldur *digri* (the stout) Haraldsson at Stiklastadir. He was seriously wounded and went for help in a cabin where a woman was looking after the wounded. Thormódur recited famous verses and gave her a ring just before he breathed his last. Clearly, he always wanted to be prepared wherever there were women, and ended his relations with women by putting down a deposit with this doctor before dying. As the saying goes, no one knows where he'll be spending the night. It can be a good idea to put down a deposit for a night's lodging, even when you're dying.

Thorgeir

It has been said that Thorgeir Hávarsson of *Fóstbrædra saga* was not interested in women and quite the opposite of his friend Thormódur *Kolbrúnarskáld*. Thorgeir Hávarsson was a sullen, seclusive young man and unsocial, while Thormódur was everywhere the life and soul of the party. Thorgeir's journey through *Fóstbrædra saga* was tumultuous, with him killing people right and left until he himself was killed. He was his parents' only son. His father, Hávar, was a violent criminal always on the run around the country because of killings. His mother, on the other hand, was a good woman. Thorgeir was a teenager when Hávar was killed due to some foolish dispute about borrowing a horse. Thorgeir, at the age of only 15, took revenge by viciously killing his father's slayer. Thorgeir and Thormódur became great friends early and rode around the district like a malicious two-man teenage gang, picking on farmers and being generally mischievous. They delighted in this lawlessness and considered themselves invincible heroes. It was soon apparent that Thorgeir had serious personality disorders, was psychopathic, unintelligent and evil-minded. Thorgeir was always searching for a father figure that he could follow blindly, first Thormódur, later the king. He made no emotional attachments, rather based his relations with others on either limitless admiration or hate.

The Saga's author speaks often of Thorgeir's lack of interest in women and how deeply he feels they are unworthy of his heroic nature. Was Thorgeir homosexual? As a character in the story he is asexual and he

probably lived and died a virgin. His fondness for Thormódur might thus have had deeper roots than just his admiration for his poetry and his friendship. There is no mention of Thorgeir having had sexual relations with another man, which would anyway not have fit in with the heroic image built up around him. Thorgeir, like many heroes of the time, was extremely devoted to his king, who became his role model, in whom he had faith. At times his pining and longing for the king was so intense that one feels that the relationship was sexual.

The slave Kolbakur

In *Grágás* there is provision for a woman to free her slave in order to marry him. This is included because otherwise any children they had would not inherit. Thormódur *Kolbrúnarskáld* Bersason frequented the home of Gríma and her daughter, Thórdís. No reader is in doubt that he was soon sleeping with Thórdís against her mother's wishes. One member of the household was Kolbakur, their slave. Prompted by Gríma, he attempted to kill the poet, but the assault failed. They fought, but Kolbakur had wound round him a magic band that protected him from the blows of the sword, Gríma's way of protecting him before sending him to this duel. Poor Thormódur was completely disconcerted by the fact that his sword was like a woollen mitten, that harmed the slave not at all.

Thormódur's father tried to get Kolbakur punished for the injuries he dealt but was unsuccessful due to Gríma's magic. When Bersi came to arrest the slave, she clad him in a helmet of invisibility, so nobody can see him. Not long after that she helped him escape to a Viking ship. It's pretty obvious from this account that Kolbakur must have played an important role on the farm. When Kolbakur was fleeing from Iceland, Gríma accompanied him to the ship, giving him his freedom and many good gifts at parting. When the steersman didn't want to take him aboard because of the offenses he was charged with, she pulled out a pile of money and paid his full fare. Clearly Kolbakur had been the woman's lover and she was rewarding him for his faithful service by freeing him and paying his fare. The slave Kolbakur must have considered himself blessed to have ended up with these good-humoured women when he arrived in Iceland.

The discerning reader can easily imagine how the slave must have provided the mistress of the house with warmth and affection, isolated as she was on her farm in a deep fjörd. He was lucky that she was alone with her daughter, because elsewhere in the Sagas it is implied that an angry husband was allowed to castrate his slave if he had had relations with the wife. We hear no more about Kolbakur after this.

Adultery and Infidelity

Sexual intercourse between unmarried people was against the law, punishable by death for the man. It was deadly dangerous to get into a woman's bed even though she was perfectly willing. Any man close to the woman had the right to kill the perpetrator without recourse to the courts. A man was duty bound to take revenge for such an offence against his wife, mother, daughter, sister, foster mother. This right to take revenge faded away little by little as the laws developed and an executive began to develop.

Sex with an unmarried woman was first and foremost an insult to her relatives. The woman's husband was mentioned first, then her father, then a son over 16 years of age. The woman's infidelity was an offence against these men and they sought redress by either prosecuting the lover or killing him. Sex with a slave woman was an offence against her owner. Sex with a woman in debt-bondage was an offence against the man she was in debt to. These provisions all focus on the proprietary rights of men over women.

A married woman cheats

There was a man named Sigmundur Lambason, a close relative of Gunnar of Hlídarendi, in *Brennu-Njáls saga*. Gunnar invited him and his companion to stay for a while. This Sigmundur was a happy-go-lucky lady's man and poet, utterly different from Gunnar. He and Hallgerdur soon fell in love and it was said that Hallgerdur did not attend to Sigmundur any less than to her husband, which obviously means they had sex. Their relationship is described in detail. Sigmundur was captivated by the lady of the house at Hidarendi and did everything he could to impress her. Sigmundur went and killed Thórdur Leysingjason, the foster father of the sons of Njáll, at Hallgerdur's instigation. For her he composed malicious verses about her enemies at Bergthórshvoll, emphasising the beardlessness of Njáll and his sons, the so-called manure-beards. Hallgerdur called him a gem and praised him for being so tractable. Some travelling women quoted these verses to Bergthóra, who then recited them to her husband and sons. Skarphédinn said his nature was not so womanish that he would get angry at just anything, but then he went and avenged his foster father by killing the ladies' man. He struck off Sigmundur's head, then got a shepherd to take it to Hallgerdur. Skarphédinn must have found this particularly sweet because he was half in love with Hallgerdur himself, and knew of her relationship with Sigmundur. He killed several flies with one blow, avenged his foster father and got even with the beautiful Hallgerdur. Much later on he killed another lover of hers, Hrappur Örgumleidason, which clearly demonstrates what a fixation he had on her. Today we would say that Skarphédinn was like a stalker in Hallgerdur's life, who watched her constantly and did everything he could to harm her.

The description of the relationship between Hallgerdur and Sigmundur is reminiscent of many passionate affairs where the couple are so drawn to each other that they throw caution to the winds. Sometimes they get so careless that it's as if they want to get caught so everything will come to light. This is quite common nowadays. Sigmundur chose to tempt fate by killing the foster father of Njáll's sons. No doubt he underestimated their strength and relied on the support of his relative, Gunnar, which he didn't in fact get. Sigmundur appears to have been beside himself, blinded by Hallgerdur's beauty and his relationship with her. One can easily admire Sigmundur's daring and recklessness. He had an affair with the wife of his close relative, who was also the most valiant man in the country, right in his home. He was so bemused by Hallgerdur's beauty and elegance that he didn't hesitate to provoke the brothers at Bergthórshvoll just to gain her approbation. Sigmundur is another good example of a man who allowed his penis to lead him into the quicksand, and he did indeed pay for his transgressions with his life. In our day, this love triangle would probably have had a more peaceful ending. Hallgerdur would have divorced Gunnar and gone to live with cousin Sigmundur. They would have lived together for some months in a passionate and stormy relationship, and then left each other after a dramatic conflict.

Ögmundur *sneis* and his married mistresses

This story comes from elsewhere, *Gudmundar saga dýri* in *Sturlunga*. A man named Ögmundur *sneis* (hook) Thorvardarson came to stay with his half-sister Ingibjörg and her husband, Brandur, in the Fnjóskadalur valley. Brandur's sister, Thurídur, also lived there. She was a handsome woman and "very brave as to temperament" (i.e. a real harridan). Ögmundur had this woman in his bed over the winter. This was unfortunate because she had a husband, Björn Hallsson. As they were both known for their strong will, Ögmundur and Thurídur did not get on even though they shared a bed. Thurídur got pregnant and it was Ögmundur's doing.

When spring came, Brandur wanted to get rid of this long-term guest and sent him away, and he went to Thórdur, the farmer at Laufás. Before long it was common knowledge that Thórdur's wife, Margrét, was spending time in Ögmundur's bed. That summer, Björn Hallsson came back to Iceland, and Ögmundur *sneis* brought his wife to him and offered him to name the amount of the penalty he should pay for having slept with his wife and the pregnancy. There was a further aftermath in that the sons of Thórdur at Laufás ambushed Ögmundur and tried to kill him. He was badly wounded but recovered and lived to a ripe old age. One can only admire Ögmundur's determination to commit offences. He seems to have constantly been on the look-out for willing women, whether married or not. Such skirt-chasing was extremely dangerous, since husbands could punish their rivals in cruel ways.

Violent men and sex

Many of the Sagas tell of warriors or berserkers who had their own way on the basis of violence. These were the mercenaries of the Saga age, men who travelled around fighting for the highest bidder. It was said that no weapons could harm them. *Vatnsdæla saga* mentions two berserkers who came to Iceland, both named Haukur. They were said to have offered men "compulsion to women or money, otherwise single combat." This meant that the farmers were required to give the berserkers access to their daughters or maid servants for their entertainment, otherwise they would have to fight them in single combat. This describes well how for many ordinary people, the reality was having to accept the fact that these violent men took their women as playthings. Often the farmers were old and infirm and had no hope of resisting the berserkers. Doubtless many women went to bed with berserkers or murderers after their husbands or fathers had been killed. Occasionally there is mention of some Icelandic champions who offer to fight the villain and free the woman, and they almost always win. These berserkers are always said to be foreign, but violent Icelandic men will of course have been equally active in this. They will have preyed on farmers, their daughters and wives, with sexual aggression, choosing their victims according to their position in society.

Fatal love

Both *Heidarvíga saga* and *Eyrbyggja* tell the story of the Swedish berserkers Halli and Leiknir. They came to Iceland and worked for a while for Vermund *mjóvi* (the slim) at Laugarból, but then went to work for his brother, Styr, at Hraun on the Snæfellsnes peninsula. Styr had a beautiful daughter named Ásdís. The berserker Leiknir asked Styr for her hand. Styr was not very happy at the idea of having this migrant worker as a son-in-law, considering such a marriage to be problematic. The berserkers were determined and assertive and went on badgering Styr. After a good deal of fuss and negotiation it was decided that Leiknir and Halli should clear a road through the lava by the farm. It was rough a'a lava, so this was not exactly an easy task, as anyone who has driven along the north of the peninsula will know.

The berserkers went to work and with their bare hands and, armed with Swedish organisation and ingenuity, cleared a path through the lava, which was seen as a Herculean task. The following day, Leiknir and Ásdís were to be married. Styr invited the brothers into his bath house to rest after a difficult job well done. They accepted with some reluctance as they suspected a plot was afoot. Ásdís had walked past them during the day and they had felt some evil foreboding had accompanied her. Styr attacked them in the bath once they had become weak from the heat, and killed them both. These young men had to pay for their love of Ásdís with their lives. She later married Styr's advisor in this matter, Snorri *godi* (priest/chieftain) Thorgrímsson from Helgafell. Styr would definitely have thought it more honourable to have Snorri as a son-in-law than the young Swede.

People have used the place names Berserkjahraun (Berserker's lava field), Berserkjagata (Berserker's path) and Berserkjadys (Berserker's mound) ever since, the last being where the Swedes were buried. Styr made the burial mound extra large (just under three meters) so it should be plain to see that these berserkers were not human, but descended from giants. The actual slaying was especially ignoble and it showed little hero-

Í Berserkjahrauni.

ism to confine two men in a tiny bath house and then kill them when they were unwary. The Saga describes the berserkers' desperation when they realised the farmer had betrayed them. They were locked in like rats in a cage, unable to reach their weapons or otherwise defend themselves.

The berserkers' civility in their interaction with Styr and his family is of particular interest. They made no attempt to use force on the girl but agreed to the farmer's harsh conditions to get her to the marriage bed. Ordinarily a berserker would use his superior strength, take the girl by force and give farmer Styr the finger. Leiknir and Halli were probably quite ordinary, polite Swedish migrant workers, who wished to follow the laws and customs of the society, not berserkers at all. There is no sign of any sexual relations between the lads and Ásdís, just young folks flirting. The story does not describe the reaction of the farmer's daughter to the cruel murder of the two lads on her account. She lived on in the

Helgafell district so she would constantly be faced with the lava field and path the brothers made. Perhaps she occasional thought of these pleasant, innocent Swedish brothers during her marriage to the politician and shyster Snorri *godi*. He was probably as boring and stuffy as they had been lively and cheerful.

An unsuccessful rape

In the rather mythical Saga of Bárdur Snæfellsás, who was said to be descended from giants, we are introduced to his daughter, Helga. She drifted on an iceberg from Iceland to Greenland and was never the same after that. Helga set up house with Midfjardar-Skeggi and moved to Norway with him. Her father was displeased by this and brought her home from Skeggi's, who was married anyway. She recited a poem to describe her grief at the separation. The Saga says she dwindled and dried up with grief, which is how the Sagas usually describe severe depression. After this she became a wanderer, quite unable to settle with her father or her family. A number of caves in the country bear her name after these wanderings. One time she accepted a winter's stay at Hjalli in the Ölfus district and behaved very strangely; she would lie all night strumming her harp. An easterner named Hrafn tried to get into her bed, she being an unusually beautiful woman. They fought and Hrafn ended up with both his right arm and left leg broken. The fight in the bed when the easterner wanted to have sex with Helga must have been pretty ferocious. The story ended with Hrafn having to go off with two broken limbs. There is no mention of any repercussions; he was not punished and Helga kept on wandering. The rapist got his just desserts and the woman escaped from his clutches. Hrafn was probably disabled for the rest of his life, after this struggle. It is clear in the Saga that Helga was driven mad by her experience of drifting on an iceberg over such a long distance. Being separated from Skeggi brought on heartbreak and depression. However, it is most likely that she had some serious mental illness such as schizophrenia, which would explain the role she had in society. Hrafn clearly thought this insane woman would be easy prey, but that was far from the case, she being a robust and able-bodied woman, as her lineage would lead us to expect.

Wandering women

There was no law against having sex with unmarried women of no fixed abode if men admitted it, but the men could be prosecuted in paternity cases like anyone else because of the duty of support. A man who had impregnated a woman of that kind was supposed to take her in and look after her until the child was born and the mother recovered. If the woman was travelling with the man, the law was the same as for other men's women and the woman's partner was guilty.

There are no known instances of a man having been prosecuted for having intercourse with a wandering woman. These provisions in the laws, however, suggest that legislators were well aware of such conduct and that it was pretty common for men to take these women into their beds and have their way with them. Wandering women were usually not connected to any family and had no male relatives to protect them, so they were more or less without rights. If somebody made them pregnant, the child had certain rights that the mother did not have. The wandering woman was obliged to name the father so he could take on the duty of support and the child would enjoy certain rights of inheritance. These provisions were clearly made in the laws because of how common it was for wandering women to be made pregnant by men they ran across in their travels.

Offspring

Having children with unmarried girls or amorous advances to them was an insult to her family, because a disgraced girl was a less valuable match. Probably, though, it mattered exactly who had disgraced her.

These matters, like matters of marriage, were settled between the men, who paid each other compensation. Women themselves received no compensation and could even be deprived of their inheritance if they had a child while still living in their father's house. What they themselves might want was irrelevant. A woman's uterus and vagina belonged to her family and no wandering youths were invited to sow their seeds there. In fact, the words fornication and adultery are not to be found in *Grágás* as such matters were settled between the men alone.

Women did have some rights according to the law, but it severely limited their freedom and made them submissive to the men. Captive women were enslaved and horny Vikings bought them for their amusement in the monotony of their lives. Drunken berserkers and fighters, who knew that life was fleeting and they could be the next to lie slain, will hardly have asked a maidservant or barmaid politely for permission to violate them. The laws were, however, in many ways solicitous. Women's rights tended to depend largely on their social status.

The legislation was primarily designed to decide things for women who were quite incapable of making their own decisions. Aristotle said that women were some kind of accident of nature. Some theologians of early Christianity maintained that women's problems came from the fact that they were made from a curved rib which curved in a different direction from the rib of a man. Thus the woman was submissive to the man and could not expect to have the same rights as he did. Men were in agreement that the woman was an inferior being whose only excellence lay in the fact that she was equipped with a uterus and vagina which were necessary to ensure the future of mankind on the earth. This attitude is reflected in *Grágás* where the main focus is on protecting the man's rights of property over said uterus and making decisions for women because they couldn't do it themselves.

The mute girl and the traveller

In *Thorsteinns tháttur* (episode) *uxafót* (ox-foot) we are told of a visitor from Norway who was named Ívar and was called Ívar *ljómi* (luster). He is described as a man of excellence and a warrior. Ívar was unmarried and in fact considered no woman worthy of him. He came to Iceland, landing at Gautavík in the Eastern Fjörds. Thorkell Geitisson rode down to the ship and offered Ívar hospitality for the winter. Ívar accepted and went to Thorkell's farm at Krossavík along with some of his companions. Thorkell asked his sister Oddný to serve the cheerful Ívar over the winter. Oddný was mute and made herself understood by carving runes on a piece of wood. She immediately made it clear that she did not want to serve the steersman because it would lead to no good. Thorkell was angry and remonstrated with his sister.

She decided to do as he said and served the steersman over the winter. Ívar must have been quite the lady's man because towards spring people noticed that Oddný was with child. Thorkell came to her and asked whether this was the case and who had caused the pregnancy. Oddný carved runes and revealed just how Ívar had repaid the winter's hospitality, he being the father of the child. She started weeping but Thorkell walked away. He went to Ívar, asked him to marry Oddný and offered a large sum as dowry. Ívar responded coldly, saying he wasn't about to marry a mute woman when he could have other more elegant women back in Norway. He suggested that Oddný had lain with her slaves and that was where he would find the father. Thorkell was furious and assaulted Ívar but that didn't go well, as Ívar wounded him badly and got away. When, in the fullness of time, Oddný gave birth to a beautiful boy, she named Ívar *ljómi* as the father. Thorkell was so angry that he ordered his men to expose the boy. He was, of course, saved like so many other children of powerful people who had for some reason been exposed.

The boy was given the name Thorsteinn and was soon a paragon among children. He was brought up by the poor people, no relations, who had found him exposed, but got to know his mother later when people realised the boy must be of a powerful family. A long time after that he went to Norway to meet Ívar *ljómi* and showed him the ring Oddný had sent him, so he could explain his background. Ívar hadn't changed, denied his paternity and said Thorsteinn's mother had lain with her slaves. He called the boy son of a harlot, which was most dishonourable. Thorsteinn accomplished a number of valiant deeds in Norway so that Ívar *ljómi* eventually admitted he was the boy's father, as he didn't really have any choice.

This story shows clearly how important it was to people that children be attributed to the right father. Ívar tried to evade responsibility with his denial and accusation that Oddný had lain with her slaves, which was of course a dreadful insult. The story has, however, a good ending. The father and son embrace one another and Thorsteinn marries his mother Oddný to the man who found and saved him after he had been exposed and left to die.

Ívar *ljómi* was a rather unattractive opportunist in this story. He immediately slept with the mute girl who was meant to serve him. He was probably happy to have her mute. He treated Oddný with unmeasured contempt, slept with her, impregnated her and ran off saying it had been somebody else. He also refused to recognise his son, so he is reminiscent of those men indebted to the local government collection offices who pretend they're not the father and want nothing to do with their children. There is in fact very little luster about Ívar *ljómi* in the circumstances. Oddný was one more of the many women in the Sagas who had to accept the patriarchy. She saw the lust in Ívar's eyes and hesitated to attend to his table and linens, but her brother was boss. She became pregnant and had to put up with the accusation that she had lain with her slaves. Oddný was even more vulnerable to the world's evil because she was mute and thus couldn't make normal contact with people. This made her easy prey for the *ljómi* from Norway.

A wrongly fathered son

It is not often claimed in the *Íslendingasögur* that a child was attributed to the wrong father, and such a thing could have had the most dreadful consequences for the genealogy and inheritance issues of noble men. *Eyrbyggja saga* does, however, describe a remarkable love affair. The protagonist of the story is Snorri *godi* Thorgrímsson. His half sister by the same mother was named Thurídur Barkardóttir, the daughter of the most dramatic character in the Saga of Gísli Súrsson, Thórdís Súrsdóttir. Thurídur had married Thorbjörn, the farmer at Fródá on the Snæfellsnes peninsula, near Ólafsvík. He was slain in some meaningless conflict, leaving Thurídur a widow.

Then Björn Ásbrandsson of Kambur in Breiduvík started visiting Fródá and would sit talking to the widow for hours. Snorri was not happy with this and made her move to his place at Helgafell to make sure Björn did not do her any harm. Snorri had no interest in his sister being married to that farmer's son so he married her to a very rich man, Thóroddur, called *skattkaupandi* (tax-buyer). With a by-name like that, Thóroddur will have been a shady businessman. There is no mention of Thurídur having been asked her opinion of the marriage. She and Thóroddur moved to Fróðá where Thóroddur became a farmer. Shortly thereafter, Björn started making regular visits and rumor had it that their relations weren't always modest. Thóroddur admonished his wife but without much success. She and Björn continued meeting, having long conversations and being immodest.

Once, when Björn left for home, Thurídur warned him against Thóroddur and his plans. Thóroddur was going to take up arms to get rid of his rival. Her prediction was right. On his way home, five men attacked him, with Thóroddur in the lead. They fought, but lover Björn won. He killed two of Thóroddur's men and got away, but he was badly wounded. Björn was convicted of these killings and sentenced to exile. This case brings out the weaknesses of the legal procedure. Björn had to defend himself against greater odds but was convicted for saving his own life. But there was more to it. Snorri *godi* backed Thóroddur up and he controlled courts by virtue of his wealth and influence. Björn took to travelling and became a mercenary with the Jómsvikings. After he had left the country, Thurídur bore a son who was named Kjartan.

After many hazardous journeys abroad, Björn came home and was called Björn *Breidvíkingakappi* (warrior of Breidvík). The book makes no secret of the fact that Björn was Kjartan's father and indeed, he admitted it in a poem he recited at a social gathering. In the poem he said the boy was Björn's spit and image but didn't know his father. There is great bitterness in the poem, as one often sees now with fathers who have no custody and don't get to know their children. He continued to meet Thurídur despite the opposition of her husband and Snorri *godi*. Thóroddur *skattkaupandi* sought the help of a woman who practiced magic, getting her to raise a great storm one time when Björn was crossing the mountain. Björn just barely made it home after four days fighting the weather, a feat that enhanced his reputation for manliness.

Eventually Snorri *godi* himself faced Björn with an ultimatum and banished him from Iceland. Björn was yet again driven away because of this affair and never returned. Much later, an Icelander ran across Björn in some foreign country where he had attained great prestige. Björn asked him about his son, Kjartan, and his mistress, Thurídur, and sent them gifts. If the Icelander was asked who sent the gifts he was to say they were from a man who was more of a friend to the mistress at Fródá than to her brother, Snorri *godi*.

This narrative asserts that Kjartan was the son not of Thóroddur but of Björn. Like so many women of the age, Thurídur was powerless as to her fate and had to accept the control of her brother, Snorri, who married her to a man she didn't know to keep her away from a man she loved deeply. Later, she had to take it when Snorri didn't let up until her lover was either driven away or dead. Snorri knew perfectly well that Kjartan was wrongly fathered because at some point he called his nephew Breidvíking.

Thurídur and Thóroddur's marriage must have been miserable in these circumstances, since the wife's thoughts were always somewhere else than on her lawful husband. Snorri's behaviour in this case is in extreme contrast to his attitude to the marriage of his daughter, Thórdís. He was not prepared to marry her to Bolli Bollason without her full consent.

The author has little sympathy for Thurídur but all the more for Snorri *godi*, for having to deal with such a difficult sister and her obstinate lover. Here we have one more instance of how hostile the legal framework was to women, so they were effectively the legitimate property of the men closest to them. The story emphasises the fact that Björn got what he deserved for his disobedience. He was driven from Iceland and achieved influence elsewhere but his heart was always at home with Thurídur and his son, Kjartan. Thurídur and Björn's trysts are not described in detail but it's clear that strong emotions were at work between them. Thurídur and Björn must be admired for their persistence in meeting and loving when faced with such a hostile environment. Their story is one of the most beautiful love stories of the Saga period.

Thurídur was brought up in the unhappy marriage of her parents, Thórdís and Börkur *digri*. She witnessed her father constantly chasing after her uncle Gísli Súrsson, the bane of her mother's existence. Their home life was a family therapist's nightmare. Once Börkur had managed to destroy Gísli they divorced, as if they had been united by Gísli's miserable existence in hiding. Thurídur's life was very dramatic, her first husband was slain, her lover Björn *Breidvíkingakappi* was driven out of the country and businessman Thóroddur drowned and returned as a ghost. Her son, Gunnlaugur Thorbjarnarson, went mad after having sexual relations with two older housewives in the district. Thurídur is described as a particularly tough woman and very avaricious. Everything repeats itself in the Sagas. Her defeat by the patriarchy is as complete as her mother's was.

Snorri *godi*, his women and his character

Snorri was himself quite a lady's man. He was thrice married and had 19 legitimate children who lived, and three illegitimate. There are many families in Iceland and elsewhere who consider themselves descendants of Snorri *godi*. He was probably the greatest politician of his day, very persistent, a sly businessman and well versed in law. He would stop at nothing to achieve his goals, and was greatly respected. Even the sociopathic hero Grettir Ásmundsson feared him. Snorri entered adulthood with emotional problems. He was still in the womb when his father was murdered, at the age of 25, by Gísli Súrsson. As a child he was fostered by the most prominent farmer in Álftafjördur. Descriptions of his childhood clearly indicate that he suffered from serious hyperactivity and oppositional-defiance disorder. He was so unmanageable as a child that he was given the by-name *Snerrir* (unruly person) which changed with time into Snorri. After that he was never called Thorgrímur, which was his original name.

Psychologists would doubtless consider Snorri a man with attachment disorder, who never managed to form normal, long-lasting, emotional attachments with other people. As he grew older, these disorders became clear. His self-image was twisted and strange. He was incapable of showing emotional empathy or putting himself in another's place. Snorri hated his foster father Börkur *digri*, and probably hated his mother also for having abandoned him. This would explain his cruelty in his dealings with his sister Thurídur among others. What we clearly have there is transference, Snorri taking his anger at his mother out on Thurídur. Little is said about Snorri's relationship with his wives but they were most likely superficial and violent.

Björn and Thórdís

Droplaugarsona saga tells of another Björn who regularly visited the farm Desjamýri in Borgarfjördur East to meet Thórdís, the mistress of the house. *Droplaugarsona saga* is mostly about the adventures and heroic deeds of the brothers Helgi and Grímur Droplaugarson. This story of Björn and Thórdís is inserted into the Saga almost like a filler. Björn was actually a married farmer at Snotrunes. Thórdís's husband, Thorsteinn, was old and it was said she had been married to him for money. Farmer Thorsteinn appealed to his relatives and asked them to speak to Björn and get him to stop these visits to Desjamýri. Björn refused categorically and continued to meet the lady completely against her aged husband's wishes. People did all they could to persuade Björn, but he didn't even answer, just continued to regularly visit the housewife's bed.

Rumour had it that Thórdís was pregnant by Björn, so he clearly was of some use to the woman. It didn't occur to anyone to think Thorsteinn was the father so everyone knew what was going on. Helgi Droplaugarson took on the case and demanded that Björn pay compensation for the pregnancy. He refused and was therefore killed by Helgi. There is no mention of what happened to Thórdís and her husband Thorsteinn, or how they got on with raising the child she bore.

The Saga is silent as to the housewife's feelings when she had to return to her husband after her robust lover had been slain. Nor is there any mention of Björn's wife at Snotrunes or her fate. Sex is a great determiner of fate and causes the death of this philanderer. The story is included to highlight Helgi's heroism as he takes on his relative's case and kills the lover without batting an eye. The aftermath of these events was serious, Björn being related to other leading figures in the region.

Helgi Droplaugarson never married but had a mistress, Tófa at Torfastadir, who was called *hlídarsól* (sun on the slopes). The book calls her Helgi's chat-woman, yet another example of the verbal camouflage so popular with the authors of the Sagas. Helgi and Tófa are said to have chatted a lot but it's clear she was his mistress. We are told about their night together shortly before Helgi was killed. Tófa suspected she would never see him again and walked along with him as he was leaving. Helgi gave her a knife and belt as they parted and she wept bitterly. She turned out to have predicted correctly: Helgi was killed on this journey so that night with Tófa was his last shag in the sexual lottery. It is tempting to interpret Helgi's final gift to his mistress as a phallic or masculine symbol that he left behind. Helgi is one of those violent men who appear in the Sagas showing complete lack of mercy or consideration for other people. He solved all problems by killing his antagonist. His father died while he was very young and he was brought up by his mother. He obviously has attachment disorder, making him incapable of imagining what it was like to be in another's situation. Freud would have said he had a serious Œdipus complex and saw a mysterious father figure in everyone he killed. In fact he succeeded in reaching the ultimate satisfaction of all Œdipuses because he managed to kill his mother's lover, Hallsteinn, an a rather disgusting manner.

A woman's initiative

In the provisions for punishment in *Grágás*, women have neither responsibility nor will in sexual matters. They, their relatives and their husbands are always the victims in such cases. But should a woman lie with a man on her own initiative, the prosecutor may take a certain amount of her money, if she has any. The penalties for women, then, are a good deal lighter than for men, since they lack free will or responsibility when it comes to sex.

In *Sturlunga* there are a number of examples of women who cheat on their husbands and have assignations on their own initiative. The married couple Bergthór and Helga lived at Breidabólstadur in Steingrímsfjördur. She had a child by Bárdur Snorrason, brother of Thorvaldur Snorrason of Vatnsfjördur, that famous womaniser and man of violence. Bergthór and his brothers were extremely upset about this impregnation though the story doesn't explain how he knew the child was not his. They asked for Snorri Sturluson, the great specialist in cases of adultery and the relevant laws. He came to the west and used the opportunity to incite the farmers there against Bárdur's brother Thorvaldur. He said that Bergthór would never get any compensation from Bárdur while Thorvaldur was in the area. This led to an attack on Thorvaldur by Bergthór and his brothers, but it was unsuccessful and Thorvaldur got away. There is no further mention of Helga in the Saga, nor of the child she had by Bárdur, but the discerning reader could try to imagine the atmosphere in the home. Bergthór is likely to have punished his wife cruelly for her adultery, though there are no records of that.

Elsewhere in *Sturlunga* we are told of the farmer Thórhallur at Hólmlatur on Skógarströnd. He had a daughter named Thórný. She was married to Thorsteinn *drettingur* (plodder) who came to live at Hólmlatur. Then it emerged that Thórný had been pregnant when she was married to Thorsteinn, and a certain Thórdur had impregnated her. He was considered pretty insignificant. There were more secrets waiting to come to light from the dark turf house hallways. Thorsteinn *dretting*ur was also expecting a baby. Not long after, a woman named Gudrún Ásbjarnar-dóttir presented herself and maintained that Thorsteinn was the father of her child, who was a few years old. When all these things had come to light, Thórhallur decided to take advantage of his superior strength, took all of Thorsteinn's money as compensation and made him work hard as a farmhand. It was said that after this, Thorsteinn was disparaged and beaten by the rest of the household. Modern people would call this bullying of this unhappy philanderer, Thorsteinn *drettingur*, who was hardly mentioned again after these fateful dealings with women. He disappeared into the mists once his unfortunate love stories had been told.

Dreadful punishments

Grágás mention wandering men or beggars who go from house to house because they are so "un-bothered" (lazy) that good men don't want them around. Such men could legally be gelded, and there was no law against leaving them disfigured or even dead after the procedure. The *Íslendinga-sögur* do not mention any wandering men who were gelded in that way, but the authorisation was there.

In *Sturlunga* there is discussion of gelding men to punish or disgrace them. Two priests, Snorri and Knútur, were gelded in Grímsey because they were on the wrong side of the battle line in the conflict between Sturla Sighvatsson and the forces of Gudmundor *gódi* (the good). Later Sturla had his cousin, Órækja Snorrason, captured and taken to the cave Surtshellir. He called one of his men, Thorsteinn *langabein* (long bone/leg), and ordered him to blind and geld Órækja. Thorsteinn was neither a surgeon nor a master torturer and this request left him at a loss. Even so, he attempted to do both, but his tools were blunt and not meant for these procedures. Órækja carried himself well while these attempts were being made, sang hymns and lauded the bishop Thorlákur. While Thorsteinn was fumblingly attempting to geld and blind Órækja, Sturla rubbed salt in his wounds, telling him to remember his wife Arnbjörg.

"Remember this, pal, you won't be any use to her once we've castrated you!" Thorsteinn did actually manage to remove one of his testicles but couldn't blind him. Órækja was disfigured but kept his virility. These descriptions are appalling and bear witness to the barbarism of the age.

A year after the burning down of Flugumýri, Gissur Thorvaldsson and another famous leader of the *Sturlunga* age, Hrafn Oddsson, made peace. Gissur had been very angry at Hrafn, who had known about the plans to set fire to Flugumýri. He had been in the wedding feast and raised his glass to the welfare of the bride and groom even though he knew enemies were on their way to set fire to the buildings. He had sat near the young groom who would never drink another toast. Later, Gissur said he couldn't understand why he had spared Hrafn, because he had immediately decided to blind or geld him when next they met. The punishments in the *Sturlungaöld* were heartless and hateful. The story of the unsuccessful gelding of Órækja and Gissur's plans for Hrafn show that these punishment must have been routine though they didn't always get written down.

In the so-called *Fornaldarsögur Nordurlanda* (Mythical-Heroic Sagas) we find the story of Án *bogsveigi* (bow-bender), a tall tale relating the adventures of Án and his skill with bow and arrow. A courtier named Ketill once impersonated and pretended to be Án. He was cruelly punished, as Án gelded him and put out one of his eyes. In this state, Ketill made his faltering way to the king, which was no better, because he was driven away in disgrace. The life of a castrated blind man must have been Hell on earth in that ultra-masculine society where revenge and craftiness were of such importance. A beggar without sight or testicles would be have been tragically laughable.

Other Kinds of Sex

Grágás contain provisions about women who are so immoral as to wear men's clothing or cut their hair as men do. Women could be exiled for such behaviour. The same applied to men who did things in the way of women. The law was clear. Both sexes were strictly forbidden to deceive people by pretending to belong to the opposite sex.

There aren't many examples of such people in the Sagas. Thórdur Ingunnarson divorced his wife Audur because she wore men's trousers, and she was in fact called Trousers-Audur. In light of these legal provisions it is interesting to consider the god Thór's cross-dressing when he went to get back the hammer Mjölnir from the giants. He was guilty of a criminal offence when he dressed as a woman.

Sex-change

In *Lokasenna*, when Loki chides the gods for their flaws and weaknesses, Ódinn answers right back. He says that Loki had lived as a woman in the underworld and born children. This is a sign of Loki's double nature, that he has children both as a man and a woman.

Svínafellsfjall.

In many Sagas there is mention of men who temporarily change into women. In *Brennu-Njáls saga* there is a long account of an attempt at reconciliation after the slaying of Höskuldur Hvítanesgodi. Njáll's sons and Kári ran across him in the field one morning and brutally killed the unarmed man. At Thingvellir everyone was involved in trying to avoid conflict and even more killing by finding a way to reconcile the two sides. After long and difficult discussions, they appeared to be about to succeed.

When they had reached agreement on the compensation and counted out the silver, Njáll laid some silk scarves on top of the money. These were very valuable items that he added in order to emphasise his good intentions. Flosi Thórdarson of Svínafell, who had argued the case for Höskuldur's family, came along and asked who had given the scarves. For some reason nobody answered until Skarphédinn Njálsson got involved and asked who he thought had given them. Flosi's interest in reconciliation seems not to have been great because he answered loudly that it had probably been Njáll, since nobody was sure whether he was a man or a woman. He was referring to Njáll's lack of a beard, which was known throughout the land. Then Skarphédinn threw some blue women's underpants at Flosi and said he had need of them, he made the hero from Svínafell change him into a woman and shag him every ninth night. Of course this exchange totally upset the reconciliation and everyone returned to the old revengeful ways. This was the spark that ended in the fire at Bergthórshvoll where Njáll and his sons were burned to death. It's rather amusing to speculate on why Skarphédinn happened to have women's underpants to throw at Flosi when everything went wrong. Did he have an underpants fetish? Did he always have women's underwear with him for his comfort?

Króka-Refs (sly fox) *saga* tells of the rumour that the hero's enemies set going in Greenland. They said Refur was called Refur the coward and that he had been driven from Iceland because of his cowardice and homosexuality. They said that every ninth night he was not like other men, but like a woman who needed a man. Refur took cruel revenge for such stories and killed these enemies. It was no joke to say of a man that he was feminine.

In the Norwegian Gulathing Laws there is a specific provision saying that it was a criminal offence to say of any man that he was a woman every ninth night and had born a child.

These allegations and assertions may possibly embody some truth. Did they refer to homosexual men who were tightly locked in their closets and occasionally popped out to serve their sexual needs? Clearly some people were of the opinion that such things occurred every ninth night, which must of course have been a made-up fact. These things reinforce the assertion that Njáll was homosexual. As for Skarphédinn's accusations, little is written of Flosi's love life. He was married to Steinvör Hallsdóttir but they had no children. There are no stories about his wife, so Flosi's marriage must have been uneventful. Do these accusations imply that these men were bisexual?

Incest

The sexual urge is one of the strongest forces in every person. It is intractable and often goes its own way without consulting contemporary mores. For this reason, all human societies place some restrictions on sexual activity. There is one completely mandatory rule to be found everywhere: close relatives do not have sex. Indeed, many people believe that it is in human nature not to want sex with one's close relatives. But lust can sometimes be stronger than this natural inclination so parents have sex with their children, siblings sleep together and close relatives lie with one another. There are many such instances to be found throughout history.

Restrictions on sex among the Nordic peoples referred primarily to siblings and relatives in direct line of descent. According to *Landnáma*, Hjorleifur Hródmarsson, one of the first settlers in Iceland, was married to Helga Arnardóttir (sister of Ingólfur Arnarson, first settler in Reykjavík), and they were second cousins. Sexual intercourse between relatives is forbidden in *Grágás*, on pain of severe punishment. *Grágás* clearly defines sexual relations between relatives and divides them into three groups. They distinguish between: *frændsemi* (kinship), i.e. with close relatives; *sifjar* (connection), i.e. with individuals with whom relatives had had sexual relations, and *gudsifjar* (godly connection), i.e with people who were connected through actions by a priest. The division into groups was based on how severe the infraction was, which again depended on how closely related the parties were.

In the doomsday prophecy of *Völuspá*, a terrible picture of the world is drawn:

> Brothers shall fight
> And fell each other,
> Sisters sons
> Shall kinship stain;
> Hard is it on earth,
> With mighty whoredom;
>
> *(translation from Völuspá.org)*

This prophesies brothers killing each other, close relatives having sex and the whole world infected with adultery.

In Norse mythology, it is often implied that the gods have children with each other and practice free-love with their close relatives. The same behaviour is found amongst the gods in Greek mythology. Njördur had children with his sister and in *Lokasenna,* Freyja and other goddesses are accused of love play with their close relatives. It is probable that heathens laid restrictions on sex with relatives, but we don't know how closely they had to be related for restrictions to apply.

Sex with animals

Sex with animals is mentioned in older laws and was strictly forbidden. The Frostathing Laws state that a man who has sexual intercourse with a sheep shall be gelded and driven into exile, while the animal is to be drowned. This fits in with the directions in the Old Testament which says that anyone having intercourse with an animal should be executed and the animal must also be killed. The Gulathing Laws have a similar provision where it is decreed that men who have sexual intercourse with animals are to be driven into exile and all their possessions go to the king. There are no instances in the *Íslendingasögur* of men having sex with animals but the fact that it is mentioned in the laws tells us that men knew of such activities.

There are provisions in the Holy Thorlákur's penitential canons that show what a serious crime we are talking about: "Should women touch one another until their lust be released they are to have the same punishment as men who commit the most foul adultery between them or with four-footed beasts." This is unambiguous and the crime considered very serious.

Actually, in the Tale of Sneglu-Halli there is an implication of forbidden conduct. The poet Thjódólfur intended to give King Haraldur *hardráda* an untamed horse and led it before the king. The horse was

very large and fat and had a conspicuously big penis. Then Sneglu-Halli recited a verse:

> Always a sow -
> Thjódólfur's horse has
> Wholly befouled his penis;
> He's a master-shagger.

This can be understood to mean that the giver has had sex with the horse. Thus the king refused to accept the horse.

Ergi *(Homosexuality)*

In the masculine society of the time, intercourse between individuals of the same sex was condemned. In the medieval sagas and legal texts of the time, the word "*ergi*" is used extensively, a word that has a variety of meanings in the Icelandic language. It can mean lack of courage, cowardliness, homosexuality and evil. In *Grágás* it was strictly forbidden to accuse men of *ergi* at the risk of exile/outlawry. Neither was it allowed to say of a man that he was "*strodinn*" (shagged, fucked) since the word implied sexual intercourse with another man. The noun *ergi* and adjective *argur* appear to have the same root as the word *ragur* (craven, cowardly). Those men were called *argur* who dressed in women's clothes or behaved like women or had sex with other men. Again we are dealing with feminine or masculine nature. Men were not to adopt women's customs, or they would risk punishment. The provisions in *Grágás* dealt mostly with defamation, the disgrace of accusing another man of sex and behaviour in the manner of women. Elsewhere, the word *rassragur* (arse-craven) was used to intensely insult a man. The man in question was unmarried and childless so it was clear what people thought about his sex life.

On the other hand, there is no prohibition in *Grágás* against sexual intercourse with a person of the same sex nor are there any punishments related to such conduct. The church, of course, condemned all sex that was not between a man and woman who were married to each other. Sex between unmarried people, sex between people of the same sex and masturbation, all were on the church's list of what was forbidden. Condemnation of homosexual sex appeared on the church's penitential canons at this time. The eldest, associated with the holy Bishop Thorlákur Helgason, considered the fornication of two men a deadly sin. The corresponding provision relating to women appeared later in penitential canons.

It is noteworthy that the Sagas never actually mention any man that definitely has sex with other men. The letter of the law is so clear that these problems must have been known to everyone, though they didn't find their way onto the pages of the *Íslendingasögur*, any more than so many other aspects of people's daily lives. The Sagas mostly deal with related insults and accusations. It was deadly dangerous to accuse one's adversary of being *argur* or *sordinn*. The Sagas mention a good many men who lost their lives due to careless words about some dignitary's sexual conduct.

Some proportion of young men and women must have inclined towards their own sex but had a tough struggle with their environment and conscience. In the Saga age, there were many closed male communities. Men would ride long distances together to assemblies or to attack their enemies. Men sailed together across storm-tossed seas in very close quarters to harry distant peoples, burn, sack and enslave them. No doubt in these expeditions various things will have happened that never found their way onto the pages of the *Íslendingasögur*.

Homosexual relations will have blossomed in these conditions whatever *Grágás* or other Laws might have had to say. Lust doesn't change and it was not so easily suppressed by young men, bursting with testosterone, on their way to a dangerous mission in distant lands. It's not unlikely that somebody might have chosen to snuggle up to another man, in the loneliness and fear of the moment, the night before some big battle where death awaited, his icy skull leering. The masculine society of the age provided a close community of men to which women had no access.

Gudmundur *ríki*

There are occasions in the Sagas where men accuse their enemies of *ergi* or homosexuality with disastrous consequences.

One of the most powerful leaders among the Northerners was Gudmundur Eyjolfsson *ríki* (the rich) at Mödruvellir in Eyjafjördur. He was a priest/chieftain and it was said he had a hundred servants and a hundred cows. He gathered around him the young sons of other dignitaries, lads who had nothing else to do than be around Gudmundur and entertain him. It is clear that it was soon whispered that Gudmundur was fonder of his own sex than of women, and wanted to have as many pretty boys around him as possible.

In the tale of Ölkofri, Broddi Bjarnason says to Gudmundur, in the heat of battle, that he finds it strange that Gudmundur should wish to prevent him from going through the Ljósavatn pass but doesn't worry about the pass between his buttocks. Broddi was accusing Gudmundur of letting men into his backside and everyone could see what a serious allegation that was.

Gudmundur *ríki* also appears in *Ljosvetninga saga*. During a wedding feast early in the book, Gudmundur's wife, Thórlaug, and Geirlaug, the wife of chieftain Thórir Helgason, have a bragging contest as to which has the better husband. Geirlaug accuses Gudmundur of homosexuality, saying everyone was talking about it. The author describes Thorlaug's dramatic reaction to this charge. She stopped eating, fell back onto the bench and then went to her bed, with dramatic gestures. She was clearly outraged but at the same time desperate because of the rumour that she must have suspected was true. The description of Thórlaug's reaction could have been taken from a textbook on hysteria. She and her husband

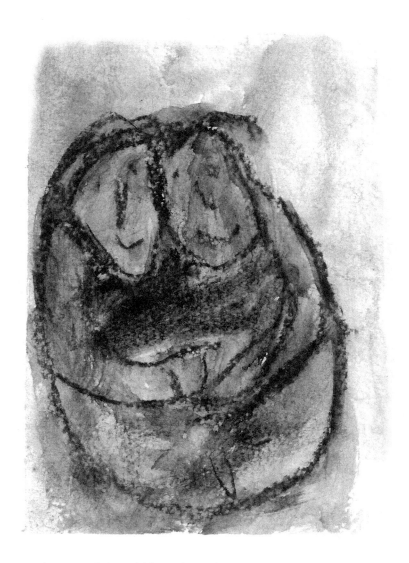

went home and she told him about this gossip. He took it seriously and considered it a grave insult.

Elsewhere in the book a great battle is described. Gudmundur made an armed attack on Thorkell *hákur* (glutton) Thorgeirsson (son of Thorgeir chieftain of the Ljósvetnings). In the fight, Thorkell defended himself well but soon had an open wound in his abdomen. Gudmundur stepped back after wounding him and fell over a milk container. Thorkell laughed, though his entrails were out, and said; "Now I would say your ass has sought most other streams, but I rather think it hasn't drunk milk before." Thorkell's unambiguous implication was that various fluids had gone into Gudmund's backside. These turned out to be his last words because at that he was killed and the rumours of Gudmundur's homosexuality stifled.

This glimpse of the battle is pretty ridiculous. A chopped up, laughing hero goads a floundering, wet-assed chieftain to have a go at him. At the moment of death, Thorkell makes fun of the big shot for his sexuality. The author of the book doesn't have much respect for Gudmundur and makes him pitiful in his misery. He clearly has a lower opinion of Gudmundur than of other heroes because of the rumours of *ergi*.

Sneglu-Halli

In the episode of *Sneglu-Halli*, accusations of homosexuality are taken more as jokes than insults. Halli lived at the court of King Haraldur *hardráda*. Once when they were walking together, Halli looked longingly at an ax the king was carrying. The king asked Halli whether he would let himself be *sordinn* (let someone shag him) to gain the ax. Halli answered that the king wanted to sell the ax for the same price he had bought it for, which was a crude insinuation as to the king's masculinity. The king took it lightly, for which he was scolded by the queen, who did not want to put up with this kind of idle talk. The lady was clearly more sensitive to gossip than the king himself. In normal circumstances, such implications would have cost the king's courtier his life, but in this story Halli is made out to be a clown, or court jester, who has more license in the court than anyone else. He was allowed to babble as he wished and say out loud what others had to keep to themselves. The king even ordered Halli to speak suggestively to the queen, at which he recited this verse:

You deserve more than most,
it makes a big difference, Thóra,
to stretch all the way to his brow
the leather on Haraldur's penis.

(You deserve more than anyone to push the foreskin on Haraldur's
penis up above the glans. It makes all the difference, Thóra!)

The Tale is set up as a comic story in which authors were clearly granted
more license than in the usual *Íslendingasögur*. The verse is both explicit
and insulting, and the queen wanted to kill the poet. The king came to
Halli's rescue, saying the queen had misunderstood the poem. It was great
praise of her, not an insult. Obviously the king secretly enjoyed Sneglu-
Halli's blunt language, which was coarser than most. Probably there were
all kinds of verses and stories about people's sex lives that never made
their way onto the vellum manuscripts in the sober monasteries of the
Sturlungaöld. That will have been the pornography of the times, stimu-
lating the imagination and providing people with a sexual fantasy world.
Almost all of this obscene poetry has unfortunately been lost to the world.

A militant missionary

When Christianity was winning over Iceland, the struggle was in some
ways sexual. Christianity was feminine and paganism masculine. One of
the pagan's main weapons in the struggle with missionaries was derision,
where the main ingredient was feminisation and allegations of *ergi*. The
following verse was composed about the two first Christian missionaries
in Iceland, Thorvaldur *víðförli* (widely travelled) and Bishop Fridrekur:

Born he has children
The bishop nine.
Of them all is
Thorvaldur father.

Thorvaldur was originally from the county Húnavatnsýsla, one of the two sons of Kodránn and Járngerdur. It was said that farmer Kodránn loved his other son Ormur like the apple of his eye while Thorvaldur was neglected. He was dressed like a peasant or a pauper and always in the shadow of his brother. A neighbouring woman, skilled in magic, noticed this and intervened to get Kodránn to give his son enough money to go abroad. Thorvaldur gained much success with kings, became a Christian and decided to return to Iceland and preach the faith.

Thorvaldur proved his manliness by killing two men over that verse. Then he went to the bishop to tell him the news. Fridrekur, a man of peace, was sitting in the common room reading a book. Before Thorvaldur entered the room, two drops of blood fell on the book so he realised something had happened. When the bishop asked why he had killed the men, Thorvaldur answered: "I could not stand that they called us *ragur* (cowardly, related to *ergi*)!" The bishop asked him to show Christian patience, which was far from Thorvaldur's mood. Christ's message of forgiveness had not deeply impressed this man of God.

His father's dreadful parenting had brought him to adulthood with an immense sense of rejection and sensitivity. The derisive verse reminded him of his youthful sense of inferiority and disrespect, when he was constantly fighting for his very existence. Perhaps we could also see the story from a different angle. Were his father's parenting methods rooted in a feeling that Thorvaldur was a bit too feminine, so he feared he was homosexual? Was he maybe homosexual? Bishop Fridrekur left Iceland and Thorvaldur took to travelling, went to Greece and all the way to Constantinople. He entered a monastary and died there. Hopefully, Thorvaldur *vídförli* found peace of mind in a foreign monastary in his old age and a beautiful lover to enjoy after an eventful life.

Promiscuity

The *Íslendingasögur*

During the Viking age there was much license, even polygamy throughout the Scandinavian countries. A remnant of this can be seen in *Grágás*, which makes provision for a man to have one wife in Iceland and another in Norway. People in the Middle ages were in part lighthearted revellers that loved singing, dancing, drinking and making love. They tried to forget the monotony of their daily lives, plagues and all kinds of difficulties.

When reading the *Íslendingasögur,* one discovers a nation that is more interested in killing and revenge than love and bed games. Other sources reveal that people's love lives were more lively than the Sagas suggest. Many great men in Iceland had concubines or mistresses (one or more) besides their wives, and had many children with them alongside the children of the marriage.

Landnáma tells of the settler Kalman who was of Irish descent. He settled in Borgarfjördur where we now find the farm Kalmanstunga. Two of his sons drowned in Hvalfjördur, but he himself drowned in the Hvítá River when he was walking south across the lava field to meet his concubine. This could just as well be a modern story where a respected farmer sets out to meet his mistress and doesn't return alive. The author finds it natural to say where Kalman was going in order to explain his death.

It was common for these men to be married to rich women but have a lower class concubine. This was in accordance with general morality and nobody objected to it except perhaps his wife's relatives, if they were sufficiently powerful. This was, in fact, common throughout Europe at the time and fit nicely with the theory of the ancient Greeks that each man should have a woman for enjoyment and a wife for bearing children. The Sagas don't mention many relations with concubines, but provisions in the law books and the church's authority in its fight for improved morality fill in the blanks. Heroes and arrogant men must have ridden through the regions, having sex with women who were socially weaker and didn't have the protection of a powerful family. The *Hávardar saga Ísfirdings* (of Ísafjördur) tells of the arrogant Thorbjörn Thjódreksson at Laugarból. "He took men's daughters or female relatives and kept them by him for a while and then sent them home ...". The reader assumes that Thorbjörn sent his servants to collect these girls, and didn't go himself. This is clearly violence against women. The age of the Sagas was the era of the strong and they took women as they took any other spoils of battle. This violence against women can clearly be seen in *Heimskringla* where Snorri tells of Hákon *jarl*, who in his old age became "immodest in womanising" and had his men bring to his home the daughters of powerful men in the Thrændalög area of Norway. He would lie with these girls for a week or two and then send them back home. Hákon here shows his power and amorality, as well as a complete lack of respect for the leaders and their daughters.

Other concubines are mentioned. In *Droplaugarsona saga* we meet the berserker Gaus. He is described as difficult to handle and the worst of brutes. Grímur Droplaugarson killed him in single combat but was himself wounded on the leg in the fight. The wound was serious. A woman came along and said she was a doctor, though she presented no credentials. She dressed the wound but Grímur died shortly thereafter. It turned out that this woman, Gefjun the sorceress, had been the berserker Gaus's concubine. She avenged her lover by corrupting Grímur's wound so much that it killed him. Perhaps she infected the wound in some way, having worked out how bacteria could cause infection a few centuries before Semmelweiss.

The authors of the *Íslendingasögur* were Christian men who perhaps wanted to make it look as if morality in the country had, in the old days, been quite different from what it had become.

Contemporary tales

In *Sturlunga* and the Sagas of the bishops, a good many more concubines are mentioned than in the *Íslendingasögur*, which underlines the value of *Sturlunga* as a source. The events were closer in time to the writers, so the concubines were still memorable. The authors and recorders were describing events that they had actually witnessed themselves or heard about from contemporaries, whereas the Sagas were written down several centuries after the events took place. Unlike in the sagas, no attempt is made to soften the stories or the sexual behaviour of the heroes. In *Sturlunga*, adultery flourishes and most of the important heroes have more than one woman and various children with them.

Here and there in *Sturlunga* we find brief and penetrating descriptions that give an interesting glimpse into people's home lives. In one of the many assaults of the period, Maga-Björn and Thorkell Eyvindarson were attacked. The two of them had done something vexing in the complex disputes of the powerful. It was decided they should be killed but be taken to a priest first. When they went to fetch them, they were both lying in the same bed far from the door and Jóreidur Konálsdóttir, Maga-Björn's concubine, lay between them. They were torn from the bed, told to make their confessions to a priest named Thorgeir who was called *Strandasvin* (pig of the coast), and then killed.

Another time, a group of men went for Thorvaldur of Vatnsfjördur with bad intentions. When they found him, he was lying in a closed bed with two of his concubines, Halldóra Sveinsdóttir and Lofnheidur. Thorvaldur got away through some ruse or another and was not harmed by the assault. There he seems to have lain with both the concubines at the same time as if nothing were more natural.

These two accounts show how shameless powerful men were about their concubines. Thorvaldur had two with him, the other two were sharing one man. This is what my generation used to call "an erotic triangle", referencing Danish. The sex lives of the powerful must have been public knowledge since they didn't try to hide their activities even though everyone knew that they amounted to a crime against the church's moral teachings. Thorvaldur was one of the best-known and most womanising leaders of the *Sturlungaöld*. He had eleven children with seven women, none of whom was a secret. In 1213, Thorvaldur killed the doctor and humanitarian Hrafn Sveinbjarnarson at Eyri in Arnarfjördur in a cruel manner. Icelandic doctors have had a grievance against him ever since, considering him to have been an amoral, sex-mad criminal. It is thus the duty of the author of this book to emphasise the ruthlessness of Thorvaldur Snorrason.

The practice of adultery by prominent men in the 12th and 13th centuries was particularly lively. *Gudmundar saga dýri* (costly) says of the main hero: "Gudmundur was afflicted by the character flaw of loving more women than the one he married." A real womaniser could hardly be described better than that. The author says Gudmundur was in no way responsible for his philandering, it was rather due to a character flaw over which the hero had no control. This is not unlike the justification offered by many modern men that before they knew it they were in bed with a strange woman; some magic had made them careless so they lost all control of their unruly penis.

In *Hrafns saga Sveinbjarnarsonar,* a short story is inserted into the main account. There was a member of Hrafn's household named Símon Bjarason. He had an unnamed concubine and child at the nearby farm

Kúla, the home of Jón Thorsteinnsson, who also slept with this concubine. Once, when Símon was visiting at Kúla, Jón snuck up on him with an ax and killed him. Hrafn was angry at this slaying of his good servant and got Jón sentenced to three years' banishment. Jón's response was to go to Hrafn and put himself at his mercy. The magnanimous doctor Hrafn decided to pay the fine for the killing and fight for Jón's right to be free man. Jón paid ill for this gift of life, because he was one of the men who went with Thorvaldur of Vatnsfjördur to attack and kill Hrafn. He got his just desserts, however, because one of his legs was cut off as punishment for his part in the attack. There is no information as to how well he managed to serve the concubine at Kúla with only one leg.

The patriarch himself, Sturla Thórdarson at Hvammur, had 14 children, seven with his two wives and seven illegitimate children with two or three mistresses. His contemporary, Gissur Hallsson at Haukadalur, had five children with his wife and another four with three other women. Sæmundur Jónsson at Oddi was head of the Oddverji family around 1200. He had eleven children with four women but never married. The sons of Sturla, Thórdur, Sighvatur and Snorri all had many children both with their wives and mistresses, and indeed, a large proportion of modern Icelanders trace their heritage back to the Sturlungs.

The greatest leader in the land in the *Sturlungaöld* was Jón Loftsson of the Oddverji family. He was said to have been fond of the love of women. He had a wife named Halldóra but he also had many children with other women. His most famous mistress was Ragnheidur Thórhallsdóttir, the sister of bishop Thorlákur *helgi* (holy). With her he had two sons, Páll (who was later bishop) and Ormur at Breidabólstadur. She actually had children with other men but her relationship with Jón was very strong and close. Ragnheidur and Jón had grown up together because both she and her brother Thórlakur had in part been brought up at Oddi. It was said that they had been in love from early childhood.

Thorlákur was a highly moral bishop and had a serious quarrel with Jón over the control of a church which Jón had renovated. In these arguments the bishop had things to say about his "brother-in-law" Jón, both about his high-handedness toward the church and the adulteresses he kept. The bishop threatened Jón with excommunication if he didn't mend his ways. Jón's answer was to threaten to go and live in Thórsmörk along with the woman they were arguing about. He also hinted at the possibility of physically harming the bishop. The quarrel grew and the bishop was on the verge of excommunicating Jón, but decided not to. This was a relief to people because the bishop might have been in danger of his life. Jón got rid of Ragnheidur and got absolution from the bishop. Ragnheidur was later married to an Easterner named Arnthór and they had several children. People have wondered why Jón gave in so easily after his boastful talk. Another of Jón's mistresses was his second cousin, Valgerdur Jónsdóttir.

Sturla Sighvatsson on his travels

When Sturla Sighvatsson married Sólveig Sæmundsdóttir from Oddi in the Rangárvellir district, she came to be the housewife at Saudafell. Sturla's mother, Halldóra had his concubine, Vigdís Gísladóttir, taken north to live in Midfjördur in the county of Húnavatnssýsla. Vigdís and Sturla had a daughter, Thurídur. Somewhat later, in 1229, one of the most famous events of *Sturlunga* took place, the so-called Saudafell raid by the sons of Thorvaldur of Vatnsfjördur. The brothers decided to move in on Sturla and kill him. His wife, Sólveig, was in bed, having newly given birth. The attack is described dramatically. The brothers strode around the house, bellowing, stuck their swords into people's closed beds and searched for Sturla, whom they called Dala-Freyr. Freyr was the god of love and fertility so that these words referred indirectly to Sturla's well-known womanising and adultery. However, the sons of Thorvaldur didn't find Sturla, who was over in Húnavatnsýsla looking to his property there. Some suspected, though, that his business there was to have a love tryst with his concubine, Vigdís. The brothers had been on a wild goose chase and set off home, after ruining the home with their belligerence and killing a few wretches for the fun of it. When Sturla got word of the attack, he immediately asked after Sólveig. They said she was unharmed and he asked no further questions. Imagine Sturla's state of mind at that moment. He had a guilty conscience after his nights of pleasure with his concubine while Thorvaldur's sons shook their bloody swords in the faces of his wife and new born child. He also realises that this trip saved him from sudden death. He was relieved but the anger simmered inside him.

The following year, 1230, Sturla went to the Western Fjörds to retaliate. Various people came to support him. They met and negotiated a reconciliation including payment of penalties, but it didn't last long. When Sturla accepted the hospitality of the priest Steinthór Steinthórsson at Holt in Önundarfjördur, he had with him 100 men. He had 18 men on guard over night. One of them, Ólafur Brynjólfsson of Ljárskógar, recited an eight-line poem in the skaldic tradition, whose basic meaning was clearly: "We stand guard over the wise and generous warrior while he happily lingers in the bed of his tender mistress." The poem is candid about how their leader behaved on his travels. Did Sturla borrow a maidservant from the priest to enjoy during the night? Was that part of the usual hospitality for dignitaries?

Two years later, Thorvaldur's sons returned to Saudafell, thinking there was a truce. That was definitely not the case and they met a dreadful death.

In the *Sturlungaöld,* men formed political connections through adultery. They would increase their influence by taking as a mistress the daughter of a powerful family. Thórdur *kakali* (who stammers) made Kolfinna Thorsteinnsdóttir his mistress. She was the daughter of a prominent farmer who was important to Thórdur in his machinations. Her brother, Eyjólfur, who was called *ofsi* (the fierce), was Thórdur's agent when he visited the king. Eyjólfur had important connections, being married to one of Sturla Sighvatsson's daughters. He attacked Gissur and his family at Flugumýri, putting an end to the wedding of the century by fire. Thus Thórdur *kakali* built up his power like other Sturlungs. Many complex impulses lay behind men's promiscuity then as now. Sex drive and lust played their part along with the opportunities open to the elite to take any mistress they chose. A girl becoming the concubine of a powerful leader was acceptable to her family because it brought wealth and more influence.

Thórdís Snorradóttir

Snorri Sturluson married his daughters to the most important leaders in Iceland, thus strengthening his position in the domestic conflicts of the age. Thórdís Snorradóttir married Thorvaldur Snorrason of Vatnsfjördur in 1224 and they had two children, Einar and Kolfinna. After four years, their marriage ended suddenly when their house was set on fire and Thorvaldur died, while Thórdís just barely managed to be rescued through a hole in the wall. Thorvaldur had four sons from a previous marriage who ran the farm in Vatnsfjördur after that until 1232 when, as we have seen, they were killed in battle by Sturla Sighvatsson, a close relative of Thórdís. Thórdís took over the farm. That same year she gave birth to a child by her lover, Ólafur Ædeyingur. Her father, Snorri, was furious and Ólafur agreed that Snorri himself could determine the fines and compensation for this insult. Snorri took Ólafur's family home and property, the island Ædey. There is no record of Thórdís having received any part of these fines to compensate for her honour. Snorri pocketed the compensation and added it to his wealth.

After this, Thórdís took up with Oddur Álason who had taken over the farm at Eyri in Arnafjördur. Oddur visited Thórdís in Vatnsfjördur and ran up against Ólafur of Ædey, but it didn't end with a battle. That same spring, Snorri sent his son Órækja to take over the farm and workforce in Vatnsfjördur, while Thórdís moved to Dýrafjördur. Not long after that, she went to Stadarholl in Dalir where she bore a daughter, the fruit of her relationship with Oddur. Unfortunately Órækja Snorrason,

Thórdís's half brother, killed Oddur shortly thereafter. So Thórdís had two children from marriage and two from her lovers. We hear nothing more about these children that Ólafur and Oddur had with Thórdís. She resembled her father in her skills as a political strategist and thus she was perhaps the most fortunate of Snorri's children, all of whom had rather erratic lives. This account is a good example of the insecurity women of the period had to put up with. Their husbands were in constant danger of their lives, whether they were of lower or upper classes. Endless hostilities plagued the elite, who could at any moment expect a blood-spattered visit. Ordinary farmers and workmen never knew when they might be called to make some fatal journey over hill and dale to harass the leaders of enemy families.

A widely travelled adventuress

Stories of the promiscuity and immorality of the elite are usually about men. But there were some women who lived an independent life in this male-dominated society.

There was a woman named Yngvildur Thorgilsdóttir who lived in the Dalur district with her husband, farmer Halldór Bergsson. They didn't get along well and Halldór went all the way to Rome to get good advice and absolution for his sins. Unfortunately, he died on the journey, which was not uncommon. The widow Yngvildur then went to run a farm co-operatively with her brother-in-law at Tunga in Sælingsdalur valley. Enter a young man, Thorvardur Thorgeirsson, 18 years of age. He was a neighbour and closely related to Yngvildur. On his way to the pool in Sælingsdalur he fell off his horse but was not badly injured. He did have a cut and bled quite a lot so he was taken to stay at Tunga where Yngvildur nursed him. Love clearly bloomed between patient and nurse as sometimes happens. They moved to the north but never lived far apart.

Later on a young girl came from the north, stayed for a while with

Yngvildur and then gave birth to a daughter who was named Sigrídur. The author makes it plain, indirectly, that the child was Yngvildur's and Thorvald's and they had got the girl to come and pretend the child was hers. The reason was how closely they were related, which made it difficult for them to have a child together without punishment. People had their suspicions, however, and in the end it was decreed that the case should be judged by God through the carrying of hot iron. In such circumstances, a party to the case was to handle a piece of red-hot iron, after which the state of their hand would be evaluated. If the hand was burnt the suspect was guilty, otherwise not. However, in this case, it was not Thorvardur who was made to carry the iron, but a man from the north, Grímur by name. It is hard to see any justification for that. Bishop Klængur Thorsteinnsson decided, after studying Grímur's hand, that Yngvildur and Thorvardur were innocent of the charge. The bishop was, in fact, a close relative of the couple, so he would have been disqualified in a modern court. The conduct of this case was altogether weird.

Thorvardur decided to go abroad and so did Yngvildur. She left her property with a dependable man, headed north, dressed in men's clothing and cut her hair like a boy's. Thus prepared, she left with her lover, Thorvardur. Yet again the rumour grew that the child Sigrídur had been both fathered and mothered wrongly and that the whole business was a web of deception with the help of both temporal and spiritual leaders. The case was taken to court but there was no judgment. There is no evidence as to whether Yngvildur and Thorvardur were living together in Norway, but it can be assumed.

Twelve years later, Thorvardur was back in Iceland where he married and had a great many daughters with his wife, another two children with his concubines and one daughter in his old age with a married woman. Yngvildur appeared again in Iceland as the mother of a child with her cousin, Bishop Klængur. They had Jóra, who became the first wife of Thorvaldur Gissurarson, who was the father of Gissur *jarl*. Klængur made serious mistakes in this matter. Not only did he have a child with his close relative but was also an accomplice in the matter of the child Sigrídur.

This is a significant story about the love of a grown woman and a young adventurer. They were incredibly bold in the context of their age, had a child, got a girl to claim the child and moved to Norway in disguise. Later, Yngvildur had another daughter with her cousin the bishop. She must have been a brave and forceful woman, who scorned public opinion and lived life to the full.

The abduction of women

In *Grágás* there is a clear and unequivocal provision regarding the abduction of women. If a woman is taken away, the punishment is exile/outlawry for the one who planned it and everyone who took part in it.

In the political turmoil of the 12th and 13th centuries, the chieftains would seize women to challenge and humiliate their enemies. As has always been the case, women were victims of men's war games. *Sturlunga* sites several instances of women being abducted from their homes by the powerful of the time. Sturla Sighvatsson had the woman Jóreidur Hallsdóttir stolen from her home for a friend of his who had proposed to her but been rejected. The woman went on hunger strike and in the end Sturla returned her to her home and paid some fines. The rights of a woman were determined by the power of her family. If her family was weak, a beautiful woman was like a piece of land that men could simply lay claim to.

Promiscuity and the moral teachings of the church

Promiscuity was not condoned according to the moral teachings of the church, yet the church mostly tolerated the fornication of Icelanders to begin with. Towards the end of the 12th century, bishop Thorlákur made a start on improving the morals of the population. In 1173, bishop Eysteinn of Nidarós in Norway wrote to bishop Klængur Thorsteinsson of Skálholt, where he rebuked the prominent men of Iceland for promiscuity, saying some had sent their wives away and taken in adulteresses. Some even had both under the same roof. Bishop Klængur had himself been guilty of having a child out of wedlock with his close relative, Yngvildur, so it was rather difficult for him to start preaching morality.

This letter of bishop Eysteinn's bears witness to the fact that news of the godless promiscuity of Iceland's leaders had made its way to Norway. *Sturlunga* further confirms the truth of this. It was the job of Klængúr's successor, bishop Thorlákur, to act on the message from the archbishop. A few years later, Eysteinn sent another letter to Iceland, a good deal more heated than the last. There he accused Iceland's elite of living profligate lives and not applying themselves to their marriages. Obviously people were behaving according to previous custom and habit and blatantly ignoring the dos and don'ts of the church.

These letters mark the beginning of the church's battle to improve morality in Iceland. The church's doctrine on marriage was unfamiliar to Icelanders. Marriage was, according to the church, one of the seven sacraments and thus holy. Divorce was subject to the bishop's permission and demanded celibacy of the parties afterwards, since all sex was condemned unless it was between man and wife for the purpose of having a child. It's clear that many married men kept concubines or mistresses and their transgression was considered a good deal more serious that that of those who were not already in a marriage, sanctified by the church.

Old sermons from this period have been preserved in *Hómilíubókin* (the Old Icelandic Book of Homilies). There we find warnings against whores and concubines. A very harsh sermon against adultery has been preserved in *Hauksbok* (The book of Haukur). It says straight out that those mistresses who give their lovers a drink to increase their love, will burn in fire and eternal agony unless they make confession. Yet again we get a connection between sex and magic. Elsewhere we are told that people should love the life of celibacy because it is the life of angels. Men must suppress physical lust so they can be sure of going to heaven.

Bishop Thorlákur decided to undertake the task though it would clearly be easier said than done. He gave out directives on various of the church's disciplines, especially on adultery, that had hardly ever been practiced in Iceland. Thorlákur placed the main emphasis on preventing marriages where there were obvious shortcomings and on keeping husbands and wives apart who were living in such a marriage. In the laws of inheritance they distinguished between children who were conceived with a concubine outside any marriage and those conceived in adultery.

But there could be reasons for sex outside any marriage. Many couples could not afford to marry, it being demanded in *Grágás* that people have a minimum amount of possessions to marry. Others found nobody of their stature to marry and chose unmarried relationships with many women instead, as many prominent men did. Also, people realised how practical it could be to have many mistresses so as to greatly increase their power and influence. Many leaders in the *Sturlunga age* chose mistresses over marriage. Most importantly, some were unhappy in their marriages and decided to have a mistress to make it easier to accept that unhappiness.

When the time came for marriage, the father of the bride was in charge. It seems likely that marriage choices will often have been based on the same wishes and interests as lay behind connections with mistresses. A girl's father could decide whether she should become the mistress of a particular man. He would decide with reference to the social standing of the man who wanted his daughter. We are once again back to the woman as trade goods like any other, who could be bought or sold according to the power games of the moment. This can be clearly seen in *Svarfdæla saga* when Yngvildur *fagurkinn* became the mistress of Ljotólfur *godi* with her father's full permission.

Many a noble woman of great family became the mistress of prominent men to the advantage of both themselves and their families. Such relationships were, like marriages, often based purely on vested interests where a deal was made as to mutual obligations. Many chieftains such as Snorri Sturluson and Thorvaldur of Vatnsfjördur systematically set about establishing a net of allies by keeping as many mistresses as possible, so as to build connections with other powerful families that could aid them in the constant conflicts of the age. Thus reason prevailed in these matters and strong emotions were rare.

Intuitively it may seem that adultery went against the provisions in *Grágás* that ensured the rights of young, unmarried girls. Impregnating an unmarried girl was an insult not only to the girl but first and foremost to her family. A deflowered girl was, of course, much less valuable to her father and other relatives than a virgin. But the most important thing was probably not so much the letter of the law as exactly who had deflowered her.

As time went on, the church fought for the advancement of marriage and would not accept married men sleeping with other women, rather demanded that men choose between marriage or promiscuity. It wasn't until after the King of Norway took over Iceland in 1262 that the church started to make some headway in that battle. Up until then, double standards prevailed in Iceland, the official ecclesiastical standard, characterised by morality and respect for marriage, and the actual, worldly standard, characterised by promiscuity and infidelity.

Snorri Sturluson and Egill's Saga

Snorri Sturluson was famous not only for his secular power and his writings but also for the women that touched his life in various ways. He was very determined and well understood that his daughters provided a convenient way to increase his power and influence through the right marriages. He married his daughter Hallbera to Árni *óreida* (the disorganised) and then to Kolbeinn *ungi* (the young), the greatest leader in the North. His second daughter, Ingibjörg, he married to Gissur Thorvaldsson himself, leader of the Southerners. His third daughter, Thórdís, he married to Thorvaldur of Vatnsfjördur, the most powerful man in the Western Fjörds. All these marriages had this in common, that they were stormy and unhappy.

Snorri himself was very promiscuous, and had two daughters with his concubines. He married twice for money, first Herdís the daughter of Bersi *hinn audgi* (the rich) at Borg, where he lived for several years. He and Herdís divorced. Later on, long after he settled at Reykholt, he was once travelling on horseback when he saw, riding in the opposite direction, a woman he thought rather rough-featured and not at all beautiful. He made fun of her looks to his companion, but was told that she was

Hallveig Ormsdóttir, the richest woman in the land. Some say Snorri turned his horse around on the spot to get to know her better. True or not, they were married two years later. Snorri understood better than anyone how important it was was to strengthen one's influence as much as possible through marriage and other love relationships. This short account of Snorri's life shows what a sly politician he was. He used both his own marriages and those of his children to increase his power and influence. On the chess-board of Snorri and the other Sturlungs, women were pawns to be played for victory in the game. Many other powerful men of the time used similar moves, though none nearly so shrewdly as Snorri. No doubt Snorri did actually love some of his women for a while.

Snorri was the most skilled writer in Scandinavia and rescued great cultural treasures from destruction. If there had been no Snorri the kings of Norway would be men with no lineage who knew nothing of their roots nor illustrious history. Without Snorri's writings we would know next to nothing about Old Norse mythology. Without him, that aspect of our history would probably have suffocated in the arms of the church. Most scholars consider Snorri the author of *Egils saga Skalla-Grímssonar*, the only Saga that can at all be attributed to a particular person. It is singular that the great womaniser Snorri should have written one of the most sex-less of the *Íslendingasögur*. Egill and Snorri have little in common, apart from their poetic skills. Snorri portrays Egill as very rough. He was a tall, large, drunken man of violence who fought against great odds and usually won. The descriptions of Egill's drinking habits are swashbuckling and derisive and probably describe in part the behaviour of Snorri's contemporaries. Egill is most similar to Grettir except that Egill had better luck so he didn't end up in the tight situations that characterised Grettir's life. They were both, on the other hand, willful, strength-oriented warriors who bulldosed their way through life with reference to nothing but their own needs and wishes. Egill's brother, Thórólfur, is presented as a much more charming and likeable person.

Snorralaug at Reykholt.

Egill clearly showed signs of behaviour problems from early childhood: he was excitable, naughty and undisciplined and had attachment disorder like so many others in the Sagas. His closest attachment was to his foster mother, Thorgerdur *brák* (trousers), when he was a child. Once his father was about to kill him in a fit of rage but *Brák* intervened. Skalla-Grímur responded by killing Egill's foster mother with the boy looking on. Thus she disappeared from the Saga, but she did gain geographical immortality, because the the little channel in Borgarnes where she died bears her name.

Egill learned at a young age not to trust anybody and it's likely that he always blamed himself for Brák's death. He disliked his father and seems to have been a good deal closer to his mother. His father, in another fit of rage, killed Egill's best friend in front of him. He learned painfully that a man's life was worthless and people's feelings made no difference.

Women don't get much space in the book. Thórólfur married a woman named Ásgerdur according to the traditional betrothal routine, where her father's consent was sought. Her father's name was Björn Brynjólfs-son, and he had himself been in serious trouble over women. He fell in love with a certain Thóra *hladhönd* (adorned hand) and proposed, but her brother wasn't in the least interested in such a marriage. Eventually Björn decided to steal her away, and did just that. They married and had Ásgerdur, who had in fact been brought up at Borg with Skalla-Grímur and Bera. So Thórólfur married his foster sister, whatever people may think of that. When it was time for the wedding feast, Egill suddenly felt ill and not up to attending. He was left to stay at the home of Thórir Hersir and his friend Arinbjörn, but once the guests had left he got up and set off for adventures with some of Thórir's men. The clear implica-tion is that Egill was so jealous that he didn't trust himself to attend the wedding. Both the brothers were in love with this foster sister of theirs.

Some time later, Thórólfur fell in battle and Egill married Ásgerdur after the appropriate preparation and negotiations. In this instance, Egill showed his humanity. He had been depressed from love-sickness but became most cheerful once they married. In his depression he composed melancholy and obscure love poetry that few could understand. This marriage was not entirely legal because of various provisions in the law about the marriage of people who were as closely connected as Egill and Ásgerdur, but they managed to get around them. They had some children together, but Snorri doesn't describe their relationship much. Ásgerdur does not take up much space in the story, considering she was married to both its main heroes. She appears to be perfectly satisfied with the fact that her husband spent long periods of time abroad, killing men and composing deathless verse. Perhaps this was Snorri's message to his own wife, to leave him in peace with his vellum and travels while she concentrated on child-rearing and care of the household. Egill's name was never linked to another woman, and he clearly had a major problem with human relations.

When Ásgerdur died, Egill moved from Borg to his niece, Thórdís, at Mosfell, whom he loved more than others. The message is clear. Ásgerd-

ur was dead and Egill had no further business at Borg with his son Thorsteinn. Clearly Ásgerdur must have been a good mediator and kept everything smooth while she lived. Once she was gone, the father and son could not live under the same roof. This could be part of a modern day family saga.

Women were usually silent behind the scenes except for the malicious Gunnhildur, one of Egill's greatest and most powerful enemies. It is implied that she had seduced Egill's brother Thórólfur, but there was no sexual connection between her and Egill. He hated her and her husband, King Eiríkur *blódöx* (blood-axe), with all his heart, and much of the Saga is about their dealings. Egill raised a *nídstöng* (a tall pole with runes carved in it and the head of a recently killed horse on top) to curse them both. The *nídstöng* could, at a stretch, be interpreted as a phallic symbol.

Egill was no womaniser like Snorri. He was sly as a fox about money and he ended up with a whole lot of it, so the author and his protagonist were alike in this. Egill was unlike Snorri in every other way. He was violent and a bully and always got what he wanted, whatever it might entail. In his old age, Egill composed a remarkable verse where he described himself as old, deaf and weak, and especially mentioned that he felt dizzy and his "procreative member" had gone soft. This is the only directly sexual reference in the book and perhaps it mirrors the womaniser Snorri's anxiety about the impotence of old age.

Poems and Penitential Canons

Hávamál, which can be found at the beginning of the *Konungsbók* (Codex Regius), is the most famous of all *Edda* poems. It is spoken by Ódinn himself and provides the life precepts of an ancient golden age. It is still frequently quoted by long-winded speakers and politicians who wish to call attention to their own erudition and love of country. It has also been popular to quote *Hávamál* in obituaries, when men wish to speak with some depth of wisdom about the meaning of human existence.

People have long defined *Hávamál* as a pagan poem from the 9th century. Now, however, there are hypotheses to the effect that there are some Christian attitudes to be found in the poem, and that it may have been put together by a sort of editor who put it in order and may even have filled in gaps with poetry of his own. Some find what might be influences from Christian Latin words of wisdom about similar subjects.

Hávamál is diverse in content and form and is probably a conglomerate of poetry from various sources. The first section, which has 77 verses, is a poem of advice which deals with innumerable areas of human existence, such as friendship, discretion, greed, drunkenness, diet and more. One could say that it is a collection of advice-verses that encourage people to live honestly and adopt nobility and modesty. A great deal of emphasis is placed on honour and reputation and how important it is that a person's exploits be reported after death, because reputation never dies.

This advice section deals first and foremost with every day matters and the ordinary problems of life, but very little with religion. The message of the poems is neither Christian nor pagan, but above all practical ethics. Followers of today's *Ásatrú* (Norse paganism) have appropriated *Hávamál* as the main source of pagan moral teachings, and are in no way prepared to accept that there is any Christian influence to be found in it.

The best verses in the advice section of *Hávamál* resonate with wisdom and humility towards the problem of being a human. This wisdom is expressed in a concise and entertaining way and many count this poem one of the highlights of Nordic literature. It is impossible to summarise the message of the poem, since it touches on most areas of human existence. Friendship is important and *Hávamál* urges men to tend well to their friends; the poem is a eulogy to life, since "none have use for the dead." *Hávamál* contains no religious beliefs, only timeless principles.

Hávamál was preserved orally for a long time before it was written down. No one knows how it was passed on nor how popular it was with people. The *Íslendingasögur*, apart from *Fóstbrædrasaga*, do not refer to it but it can be assumed that people were familiar with the poem and many will have known it by heart. Perhaps it was repeatedly recited, whole or in parts, to children, who thus learned it by heart, as my generation learned the maxims of Hallgrímur Pétursson.

What, then, was the message of the poem to the young folk that were growing up in Iceland around the year 1000? What were the teachings of *Hávamál* to the sexes? It must have been difficult for young girls to hear in several places that the most important thing was to have a son who would keep your name alive. A son would raise a memorial stone to his deceased father, thus ensuring that his memory would live. Daughters are never mentioned, as they are unlikely to contribute to their fathers' immortality. Obviously young girls will, like the boys, have learned the poem and understood its message.

This verse describes well *Hávamál's* attitude to women:

> A virgins words
> should no one trust
> nor that which a woman speaks,
> for on a potters turning wheel
> were their hearts shaped,
> fickleness placed in their breast.

No one should believe women, they are dangerous and deceitful. This is perhaps the main message of *Hávamál,* as far as women are concerned.

Hávamál warns young men of this insincerity of women. Nobody should ever believe the words of a woman because treachery is in their blood. Moreover, it warns against "the peace of women", which it compares to riding on ice on an unshod horse, comparable to driving on summer tires on icy roads. The message of *Hávamál* regarding women is similar to the warnings of the Old Testament. Women were not to be trusted.

The poem continues and gives young men good advice regarding women. They are advised to give women money, speak prettily and praise their beauty, if they want to have their way with them, which is actually strange advice in light of the contemporary laws that pretty much forbade men to court a young girl without the permission of her father and relatives.

Hávamál warns against unnecessary chatter and careless words. "The tongue will kill the head", it says somewhere. But the most dangerous speech is the idle talk of women, as we have seen so often. "A virgin's words/ should no one trust/ nor that which a woman speaks." Elsewhere men say that the words of a woman and a treacherous tongue can bring men to their death. This is a theme in many of the Sagas which point out what dangers may arise from the idle chatter of women.

Hávamál is remarkable poetry. Clearly the verses of advice are directly aimed at young men. They are given advice on most aspects of life so they can have an enjoyable and honest life. Men should eat and drink in moderation, guard their friendships, be careful of their reputation and honour and last but not least, beware the treachery of women. *Hávamál* is a misogynistic poem where all the emphasis is on the honour, values and concepts of manhood, while the woman seems at times to be just another evil that lusty lads must avoid. The message of this poem to young people was very clear and young women who learned the poem and thought about it must have been hurt by the writer's opinion of women and what role they should play in the lives of heroes.

Mansöngvar (love poems) and *manvélar* (woman-catchers)

The *Íslendingasögur* are in many ways intensely moral, but there is every reason to believe that people will have known plenty of bawdy poetry which is now mostly lost. The story of bishop Jón *helgi* (holy) mentions that people were reciting salacious poetry, but Jón stopped that practice and banned it. He did not want *mansöngvar* sung or listened to and did everything he could to ban them.

Mansöngvar were banned in *Grágás* on penalty of exile. This probably explains why so few such love songs have been preserved, though men will have composed them for their women. They considered *mansöngvar* likely to seduce women from the path of virtue, so their guardians would lose control of their lives. Not all *mansöngvar* will have been bawdy, more likely innocent love poems.

In this context it is fitting to mention the love poem that Thormódur Kolbrúnarskáld composed to Thorbjörg *kolbrún*. It is nowhere preserved. The same is true of many other *mansöngvar* that the Sagas mention but do not specify further. Some of Hallfredur's verses to Kolfinna could be defined as *mansöngvar* with very physical declarations of love.

Some of the authors of the Sagas mention that though men composed poetry to their mistresses, they cannot quote them, so they clearly self-censored what they wrote on their vellum.

Probably the love poems contained the sexual expression that is totally missing in the Sagas. Men composed salacious verses that could not be published because of the laws and were later lost in the depths of time.

There are, however, a number of verses and poems in the Sagas that are quite bawdy and have very sexual interpretations. They were usually hidden within other poetry and often of such intricate composition that it will have been difficult for people to make out the meaning. In them, metaphors and *kennings* (poetical circumlocution found in Old Norse poetry) are unusually tricky as if the poets had made a point of confusing their language to such an extent that no one would be able to catch them out for indecent activity. Some of these verses are so deep and mysterious that people of today with piles of books and notes have a very hard time understanding the meaning behind the poet's tangle of words. But the sexual undertone of many of these verses can't be concealed, so they are often bawdy disguised with complex *kennings*.

Though many *mansöngvar* have been lost, *manvélar* have survived, which is the name given to advice to young men abut women. The word *manvélar* appears in the *Edda*, in the Poems of Hárbardur, and clearly indicates that Óðinn had won women through trickery. *Hávamál* shows how to win a woman to your will. The author recommends kissing and talking to a woman in the dark.

Young men are advised to speak prettily to women, offer them money, and praise their beauty so it will be easier to have their way with them. This advice is actually timeless and fits just as well with our day. It can also be found in the Roman poet, Ovid, who advised men to give women tasteful little gifts and constantly praise them, their faces, their hair, their lovely fingers or tiny feet. "Love should be nourished with tender words", said Ovid. Elsewhere in his works he said that a girl may be conquered with eloquence in the same way that one can sway the mind of the public, judges or those who sit in the senate.

But dishonesty is the most important of all for conquests in love. Men should speak beauty but think deceit, as Ódinn himself did when he managed to trick the mead of poetry out of Gunnlöd with sweet talk. The message of the poem is that men should praise women highly and not hesitate to speak what they don't think so as to have their way with them.

This advice doubtless encouraged some young men to try it on with girls, but we must remember that this was of course totally illegal and an insult to the men of a girl's family. All of which suggests that there was a good deal of hypocrisy in the nation's moral outlook.

The adoption of Christianity and bishop Thorlákur

Bishop Thorlákur Thórhallsson was the most sacred of all Icelandic bishops. He became a bishop in 1178, and promoted reforms in the Church regarding the celibacy of clergy, the marriage of prominent people and the morality of the population. He did not hesitate to harass the Icelandic elite about their promiscuity.

The so-called penitential canons of bishop Thorlákur have survived, in which he lists many moral crimes and details the church's punishment for each. The bishop himself wrote these penitential canons, which are very detailed.

He classifies the punishable sins according to their seriousness.

The most serious sin he mentions is "fornication with one's own sex and animals."

Then comes a list of sexual offences:

Fornication between married people where on the one hand both are married and on the other only one is married.

Fornication between related people, which was detailed further according to how closely related they were.

Fornication on holy days, which again was further detailed. It was thought most serious to have sex during the final days of lent, the least serious was fornication on Sundays and other holy days.

In addition he inserted comments on fornication with a woman fresh from childbirth or a pregnant woman.

The structure of these penitentials is complex but systematic and logical. The penalties for violations were of many kinds, such as fasting, kneeler-fall (slap or lay your outstretched hand on the floor/ground before falling to it), singing *pater-nosters* (prayers), being beaten and a bed and underclothing ban (a ban with using linens of a particular kind).

Many other dos and don'ts regarding sexual behaviour were woven into confession. Thus it was forbidden to abort a baby or use contraception, also it was forbidden to "look at a woman's back for intercourse", which meant to enter a woman from behind, as it was considered an animalistic way of conceiving that many clerics even considered harmful.

Sex outside marriage was to cost three years of various penances before you could make peace with the Almighty. The punishments intensified as family ties became closer. If it was a question of first cousins, then confessions, penance and prayers would have to last for nine years.

In one summary the penances are described thus: *The least shall be offered for that which is done wrong in lewdness if a waking man be defiled by languishment with a woman. More if a man be defiled by his own hands. More if he be defiled by wood drilled. Most if a man be defiled by another man's hands. For these things must be offered kneeler-fall and prayer during lent and a number of punishment fasts.*

No doubt Thorlákur was speaking from knowledge and experience and knew of all kinds of sexual activity the church was against in the common rooms of the countryside. It is worthy of notice that he knew of skillful carpenters who would have sex with a piece of wood with a hole drilled in it, which must have been a sex-toy of their day.

Those must have been difficult days for clerics, with fornication rampant. Thorlákur's penitential rules bear witness to the struggle of the church and its clerics for improved morality.

In Conclusion

I have, in this book, painted a picture of Icelanders' sex-life during the Saga age. The Sagas don't say much about relations between the sexes so it has often been necessary to fill in the blanks, using imagination and poetic license. The more one studies old sources, the clearer it becomes how bad the situation of women was. They were tyrannised and oppressed by the male dominance of their time, men having the upper hand in every aspect of their lives. Men sought their power in both the laws and the religion of the day. They suspected women of treachery and faithlessness and didn't trust them.

Life in the Saga age lacked a formal executive power, which meant it was the families themselves who sentenced and punished those who broke the law. It was a society of revenge and pointless killings, where the slightest insult could cost a man his life.

When the King of Norway took power, calm came to the country and the civil wars of the *Sturlungaöld* came to an end, little by little. The power of the church increased significantly and the morality of society's leaders improved. The laws remained largely unchanged, which meant that the absolute power of men over women remained. Women didn't break through the patriarchy's barricades until the last century, when they managed to control their own fertility.

In writing this book, I looked first and foremost to the *Íslendingasögur* and *Sturlunga* for inspiration to analyse the sex-lives of the protagonists. I studied much that others have written about love in the *Íslendingasögur* and Norse mythology and they have my heartfelt gratitude. I especially wish to mention, among others, Böðvar Guðmundsson, Einar Ól. Sveinsson, Gunnar Karlsson, Heimir Pálsson, Helga Kress, Jón Karl Helgason, Ólafía Einarsdóttir, and Torfi Tulinius. I hope I have referred correctly and not seriously corrupted their writings.

As the book ends I wish to thank my wife, Jóhanna V. Þórhallsdóttir, for her patience and support. This book has been under construction for so long that it has become part of the family. Jóhanna has taken in this difficult foster child with great kindness and helped me raise it so it is ready to leave home.

I thank my publisher, Steingrímur Steinþórsson, for great collaboration and the poet Þorsteinn frá Hamri for countless good comments and suggestions. I am grateful to Hafsteinn Michael Guðmundsson for help with the layout and design and to Andri Óttarson for good advice and discussions. The historian Magnús Jónsson has my gratitude for awakening my interest in the lore. The greatest and warmest thanks go deservedly to the patient and conscientious authors of the *Íslendingasögur* and *Sturlunga*.